ZOMBIE GODDESS

888-555-HERO

Hero De Facto
Hero Ad Hoc
Hero De Novo
A Very Hero Christmas
Hero De Jure
Hero In Camera
Hero Amicus Curiae
A Very Hero Wedding
A Very Hero New Year
Hero Ad Litem
Queer Eye for the Super Guy

Solar System Services, Inc.

Alone Is Not Lonely
Halloween Harvest
("A Place at the Table")
A Place at the Table

Millersburg Magick Mysteries

Spells and Sleuths
Fae and Felonies
Magick and Murder
Feline Navidad

Soccer Moms of the Apocalypse

Pestilence in Pumpkin Spice
Famine in French Vanilla
War in White Chocolate
Death in Double Mocha
Demons Run at Halloween

The Enchanted Bakery

Chefs, Shrooms, and Sherry
Cakes, Cookies, and Conjuring

Miscellaneous

Sword and Sorceress 31
("Pig-Headed")
Sword and Sorceress 32
("Unexpected")
Practical Witches
Revenge Served Hot
The Yule Switch
Chocolate for Dinner
Silver Shoes and Pigs' Ears
Snipe Hunt

For updates, news, and giveaways, join Suzan's mailing list at suzanharden.blogspot.com/p/contact-me.html, or visit her website at www.suzanharden.com. You can also check her out on Facebook @SuzanHardenWriter.

SUZAN HARDEN

ZOMBIE GODDESS
(Bloodlines #6)

This is a work of fiction. All characters, organizations and events in this novel are products of the author's imagination and are not to be construed as real. Any resemblance to persons, living or dead, is entirely coincidental.

ISBN: 978-1-938745-65-2

Published by Angry Sheep Publishing LLC
Findlay, Ohio

Cover Design by For the Muse Design
Interior Design by JW Manus

To all the readers who send me
lovely notes that keep me going . . .

AUTHOR'S NOTE: The events in this novel take place four months after the events in *Amish, Vamps & Thieves* and *Blood Sacrifice.*

I gasped for enough air to get out, "You're welcome." If someone would have told me last year that I'd be the successful agent for three dead entertainment legends, I would have asked for a hit of whatever they were smoking.

"Samantha Ridgeway?"

Lily let go of me, and we both turned to find a cute little brunette standing next to us. "Yes?" I said.

"Your company manages the Lily Bell retro act that was just on, right?"

I took a deep breath. The scent of Fiji apples confirmed this girl was a Normal human. No honey. I'd learned to be a little paranoid since my own death in January. The fairies' contract on my head encouraged that paranoia. The actual assassination attempt last summer meant it was no longer paranoia.

"Yes." I plastered a polite smile on my face. "Is there something I can help you with?"

She smiled and held out a large envelope to me in one hand and another to Lily in the other. "I represent someone who's interested in your act."

The second both Lily and I took the paperwork, the mysterious woman's smile transformed into a toothy grin. "You've been served, bitches."

"Goddamn, mother-fucking, son-of-a—" I muttered. I wanted to kick myself. I should have known better than to take those damn papers. I'd been a tabloid reporter long enough to sniff out a process server.

For a brief instant, I considered altering her memories, but my control of my mental mojo was sketchy at the best of times. I'd accidentally left the necromancer who'd resurrected my baby zombies in a coma.

I ripped open the envelope and skimmed the contents. A cease-and-desist order along with a lawsuit claiming trademark infringement by Lily and me. The worst part was the name of the plaintiff.

"How dare you!"

I looked up from the complaint. An older woman stalked toward us. Why the hell did The Vegas Grand security let all the crazies back here? This would never have happened at the Karnak. Mainly because my vampire hunk of a boyfriend Duncan ran it. But then, most of the security there weren't Normals either.

Recognition of the screaming woman clicked. Lilianne Costas had finally given up on dying her hair black. Her short 'do was now a chic silver. Her hawk-like nose had been inherited from her crooner father Aristotle, but the dimples and eyes were pure Lily.

"How dare you profane my mother's career." She literally spat the words. I could feel the fine spray cover my face. "My mother never cursed during her act."

"I—I—" Lily spluttered. I didn't have to imagine how she felt. Her shock at seeing her daughter grated along my nerves.

I stepped between the women. "Your lawsuit's been served Ms. Costas. I'm sure your attorney wouldn't be happy about you confronting us directly. I *know* my attorney won't be."

"I want that bitch to know exactly what I think. She's a fake, and a terrible fake at that. I won't stand for her desecration of my mother's memory!" Another spray of saliva hit my face. Lilianne stabbed a finger in Lily's direction.

The process server soaked in the entire scene. An icy ball of rage froze my gut. This mess would be all over the internet gossip sites five minutes after the bitch left. I knew because I was formerly one of the people reporting on this kind of crap.

"Now, wait here just a minute, young lady." Bill stood shoulder-to-shoulder with me. "Lilianne, you can't insult your mother—"

Shut up, Bill. My telepathic warning came too late.

Lilianne's anger went supernova. "How dare you!" She exploded with enough profanity in English and Greek to seed a couple of galaxies. Finally, security noticed there was a problem. Two burly men escorted her and the process server from the backstage area. Her invectives died when the huge door slammed shut.

I turned back to Lily.

She shook her head, a defeated expression on her beautiful face. "I'm ashamed to say I taught her most of those words." Then she burst into tears.

I kept my temper under control while we took Lily back to the Karnak. Once we got the weeping comedienne into her suite, Bill promised to stay with her. I knew he'd keep Lily from doing anything stupid. The budding relationship between the two old friends was the one small favor the universe had deigned to grant me lately.

Instead of taking the elevator, I jogged down the stairs to the management section of the hotel where I'd claimed an office. No one argued with the boss's fiancée about the appropriation, especially those who knew I was a zombie.

Well, sort of a zombie. I sure as hell didn't like the Augustine chief enforcer's or my witch doctor's theory of what the damn nanites were actually turning me into. They kept me alive. That's all I cared about, even if my grocery budget rivaled a small nation's.

Alex and Bebe had to be wrong. They just had to be.

The exercise blew off some of my fury. No sense in scaring the piss out of my secretary. Not that much scared any canine were.

I burst into my office. "Staci, I need you to get Colin—"

"Shhh." Staci Warner glared at me from across her desk and held an index finger over her lips. I swear since the werecoyote had gotten married and had her pup, she'd become more of a bitch than her mother-in-law.

She stood, watching the witch in front of her desk. If his ginger scent hadn't given him away, the scarlet tendrils of energy streaming from his fingertips were confirmation. He was magickally examining a white box sitting on Staci's desk. His shoulder-wide stance gave no indication that he was aware of my presence.

I stepped inside and quietly closed the door. Mai Osaka, the head of Karnak security, watched the proceedings, and I sidled over to her.

"What's going on?" I whispered.

"You received another package." Her words were as sharp as the black suit she wore. Her almond eyes remained locked on the witch.

"I'm sure it's nothing." I wished I believed my own words.

She shot me a dirty look. "When you're head of security, you may make that decision."

"Shhhh!" Staci hissed again.

The energy tendrils sank back into the witch's dark skin. His eyes blinked and he shook out the tension from his hands. "You're right. There's a spell on the contents."

Staci looked pleased with herself.

"What kind of spell?" Mai asked.

The braided silver hoop in his left ear winked at the golden eagle in the piercing above it when he shrugged. "That's just it. It's a simple motion spell. The kind you put on a toy for kids." He ran a hand over his close-cropped black curls. "There's no blood magick or ill intent I can detect."

"I owe you one, Quinn," Mai said.

"Any time, pretty lady. It's been boring over at the Scheherazade." Ah, the casino owned by the Las Vegas witch coven. He reached out, and Mai fistbumped him.

Fistbumped.

Mai.

Who was so rigid and uptight, she made my sixteenth-century-born fiancé look like Charlie Sheen on a bender.

Staci held up a box cutter. "Let's find out what it is."

I held out a hand. "Maybe you should let me."

The werecoyote shook her head fiercely. "I'm not going to explain to Mr. St. James why you got hurt."

I scowled at the stubborn bitch. "I'm damn near indestructible. You're not." And Alex and Bebe's half-baked theory popped right back in my head, initiating a wave of nausea in my cast-iron zombie stomach. Unfortunately, other people were latching on that self-same idiotic idea, which led to the crazy gifts landing on my plate. Like the one sitting innocently on Staci's desk.

I smiled to take the sting out of my insult to Staci's abilities. "Besides, it can't be worse than the black roses or the skull jewelry." Especially considering the jewelry had been made from actual human skulls. We weren't going to talk about what the roses did to a maid.

"Maybe I should stick around," Quinn murmured.

"That would be best," Mai said. "I may need you to separate these two."

Staci and I turned to glare at the two security chiefs before returning to our stand-off. Finally, my secretary handed over the box cutter. "Fine." She practically growled the word.

"You're sounding more and more like Leslie every day." I grinned.

This time, Staci really did growl at the mention of her mother-in-law.

I held my breath and sliced across the tape. Inside the cardboard box was a Styrofoam container, a smaller version of the type vampires used to transport blood.

Very carefully, I eased the insulated package up. Staci yanked the cardboard box out of the way, and I set the Styrofoam on her desk.

My lungs reminded me I needed to breathe, and I took a huge gulp of air. Ozone leaked from the package. Steeling myself, I cut the tape holding the Styrofoam lid in place and flipped it up.

Dry ice vapor clouded my vision for an instant. Thank god, the little mass of red inside the container didn't jump out. The other three crowded closer to take a peek.

"Well, it kind of makes sense," Staci said.

"If you're a psychopath," Mai added dryly.

"Holy shit! That's a beating heart!"

Leave it to the only man in the room to state the obvious.

Chapter 2

I sighed and ran a hand down my face. Mai had a faintly amused look on hers. Staci sniffed the pulsing heart.

Quinn raced around the desk, grabbed Staci's trashcan and proceeded to vomit.

"It smells like some breed of deer," Staci offered. "But it's not one I'm familiar with."

"At least, it's not a human heart," I said.

"Or brains." Mai now wore a full-blown smirk.

I groaned. "I'm afraid that may be next. Was there a card?"

Staci handed me an ivory envelope. "I smelled the ozone when I took this off the box."

I sniffed the envelope as well. No ozone indicating magick contaminated the paper, but another scent lay underneath the wood pulp and glue. One that was all-too-familiar.

Best to get this over with. I slid a nail under the flap. The matching card had the expected cinnamon writing of dried blood. I couldn't make heads or tails of the neat script. The first two suitors had the grace to write their notes in English.

I held up the card for Mai to see. "Got a clue?"

"It's Hindi." She reached for the radio hooked to the waistband of her uniform slacks. "I'll get Kunal up here to translate."

I ignored Mai issuing orders and called, "You okay back there, Quinn?" The sound of him puking had subsided, so my attention returned to the beating heart.

"Yeah," he muttered. "Wanna tell me what's going on?"

Unfortunately, my secretary opened her giant canine yap. "There are . . . entities that believe Ms. Ridgeway is marrying below her station." She reached into one of her drawers and produced a canister. "Here."

The witch stood and yanked a couple of anti-bacterial wipes from the dispenser. "Thanks." His eyes met mine as he dabbed at his face and hands. "You're the zombie, right?"

Not *a* zombie. *The* zombie. I wasn't exactly the fresh-from-the-grave type. More like Frankenstein's monster.

If Mary Shelley's creation had been the Borg Queen.

"What? The black aura wasn't a dead giveaway?" I said sourly.

Of course, my stomach took that opportunity to growl, which meant all three of them stared at me.

Mai's brow furrowed. "When was the last time you ate, Sam?"

Before she finished speaking, Staci was on the phone, calling the kitchen. "I need three T-bones, well done, a pound of garlic mashed potatoes, a pint of peas and two loaves of oatmeal sourdough bread."

I made my best pleading face. "Chocolate soufflés?"

She relayed my request.

I could hear the chef say he was out, but he still had caramel fudge brownies. "Yes! Feed me!" I yelled. My mouth watered at the thought.

Staci placed her hand over the receiver. "You two want anything?"

Mai shook her head. Quinn shook his too, but his wide-eyed gaze shifted between me and Staci as she placed her own order.

Someone knocked on the door.

"Come in," Staci and I yelled at the same time.

As much as I wanted those brownies, I knew it couldn't be the waitstaff yet. Kunal stepped into the room. Like the rest of the Karnak security personnel, he wore a tailored black suit, white dress shirt, and a scarlet tie.

The vampire bowed to me, then Mai. "You requested my assistance, Ms. Osaka?"

She handed him the card. "Can you translate this for us?"

His dark eyes flicked over the scrawl. Instantly, his eyes glowed neon yellow, and his fangs extended. The ashy scent of fear radiated from him, and his face paled, which is no mean trick for a vampire originally from the slums of India. He threw the card away from him. "What is the meaning of this?" he hissed. "If this is a joke—"

"I'm not so insensitive that I'd open up the Karnak to a religious harassment lawsuit." I stooped to pick up the paper from the carpet and straightened. "Someone else sent it to me. I need to know what it says."

"It—" The vampire cleared his throat. His eyes had dimmed a little, but his wicked-looking canines still poked between his lips. "It asks for your hand in marriage."

Shit, someone was upping the ante in this perverse game. "Who sent it?" I snapped.

"Y-y-yama," Kunal managed to spit out.

"He's the Hindu god of death, right?" I'd been studying up on religions since this whole madness started over the summer.

Kunal stiffened. "He is subordinate to Siva, but yes." He hissed his "S"s like a pissed off cobra, but he didn't coat my face in saliva like a certain human bitch had earlier. Which brought me back to my original foul mood.

I handed Staci the manila envelope I had tucked under my armpit the entire time. "I need you to call Colin for me. Scan and e-mail this to him."

Staci frowned. "You usually scan and send your own documents. Did you fry another phone?" She yanked open a desk drawer and pulled out a box.

I resisted the urge to grind my teeth, but it wasn't her impertinent were attitude that bothered me. Since my rudimentary magickal power had manifested last spring, my cell phones had a tendency to spontaneously combust. "No, I didn't. And I told you and Duncan I would pay for my own from now on."

"What is that paperwork?" Of course, the hyper-alert Mai would butt in, but I wasn't about to discuss this in front of vampires and witches I didn't know very well, so I did my usual.

I ignored her.

I smiled at Quinn. "You sure we can't offer you dinner for your assistance?"

"That's all right." He glanced at the Styrofoam. Deep avocado tinted his dark coffee skin.

"Kunal, would you please escort Quinn to accounting?" Mai said. Leave it to her to clear the room. "They should have his check ready."

"Yes, ma'am." Another set of bows before the men departed. The whole deference thing really creeped me out. There was a certain amount of protocol since Duncan was the head vampire of Las Vegas now, but still . . .

I could see Mai mentally ticking off the time for Kunal to get out of vampire hearing range before she turned and said, "What's in that envelope?"

The barely audible *squish* and *suck* sounds of the deer heart trying to pump nonexistent blood was getting to me. I flipped the foam lid back into place. "Lily and I got sued tonight by her daughter."

"Why? *Parade of Stars* is a tribute act."

"No shit. They have Elvis impersonators, and you don't see Lisa Marie flying off the handle." I slumped into one of the visitor's chairs.

"Didn't you have an attorney check any potential problems?"

I folded my arms over my chest, irritated with her nosiness. The card with the blood ink still clutched in my hand crackled. "Yes." I couldn't just kill Duncan's head of security. Well, actually, I could, but then he'd give me that perturbed look he gets when he thinks I've really fucked up. Besides, Mai was one of the few people, Normal or supernatural, who didn't run screaming into the night over my . . . peculiarities.

"Then why—"

"Because she can. Because she has mommy issues. Because even though we'll probably win this case, she can drag it out for years to make us miserable." I rolled my head, trying to stretch out the kinks. For all the super-strength, super-speed and super-appetite, tension still sent shooting pains up my neck when I was upset.

My arms dropped to my lap, and I leaned forward. "I'm more worried about what this will do to Lily. Tonight is the first time I really understood why there are the rules about not mixing with your Normal family." My parents and older brother were rare exceptions to the rule, but unlike Lilianne who actually buried her mother, my family hadn't known I had died until after I'd been resurrected.

"Do you think she might try to tell her daughter the truth?" Mai was back in enforcer mode. Considering she was one of the very few Normal enforcers in the Augustine coven, she was totally capable of putting down Lily permanently if she believed my zombie spawn was a threat to her vampire master and his people. Nor would she hesitate to do so.

Despite my concern about Lily, I said, "I don't know. I honestly do not know."

After all of the night's bullshit, I had the kitchen send my dinner up to the penthouse. I pulled on an ancient Spice Girls t-shirt and a pair of sweatpants before I settled into the evening's meal. I was licking the last of the dozen caramel fudge brownies off my fingers when our private elevator dinged.

The doors slid open, and the familiar scent of sandalwood enveloped me. As usual since his master assigned him to Vegas, Duncan dressed impeccably. Today was a charcoal suit and an emerald tie that matched his eyes. The green silk was loose instead of its proper Windsor knot.

That should have been my first clue that something wasn't right.

But it had been such a bad day that all I wanted was to cuddle. I scooted over on the couch to make room for him.

He actually looked tired as he sat down next to me. Faint lines fanned from his gorgeous eyes. Additional lines dragged his mouth into a frown. I paused the episode of *Buddies* I had been watching while I ate and snuggled against his chest. His arms wrapped around me.

"Are you sure you do not need a new phone?"

"I told you I'd buy my own damn phones." What I needed was to get my new powers under control, but that paled compared to other issues in my life. I listened to his ultra-slow heartbeat for a while before I said, "I think this job is getting to you."

"It is not my current position that troubles me."

The weariness in his voice sank through my ugly mood. "Mai blabbed."

"She did not blab. She did her duty as head of security."

"It was nothing." I dared a peek at his face.

Which scowled down at me. "Nothing?" The neon green glow of his eyes brightened the dim room. "Someone sent you an animated animal heart."

"The latest stupid-ass rumor is getting out of hand." And it was royally pissing me off. "As if I didn't have enough problems."

"It is not a rumor, and you know it," he said softly. Ash and rotten oranges overrode his sandalwood. This *thing* was bothering him a lot more than he wanted to admit.

"Bebe's wrong," I said. "And you know better than me how Alex likes to pull practical jokes."

"What if she is not? Not to mention, Alex is not that cruel to make a joke of something like this. He still blames himself for not protecting you."

I pushed away from Duncan and sat upright. "That's ridiculous. He couldn't protect himself, much less me. Mallory had been starving him for months." I wasn't about to mention the role of Selene, Duncan's maker, in last winter's mess.

The faint glow of Duncan's eyes brightened, but he looked more exhausted than he had when he stepped off the elevator. "Are you saying Phillippa's father is lying? That the Incan god of death also lied to her and Alex?"

I glared at him. "I admit I'm a fucked-up science project, but humans can't just create a god. It's not possible."

He matched my glare. "And you know this how? What makes you an expert in what is possible?"

It would have helped my cause if my eyes glowed too. But that was one little thing missing from my growing arsenal of powers. The wonky ones I still fought to control.

And I could feel that tenuous control slipping.

I jumped up from the couch. I couldn't be this close to him. With my sketchy telepathic control, I'd accidentally transmit some thought I'd regret. Or melt his phone in his suit pocket. And I hadn't told him about the strange visit I received the day his niece Tiffany had married my brother Max. So I did what I usually do when I was scared.

I went on the attack.

"You're supposed to be on my side!"

"I am on your side, darling." He leaned forward, resting his elbows on his knees. "That does not mean I will ignore obvious truths because I am uncomfortable with them."

I threw up my hands. "Who shoved this stupid idea into everyone's head? A couple of gods who are known to get their jollies from fucking with humans."

"But you are not human, Samantha. Not anymore."

He couldn't have hurt me any worse if he'd punched me in the gut. I swiped the tears I couldn't stop. "You're a dick, St. James."

"I am not trying—" He closed his eyes, a pained expression on his face. Whatever else he was going to say he swallowed and rose. "Maybe it is best if I return to my duties." He didn't bother to use the elevator.

Once the stairwell door slammed shut, I walked over to the balcony. A push on the sliding glass doors let in the desert night. Cool, dry air brushed my skin, and I stepped outside.

The neon lights or the black shadows didn't draw my gaze. Instead the ugly stain on the pristine tile consumed my attention. It matched another stain on the street in front of Caesar's Brentwood mansion. Stains on the very fabric of the universe that I discovered only Phil's dad, the Greek god of war, and I could see.

Bebe said that crimson teeth had come through both places. That those teeth had shredded and consumed the souls of the men who had died on those spots. But she didn't see the residual scars.

I was too damn scared to fly to Peru to see if there were similar stains on the Nazca plain where Phil and Alex had fought some weird extra-dimensional demon. Because it meant Ares and my other suitor, Supay, aka the Incan god of death, were right about what the nanites were turning me into. Yama's proposal didn't help my state of denial whatsoever.

While the desert breeze felt good on my bare arms, the stain only agitated my thoughts more. I walked back inside and closed both the glass doors and the heavy drapes. Curling up on the couch, I hugged myself and ran through my options.

I needed help. Neither Supay nor Yama had a reason to be straight with me.

But maybe, just maybe, Ares would respect my friendship with his daughter enough that I could get some real answers. I reached for my smartphone and pulled up Phil's home number.

I prayed I wasn't making a big mistake.

Then a worse thought occurred. Was I even allowed to pray to a god if I was becoming one?

Chapter 3

Max Howell deleted the three sentences he'd spent the last half-hour typing. Normally, he could whip out a juicy story like this one by now. White slavery in the heart of Beverly Hills? The damn thing should be able to write itself.

But after talking to one of the victim's fathers, all he could think about was his own daughter. His wife Tiffany may be two weeks from her due date, but how the hell would he ever be able to protect his little girl?

There were things running around Los Angeles. Dark things that wouldn't hesitate to maim or kill or eat whoever got in their way. None of them were worse than a pair of sick-ass rapist brothers who chained and tortured women in their house for their own perverted pleasures.

Max glanced at the clock on his laptop. It was nearly noon. Maybe he should grab a sandwich, and maybe come up with a different slant for this story. Maybe like how these women kept each other alive until one of them escaped and brought help.

However, a knock on his door terminated his tentative lunch plan. "Yeah."

Amy, one of the staff photographers, poked her head in. "I know you've got your phone on Do-Not-Disturb, but reception says you've got a visitor."

"Who?"

She shrugged. "Wouldn't give his name, but he looks like a Flavor Flav wannabe."

"Flavor Flav?"

Amy grinned. "Yeah, white tails, top hat, and a big-ass clock on his chest. Except a lot younger and without the crack teeth."

"You're a little young to be listening to Flavor Flav."

"Don't diss my dad's record collection," she shot back. "Anyway, reception tried to get rid of him, but he said he was a friend of your sister's, and it was imperative he speak with you."

The proverbial chill raced up Max's spine and back down again. A friend of Sam's meant only one thing.

Supernatural.

It wasn't like he hadn't known about the secret side of the world from the time he was sixteen, but since Sam died last winter, the uneasy truce between the fae and the vampires had been shot to hell and back. He wasn't stupid. With his sister under the protection of Caesar Augustine, the Western U.S. vampire master, and his wife being one of the said master's enforcers, Max was an auxiliary target.

"Thanks, Amy."

She nodded, left his door open, and strode toward her cubicle.

Since the Unseelie had tried to assassinate Sam last summer, he kept a chain of steel paper clips nearby. He opened his top desk drawer, grabbed his makeshift weapon, and shoved it into his right pocket. It would hold a fae long enough for the paper's armed security to arrive.

His silver wedding ring and the silver wrist band Tiffany had bought him for their six-month anniversary would serve as a delaying tactic if his visitor was one of the rebel vampires who had tried to oust Caesar at the end of January.

The walk to the reception desk took forever. As Amy said, the man pacing the area dressed like the old school rapper. What she didn't mention was the cotton wadding stuffed up both of the man's nostrils or the odd black cane he carried.

"Can I help you?"

"Ah, Monsieur Howell!" The visitor's accent wasn't true French. It sounded like a cross between Cajun and French Caribbean. He swept off his top hat and bowed. "A pleasure to see you again."

"I'm sorry. Have we met?"

The stranger replaced his hat. "Your wedding." His voice had a nasal quality thanks to the packing in his nose. It ruined the charm of his accent. "Or I should say your first ceremony."

Shit. This was the man in the pre-wedding photo. The one that no one recognized when they had flipped through the albums Alex had retrieved from the photographer before he erased the poor woman's memory. The reminder of the zombie attack did nothing to stop the unease crawling back up Max's spine.

The visitor's jovial smile faded. "Alas, I did not come to reminisce."

"So why are you here?"

The stranger glanced at the receptionist, who did her best not to appear as if she were eavesdropping. "I apologize, Monsieur Howell, but given the delicacy of the matter, may we speak in private?"

Max turned to the receptionist. "Is anyone in Conference Two?"

She did a slow blink. "Conference One is open."

"Is anyone in Conference Two?" he repeated.

Another slow blink. "No."

He understood her confusion. Two faced south, and there was no UV film on the windows. No one ever wanted to use it. Even this late in the year, the room became a furnace.

Max gestured for the visitor to follow him. When they entered the stifling conference room and Max closed the door, the visitor broke into a broad grin.

"Are you satisfied I'm not a vampire, Monsieur?"

Max's own stiff smile tightened the corners of his mouth. "That's not my only concern." His smile fell. "Did my sister break your nose?"

The visitor started and ran fingers over the packing in his nostrils. "No." He dropped into a chair. "Actually, I am here on behalf of my father. Your sister has something that belongs to him. I have asked her to return it, but she has failed to do so."

Max sat as well. He pulled the steel links from his pocket, laid them on the table, and started straightening the first paperclip. "How do I know you're telling the truth, Monsieur . . . ?"

"You may call me Baron." The visitor inclined his head.

"Baron of which court?"

The visitor chuckled. "Not one you have visited yet. I am not of the Tuatha de Danann."

Max could hear Tiffany now. *This is so not good.* "Have you tried going to her boss? Sam's going to listen to him before she'll listen to me."

"Oh, I think she'll listen to you." Baron removed his top hat, then lifted the chain to the antique-looking clock over his head. Both pieces had the reddish hue of pure gold. "Show her this."

"No." Max tried to rise from the chair, but the aluminum and plastic flowed and trapped his forearms and ankles. He tempered the panic threatening to engulf him. Whatever this guy was, he wasn't the least bit human, but he wasn't ripping out Max's throat either. Putting the rest of the *Times* staff in danger wouldn't help. He forced out a sigh. "Isn't the poor-mortal-family-member-as-hostage routine a little old?"

"But the classics always work, Monsieur." Baron grinned.

The clock crawled from the supernatural's hands and across the wood veneer of the table, a gigantic gold inchworm. It also changed shape, growing smaller, longer. By the time it reached Max, the clock looked like a very expensive Rolex. The cool metal oozed across the back of his left hand and strapped itself to his wrist.

Baron replaced his top hat once again and stood. "Tell your sister she has until midnight tomorrow to return my father's property. Thank you for your time, Monsieur Howell." White teeth flashed against his espresso skin at his lame joke. "I'll see myself out."

The minute he departed Conference One, the chair reformed to its normal state. Max clawed at the strange watch, but the thing melded to his skin. All he succeeded in doing was dig bloody furrows in his flesh.

Dammit, he couldn't call Tiffany. Not this close to her due date. She wasn't the epitome of calm, rational thinking when she wasn't pregnant. Her idea of fixing the problem would be grabbing an RPG and go after this Baron character.

He should call Sam to warn her, but she hadn't taken Alex's theory or Bebe's facts about the nanites turning her into a god very well. What he needed was a solution before raising the alarm.

He did the next best thing by following his own advice. He pulled his phone out of his left pocket and thumbed the icon for Tiffany's doctor. "Hi, this is Max Howell, Tiffany Stephens's husband."

"Oh, Mr. Howell!" the receptionist gushed. "Has your wife gone into labor?"

"No, but I need to talk to Dr. Zachary now."

"She's with a patient. Can I take a message?"

Max rubbed his temple with his free hand at his growing headache. "Tell her it's a zombie emergency, and I really need to talk to her now."

"A zombie—oh, a *zombie* emergency! One moment, Mr. Howell." Shuffling followed by a bang echoed across the line.

In less than a minute, Bebe picked up the receiver. "What did Sam do this time, Max?"

"I'm not sure, but I've got a wristwatch magickally super-glued to my wrist unless Sam coughs up something that belongs to a guy named Baron and his dad. He's given me thirty-six hours, and I've got a very bad feeling if he doesn't get his shit back, he's going to take my soul as compensation."

Chapter 4

"Lawyers in Love" interrupted the bad dream I was having. The same one I was having more and more frequently. Something that looked like a velociraptor with tentacles tearing me apart faster than the nanites could put me back together.

Grateful for the sort-of rescue, I reached for my phone, checked caller ID, and thumbed the answer button. "Hey, Colin. What do you have for me?"

"Did I wake you?"

A glance at the bedside clock said it was just past noon. He must have stayed up well past vampire bedtime to research my problem.

I sighed. "It doesn't matter." I started to fling back the covers, but Duncan wasn't in bed with me. Where was he? He was usually sound asleep this time of day.

I settled back under the sheet and comforter. "Is there any way Lilianne can shut our act down permanently?"

"It's always a possibility, Sam. I stand by the legal team's original analysis, but that doesn't mean she won't get a sympathetic judge or jury who will do something stupid, and we have to drag this to the court of appeals. I'm calling to let you know Marshall received a cease and desist order from Lilianne's attorney, too. His attorney e-mailed a copy to me this morning. For now, Lily can't go onstage. I've got a phone hearing with the judge scheduled for this afternoon, but ..."

The urge to cry hit me hard when Colin's voice trailed off. This was going to devastate Lily, and I couldn't blame the show's producer, Marshall Wagoner. He had to look out for his own interests, not to mention the other performers.

"What can we do to fight this?" I leaned over and sniffed Duncan's pillow. His scent wasn't fresh. Nope, he definitely hadn't come to bed last night.

Great. On top of everything else, I had a pouty fiancé to deal with.

"Given Lilianne's accusation that her mother's reputation and memory are being desecrated, we need evidence Lily is being faithful to her original act since this is a tribute show."

"But I thought we didn't want to violate copyright?"

Colin's exhale whistled through the receiver. "That's the reason you're not using her original material, but Lilianne's accusing Lily of perverting the act by using off-color jokes and obscenities. We need something, a recording, a news clip, anything that shows Lily is sticking to her old style without reusing the same material."

I swallowed the hard lump at the back of my throat, unsure if the emotional crap was mine or empathy for my baby zombie. "I'll see what I can find." I really needed to change the subject before I lost it. "How's the vampire thing going?"

Colin chuckled. "I'm getting used to it. Caesar let me go back to Philly to see my family. It's unbelievable being able to talk to my nephew Evan again, even if it is through telepathy."

I smiled at Colin's excitement. The lawyer was adapting to vampire life far better than any of us expected. "Caesar must really have taken a shine to you to bend the rules."

"No, he's overly aware of the implications in the sudden disappearance of a scion of the famed Fitzgerald political family."

Envy stuck a needle in my heart. Colin had a good relationship with his parents. I had to die before my mother and I developed a strained truce. "At least, you had a choice."

After an eternity of silence, he said, "Did anyone in the coven besides me choose?"

My laugh was rather weak. "Alex, but technically, he was dying from a dozen bullet holes when Duncan offered to Turn him."

Colin's chuckle was equally uncomfortable. "Yeah, I noticed pretty quick not to ask certain questions. Thanks for being straight with me." He cleared his throat. "Anyway, keep Lily away from the showroom while I work on your case. Hopefully, Lilianne will agree to settle this before it gets too far. The last thing we want is for the case to go on for years, and people noticed you and Lily aren't aging."

"Thanks, Colin." I blew out a deep breath. "Thanks for everything. I owe you." I thumbed off the phone and ran my hand over Duncan's side of the bed. Compared to some of our epic battles, last night's tiff hardly registered on the Richter scale. But ever since Alex and Phil's little trip to Peru, things between Duncan and me had gotten very weird.

But I needed to deal with Lily's issue first. I owed her that much.

I wasn't the one who resurrected the corpses of her, Bill and Morty. No, that was pro basketball player and necromancer extraordinaire David Head. All because that asswipe, now comatose bed warmer, had a major league crush on Duncan.

But thanks to Head, I learned two very important lessons six months ago. My blood killed the living, and it restored dead things to life. The incident made me super-cautious about as small of a thing as a paper cut.

I dressed and raided the suite's refrigerator. The staff kept it stocked with hard-boiled eggs, cheese and pre-cut veggies for emergencies. The contents of the fridge and half dozen bagels I pulled from the pantry would tide me over. I definitely needed to break the news to Lily before I hit one of the casino restaurants for my second breakfast.

Fifteen minutes and a shower later, I knocked on her door. It swung open with a vision I didn't need to see—Bill Faith in Lily's pink fuzzy bathrobe.

He turned beet red, from his bare toes to his prominent nose. "Uh, I, uh, was expecting room service."

I crossed my arms and tried to hide my delight that he and Lily had moved to the next step in their relationship. "And I thought drag was part of your act, not a lifestyle choice."

Apparently, there was a color more red than beet because Bill's skin turned that shade. "Our private life is none of your concern."

I shoved past him. "I don't care if you lick honey off her ass—" I squelched the urge to wince when he went from red to an interesting shade of purple. "I'm here on business and I need to talk to Lily."

She appeared in the doorway to her bedroom, wearing a retro sweater and skirt set. "What did your lawyer say?"

I sucked in a deep breath and released it. "You're going to have to take a break from the show for a few days. Just until Colin and his team can get this straightened out."

Her stricken expression yanked at my heart as she sank down on the couch.

"Why?" Bill waved a hand in Lily's direction. "Red hasn't done anything wrong!"

"No, she hasn't." I crossed the room and sat next to Lily. "Colin says it would help if we could find some recordings of your old stand-up act. To show that you're being authentic to the original Lily Bell."

"I *am* the original Lily Bell," she wailed.

I took her fisted hands in mine. "We can't tell anyone that. Not unless you want to end up as a lab experiment."

"You were one," Bill mumbled.

"And that's what got all four of us into this mess," I shot back before I turned to Lily once more. "We need to give the lawyers everything we can in order to fight this."

Wetness shimmered in her eyes. "I don't want to fight my own daughter, Sam. We did far too much of that the first time around. Can't I just go and tell her—"

I squeezed her hands. "No, Lily. We've been over this before. Your children attended the funeral for their elderly mother. If you show up on Lilianne's front door looking like you are now, she will never believe you. She wouldn't have believed you last night."

Her expression turned downright ugly. "It's not fair. You get to see your family."

"Because my brother and I are members of the Augustine coven, and because my parents will keep their traps shut in order to see their grandchildren." Also because my Normal mother was the one person in the universe who scared a vampire as ancient as Caesar. I wasn't quite sure why.

Lily switched tactics. More tears trickled down her cheeks. "If we can convince Lilianne of the truth, she'll keep our secret."

"Do you have any idea what will happen to her if she doesn't?"

"Duncan can erase her memory."

I shook my head. "Sometimes, the vampires can't. Anne couldn't erase my brother's memory when he found out the truth about her years ago. If Max hadn't kept his trap shut, she would have had to kill him."

Colin's wife Anne had been Amish before she was Turned. Despite her attempts to stick with pacifism, she was the most dangerous out of all the vampires I knew. I'd seen first hand how efficient she could be at killing.

Lily grabbed my shoulders. "If they kill her, you could bring her back."

I stared at her. "No."

"But you did it with us." She waved her hand between herself and Bill.

"Are you honestly suggesting a horde of zombies invading your daughter's backyard is a brilliant idea? Because that's exactly how you ended up here. You were trying to eat my brother's wedding guests."

I instantly regretted the words at the pained look on her face. The antsy prickle of my conscience drove me to my feet, and I started to pace. I shouldn't have thrown the wedding in her face.

Their memories of the event were hazy; mine crystal clear. Morty had literally ripped out my throat, and they licked my arterial spray off of everything. Next thing any of us knew, the three comedians were alive and healthy.

"B-but we're human. Dr. Zachary said so." This time the tears in her eyes weren't an acting job. "And there's none of your robots in us."

"This is the same witch who has no fucking clue what these nanites are doing to me." My lie triggered a nasty ache in my frontal lobes, and I rubbed my forehead. Bebe agreed with Alex. Phil's dad had even offered a sample of his own DNA for Bebe to compare with mine. Just because I didn't like Bebe's conclusions, I couldn't take my personal frustrations out on my baby zombies.

And Lily needed to know the truth about their status within the coven. "I'm sorry, but you can't contact any of your family, much less Lilianne. You saw how she freaked out last night. We can't take that chance. *I* can't take that chance."

"But—"

"You're my responsibility. That means if you tell her and she can't handle it, I'm the one who has to put her down. And if I don't, that means Caesar will kill all of us—Lilianne, you, me, Bill and Morty."

Her eyes grew into huge, blue marbles of shock. Bill's mouth tightened into a straight line. He'd obviously suspected the stakes from the beginning.

I sat next to her on the couch again. "I don't want your daughter's death on my conscience, and I don't think you do either. Promise me you won't do anything stupid."

She slowly nodded. "I promise. I-I didn't realize . . ."

I patted her hands. "I'm sorry for not being totally straight with you. I didn't want to scare you." My stomach growled. "Feel up to joining me for breakfast downstairs?"

She slowly nodded again.

I turned to Bill. "I'll cancel room service. You need to put on a day dress. I'm not taking you anywhere in a bathrobe."

Mortimer Stern pulled into a parking spot five cars down from the dark green convertible he had followed. For decades, he would never have gotten away with tailing the attractive brunette. Now, no one recognized him. He'd gotten his long-time wish of anonymity, but he wasn't sure if it was a good thing or not.

He sipped the expensive shit kids today called coffee. Couldn't get a plain cup of joe anymore. No, it had to be creamed, steamed and sweetened until you couldn't taste the beans.

But he needed the cover. The Karnak's head of security was a smart cookie for a broad. He claimed he needed to get out of the damn hotel to think. As long as he came back with a receipt for the coffee and some notes for the Vegas show, she and Sam didn't question his whereabouts for a few measly hours.

Molly climbed out of her convertible and headed into the grocery store. She still had a set of legs and an ass any woman half her age would envy. Those nice, tight pants broads wore to yoga classes showed off her assets nicely. He recited baseball statistics in his head to get his dick under control. Damn, getting an erection the last couple years of his life had been moot with the fucking catheter.

And that memory took care of the problem. He climbed out of the SUV he'd borrowed from the Karnak's vehicle pool and arrowed for the grocery's main doors.

Learning his second wife now lived in Vegas had been the only reason he'd agreed to Sam's cockamamie plan to have him, Bill and Lily join that stupid showcase. Now, his new job would come in handy when Molly recognized him.

She would recognize him, wouldn't she?

Squelching the fear, he yanked a cart out of the rows and guided it toward the produce section. Molly was still a vegetarian, or that's what it looked like the last time he'd followed her through the store. Regret tugged his heart. Why the hell hadn't he treated her better? He even missed her eggplant lasagna.

Accidentally running into her cart might work, but it was too obvious. Ask her advice on melons? No, too desperate. But then she stopped in front of the bananas.

"Why did the banana go out with the prune?" He reached for the bunch next to the one she was reaching for.

She turned and stared at him. Her face paled the moment the recognition hit her. "I beg your pardon?"

He smiled. "It's a joke. Why did the banana go out with the prune?"

"Because he couldn't find a date," she answered weakly.

"Ouch. My best material, and you've already heard it."

"Who-who are you?"

"Walter Kinney." At least, that's what the fake ID the vampires had given him said. He held out his hand, but she still stared at him, shock imprinted on her patrician features. She made no move to take the proffered palm.

He lowered his arm. "Oka-a-ay, it wasn't my best pick-up line. I'll give you that. But why are you staring at me like you've seen a ghost?"

"Y-you look like Mortimer Stern."

He rubbed his chin. "Ah, I take it you caught my revival act at The Vegas Grand."

"No." The color flowed back into her cheeks. Her hair was still pinned up from her yoga class, and it was all he could do not to pull out the clip and bury his face in the mass. Did she still use that honeysuckle shampoo she had loved when they were together?

He grinned. "You can't tell me you knew the real Mortimer Stern."

She blinked. "Yes. I did. He was my ex-husband."

"Really?" He hoped his pretend surprise looked real enough. "And you are?"

"I'm sorry. You really threw me off." Her gorgeous lips curved into a polite smile, and she held out her hand. "Molly Weiss."

He shook it, and her touch made his cock twitch. "A pleasure to meet you, Miss Weiss. Aren't you a little young to have been married to him?"

She released his hand before he was ready. Her accompanying chuckle was tinged with bitterness. "That's how Morty liked his women, the younger the better."

God, he'd been such an insecure asshole. "Oh." He ran his hand over his hair. Since his resurrection, it surprised him to find some still attached to his scalp. "Finally get up the nerve to talk to you, and finding out I resemble your ex makes asking you out incredibly awkward."

"Asking me out?" She turned and dropped the bananas into her cart. The same duck-and-occupy-herself maneuver she used to do when she was uncomfortable.

"Yeah. I've seen you in here a couple of times. And—" He shrugged. Approaching Molly like this really was the stupidest thing he'd ever done. She was no longer the easily impressed girl fresh out of high school he'd first met, but a middle-aged career woman who knew all the tricks he could pull.

And he didn't want to use those tricks on her either.

"Sorry to bother you, Miss Weiss." Yep, definitely a stupid idea. He shoved the shopping cart toward the dairy section, disappointment thick in his mouth. Sam had warned them. He couldn't recapture his past. Couldn't rectify all the things he'd done to hurt Molly.

"Walter?" A soft touch brushed his arm.

He stopped and turned toward her, praying he didn't look too eager. "Yeah?"

"Would you like to get some coffee? Maybe? Some time?"

Paralysis gripped him. *She* was asking *him* out. He hadn't expected the switch in roles.

She withdrew her hand. "I'm sorry. I guess the whole thing about you looking like my ex really is awkward as hell."

"No," he blurted. "That's not, uh, I mean—" *Dammit!* He was making a mess of things. "I'd love to."

She reached into her purse and pulled out a card. "Here's my number."

Mortimer took the proffered card. A wild idea popped in his head. "Why don't you come to the show tonight? I can leave a ticket for you at will call and—"

Molly shook her head, and a tendril slipped from the tortoise shell clip. It took all of his willpower not to smooth the wayward lock from her face.

"That's not a good idea. Let's stick with coffee."

The pain in her expression tore at him. "Look, if my resemblance to your ex bothers you—"

Her smile was wan, a shadow of its normal brilliance. "That's not your fault. I'm sorry for the way I reacted. I'd like to get to know Walter Kinney, not the ghost of someone I used to love."

Used to love. Her remark couldn't have hurt worse if she'd plunged a real knife into his heart. But if that was all he could have of her, then he'd take it. "Coffee, then. I'll . . . text you."

Her smile brightened a notch. "Coffee, then." She turned and pushed her cart toward the pile of avocados.

Mortimer pivoted and shoved his own cart toward the grocery's main doors. The only reason he didn't text her right then and there was he needed someone to show him how.

Chapter 5

The god popped into existence in my living room after my brunch with Bill and Lily. Ares epitomized the word "god". Wavy black hair fell to his shoulders. His unadorned blood red t-shirt emphasized the sharp plains of his chest and the ripples of his abs. Black jeans hugged his lower body in all the right places. I gave him credit for trying to fit in with twenty-first century life, but he couldn't be subtle no matter how hard he tried.

He was basically sex on a stick.

Framed by his neatly trimmed moustache and beard, his full lips quirked into a cocky grin. "So you decided to accept my offer, Samantha."

Not even a fucking question. He really believed every female, no matter whether Normal or supernatural persuasion, should drop her panties at his request. He was that sure of himself.

"No." I crossed my arms over my chest and gave him my best evil eye. "Didn't Phil tell you why I wanted to meet you?"

He chuckled. "Females often prevaricate in order to experience my particular skills." With each word, he took a swaggering step toward me.

"I'm not lying," I ground out between my clenched jaws. He was too damn close. Exuded too much sensuality. "I need answers to my questions about . . . what I've become. I was hoping you'd agree to help because we're practically family."

"Phillippa should have told you I don't do anything for free. Even for family." He reached behind my head for my ponytail and playfully yanked it. "What will you give me in return for your answers?"

Anxiety and lust shuddered through me. It was worse than I imagined a vampire's mojo would feel like. Annoyance at being manipulated in such a manner cracked whatever spell or influence he aimed at me. My irritation welled, and I smacked him with a psybolt.

The combination telepathic/telekinetic stunt knocked him backwards. He landed on his well-formed ass. The floor shivered under my feet. Not sure if it was him or me that caused the vibration, I wondered if I had started something that I couldn't finish.

Again.

"If all you're going to do is play games, then leave." I tried to keep my voice level, but I was sure I wore my bitch scowl.

Ares climbed to his feet, but he didn't look pissed as I expected. His steady gaze held me, but none of the earlier leering quality lay in his expression. "This is why you need a more suitable mate." He gestured at the scuff on the carpet where he had landed. "You would have killed the vampire."

I quelled my shiver of fear. No sense in giving Ares any more ammunition. "I've smacked Duncan with a psybolt before. Worst thing I did was give him a headache."

"Your strength is growing, my lady." Ares shoved his hands in his pockets. The non-threatening gesture didn't make me any less worried about what he could do. "Yes, you knocked me down, but you would've sent the vampire through the glass." He tilted his head toward the huge plate windows and sliding doors to the terrace behind him. The terrace filled with bright afternoon sunshine. "Despite his enhanced attributes, he wouldn't survive Apollo's rays, much less the impact on the concrete below us."

Was that the real reason Duncan avoided our bed last night? Did he know how strong I was becoming? Did his Elizabethan sensibilities object to the reversal of our roles? He'd been the one watching my back since the day I died and became . . .

What? Every time I got a handle on the things happening to my mind and body, someone offered a new theory.

And I really hated the latest theory.

I cleared my throat. "Would you like something to drink?"

Ares's smirk returned. "Wine."

My irritation returned. "It's too fucking early for wine. You'll take a soda and love it."

"Of course, my lady."

His faux politeness stoked my temper while I stomped into the kitchen. I pulled two colas out of the fridge and managed to suppress the urge to shake his can so it exploded in his face.

Except I was shaking it slightly, not on purpose, when I returned and handed it to him. The reality of the answers I'd been denying for the last four months prompted what could only be an anxiety attack. My breath came in short rapid pants. Sweat prickled along my neck. This wasn't Ares's doing. Why the hell weren't the nanites compensating for my nerves?

"Would you like to sit down?" I waved toward the couch.

He sprawled across the upholstery as if he owned Las Vegas. I perched on the edge of the matching plush armchair and busied my fingers with opening my can. Carbon dioxide hissed as it escaped from its aluminum prison, but no foam overflowed.

From Ares's disappointed expression, he'd expected me to sit next to him on the sofa. He took a drink from his can before he said, "I still expect payment for my assistance."

The exasperated exhalation that escaped from me matched the sounds I often heard Duncan make when he was at his wits' end with something idiotic I had said. Or done. "Sex is off the table."

Ares's smirk shifted into another cocky grin. "Personally, I prefer a bed."

"No sex at all." I glared at him. Or tried to. His wicked humor and dark hair would be my undoing. They were the very same things that attracted me to my ex-fiancé Jake and my current fiancé Duncan.

My mental state wasn't helping my resistance to the Olympian. After spending years photographing, and resisting, the most gorgeous men on the planet while I worked for one of the top tabloids, I had thought I'd been picky. But since I'd died, I felt like a werewolf in heat. When I had asked Bebe about my revved-up libido, she admitted that it corresponded with my revved-up everything else thanks to the damn nanites. Deep down, I believed I wouldn't hurt Duncan by cheating on him, no matter how my hormones tried to convince me otherwise. But it was getting harder and harder to keep my impulses under control.

All of my impulses.

I focused on Phil's threat to put my speed healing to the test by shoving a grenade down my throat for even thinking of doing her dad. She'd made her point perfectly clear on the phone, even if he was the one chasing me.

It wasn't my fault if Ares mojo'd me, was it?

Aluminum crackled beneath my fingertips. Maybe I needed to focus on other things I really cared about. Like my unborn niece.

"I can be your personal shopper for Tiffany's baby."

Ares snorted in derision. "You believe I cannot provide an appropriate gift for my foster granddaughter?"

"I think Cerberus is a totally inappropriate choice for a mortal child's puppy," I shot back.

Glass in the windows and picture frames hummed in response to his laughter. "Not even I would be that foolish."

"Then there's my mother," I added. "You want to have access to Tiffany and her baby? You're going to need me to get through her. This is the woman who had no problem taking on the zombies that invaded my brother's wedding. Not to mention, she bitched out three ancient vampire coven masters in the hospital afterward. Mom's not going to cut you any slack because you're a god."

Ares's right eyebrow lifted. "And if I simply remove her?"

"If you came to me with that proposal while I was still alive, you would have had a deal." I shrugged. "Now that I'm dead, I find myself a little more forgiving when it comes to her behavior. So if you do anything to her, I'll have to knock you on your ass again." Somehow, I managed to keep "well-formed" out of that statement.

"How does my treating your mother with deference correlate to a favor given by you?"

"I'm smoothing the path, remember? If you want to do something stupid, oh, like give the baby a present that will cause her harm, let's say a Golden Apple from the garden of the Hesperides, that's your fault, and Mom *will* find a way to take you out."

I took a sip of my soda, watching for his reaction. For all the stories about him not being the brightest of the Olympians, I got the impression his moronic playboy behavior was mainly an act.

"I'll accept your offer with one condition—"

The carbonation in my stomach cavorted with digestive acid to produce an uncomfortable sensation. "Yes?"

"I accompany you on this shopping trip."

The vision of the Greek god of war holding my purse while I looked for onesies triggered an unfortunate response. I started laughing hysterically. Somehow, I managed to set my cola on the coffee table before I dropped it, but despite my best efforts, I could only tamper the sounds down to random guffaws.

Ares scowled. "And why do you find the thought of my company so amusing?"

"Because I can't imagine you doing the things for me that Duncan would do on a shopping trip," I said between snorts.

"And what do you think a vampire could accomplish at a market that I could not?" From the sparks in Ares's eyes and the red flush creeping up his neck, I'd pushed him too far.

With a strength of will I didn't think I had, I managed to sober myself. "First of all, he carries my bags."

"Done."

"He pays for everything."

"Of course." The wicked smirk was back.

"And he does it without complaining or whining."

A scowl chased the smirk off Ares's face. "Are you calling me a sniveler with no backbone?"

"Are you saying a vampire can do something you can't?"

"No." His tone was the same as a pissed-off werewolf. I should know. I've done my share of pissing off werewolves. And werecoyotes, too.

"Do we have an agreement?"

"Yes."

"Swear by the River Styx."

That jolted him out of his anger. "You cannot be serious! You want me to swear our most sacred oath over a shopping expedition for baby gifts?"

I crossed my arms over my chest. "It's not just the shopping and you know it. I help you with handling Mom and selecting the baby presents. In return, you answer my questions." I sucked in a deep breath. "Fully and truthfully," I added. Maybe Colin's negotiation lessons were sinking into my robot-laden brain. "And absolutely no sexual innuendos, suggestions or inappropriate touching of any kind whatsoever."

Ares was silent for so long I thought he would disagree and leave. "Did you destroy the roses I sent?"

His question was so unexpected, his voice so quiet, I wasn't sure I'd heard him right. The potted rose bush with twelve perfect, ebony blooms had been my first gift. The Normal girl from housekeeping who'd brought it to my office was still on personal leave, but at least she was out of the hospital. I was the only person the plant wouldn't attempt stab with its thorns.

"No."

"Where are they?"

"In my safe where they won't try to drink anyone else's blood." I tried not to think about the special vault in the basement. When the city had been first built, it had been a safe house for vampires immigrating to Los Angeles. Later, it became a prison for rogues. I hated going into that vault. The stench of death and despair smelled better to me than the Karnak chef's molten lava cake.

And my attraction to that odor scared the piss out of me.

Concern creased Ares's forehead. "Aren't you feeding the plant?"

"That thing drinks blood!"

"Of course." He actually looked confused at my revulsion. "Can you not conceive of a better gift from a god of war to a goddess of death?"

"I'm not—"

He looked at me askance.

The denial died on my lips, but I still wasn't ready to say the truth aloud, even in an argument. I sucked in a deep breath. "I'm not in the market for a boyfriend, Ares, and I already have one fiancé, which is plenty. This is why I want you to swear on the River Styx concerning our deal."

The sorrow in his expression made me want to cry. Somehow, I knew his emotion had nothing to do with me turning him down or my insistence on his oath concerning our deal. "Ox blood. If you are unwilling to feed my gift human blood, then feed it ox blood. Otherwise it will unpot itself and look for nourishment on its own."

Would the damned rose plant even leave if I gave it back to him? I'd read enough Greek mythology to know that gifts, or curses, from the gods couldn't be returned. Only amended.

With the supernatural races, I was learning there was always a grain of truth within their stories. I nodded once. "Thanks for the info. Now about our deal—"

He blew out a deep breath, and I suppressed a smile. It seemed I exasperated every male I encountered.

"How do I know you will keep your side of the bargain?"

I shrugged. "You can always ask Phil to be your enforcer. She's already threatened to use a grenade to disembowel me if I sleep with you."

"Is that why you won't—"

"No!" The walls of the penthouse shivered in response to my shout, and a hairline crack appeared above the kitchenette. Great. Now I needed to call maintenance, and they would tell Duncan, and he'd ask what happened, and . . .

I cleared my throat. "Do I need to repeat my terms?"

"When?" Ares looked too damn amused by my discomfiture.

I ran my tongue over my suddenly dry lips. With Lily out of the showcase and Bill and Morty prepped for the next couple of nights, I didn't have much of an excuse. Best to get this over with. "I've got time tomorrow morning to shop."

He leaned forward, not predatory, but pretty damn close. "Then I get to choose the place." He surprised me by naming the department store at the Beverly Center where Max and Tiffany had registered, though the registry itself was probably my mom's idea.

As much as I dreaded spending any more time alone with him than necessary, maybe a trip to Los Angeles would sooth my fractured emotional state. I nodded. "As long as you answer my questions here and now."

"Agreed." He leaned back against the couch.

I cough not so discreetly.

Ares rolled his eyes. "I swear by the River Styx that I will answer all your questions for the next three hours, fully and truthfully in exchange for you spending an equal three hours in my company tomorrow where we will partake of the midafternoon meal and purchase appropriate gifts for my foster granddaughter. I also swear by the River Styx I will carry all packages, as well as Lady Samantha's purse with no complaints. Satisfied?" His expression dared me to disagree.

"Yes. Thank you," I added. "Shall we begin?"

Max's right toes tapped a nervous rhythm against the kitchen tile at Caesar's Brentwood mansion while Bebe perched on a chair next to him and examined the new adornment on his wrist. She had suggested meeting at their home for some privacy. "Well?" he asked impatiently.

"I think you're picking up some of Tiffany's less endearing habits." She glanced up at him. "Do I need to give you a sedative, or will a kick in the shins suffice?"

With monumental effort, he stilled his foot. "Can you get it off?"

She shook her head, brunette curls swaying. "No, not without blowing you up in the process."

"So my visitor lied about being fae." Figured. He squelched the urge to bang the watch against Bebe's table top.

"No, it's not fae magick. It's similar to Ares and Sam's talents." She leaned back, but kept her hand over his. "Describe this person again."

Max repeated his impressions of his visitor. "He's the same guy who appeared in one of the candid shots Alex retrieved from the photographer of our zombie-interrupted ceremony. Neither Tiffany or I could identify him, and no one else we asked could either. When he was at my office, he had tissue stuffed up his nose, and he had a cross between an American Southern and a Caribbean accent. He said to call him Baron, but when I asked which court he belonged to, he said it was one I hadn't visited. Do you have any idea of who he might be?"

Bebe's face paled. "Now I do." She pursed her lips, rose from the kitchen chair, and strode through the swinging door.

Max jumped to his feet and raced after her. She'd already disappeared from the foyer, but from the sharp clicks of her heels, Bebe was headed down the hall toward her, well, magick lab was the only thing he could think of to call Caesar's former conservatory.

The heavy drapes were pulled back from the huge windows when he walked into the room. A scarlet Persian carpet highlighted with gold threads covered the black, white and gray marble floor. Antique birch chairs and tables sat on the thick wool. An ancient cedar wardrobe sat across from the windows.

Hands on her hips, Bebe stood at the back wall and examined the contents of the floor-to-ceiling shelves.

When Max crossed over the gigantic silver pentacle he knew was underneath the carpet, tingles radiated from the strange watch along his skin. Most people had no clue about the metal embedded into the marble and hidden by the carpet. Knowing the ring was there and actually feeling the power added to his fear.

Bebe glanced up from the tome she'd pulled off the shelf. Her lips tilted down as her gaze traveled from the floor to him and back. "Well, that was interesting."

"'Interesting' is not the word I'd choose." The instant he stepped out of the silver circle the electric sensation along his arm disappeared.

She turned the book so he could see the page she was looking at. "Is this him?"

The woodcut had to have been close to two centuries old, but the resemblance to his visitor was uncanny. Max nodded. "Who is it?"

"Baron Samedi. One of the Voudon loas of death."

Chapter 6

It took a few seconds for Max to process the information. "What?"

Bebe tapped the picture with her forefinger. "The question is what does Sam have that Samedi wants."

"Here's a better question. What the hell was he doing in my parents' backyard when my photograph was snapped?"

"The zombies. One of Samedi's duties is guarding the door between life and death. As a result, reanimation and resurrection come under his domain."

Max stared at Bebe. An uneasy feeling crawled along the pit of his stomach. The same feeling that accompanied his nightmares of that night. "He said she had something that belonged to his father."

"Papa Ghede. The only thing I can think of that they would care about is a soul. Maybe someone who died at your first ceremony was Voudon. In the chaos, Sam could have accidentally redirected the spirit."

"Like she did Morty, Bill and Lily?"

Bebe swore under her breath. "We may be having more visitors. A pissed-off Baron is one thing. I don't want to be facing the Angel of Death and the Heavenly Host on top of the loa." She slammed the book back onto the shelf.

"Wait. What?"

"Think about it. Morty's Jewish, and Bill and Lily are Christian. If Papa Ghede and Baron Samedi want a soul sworn to them back, what're Yahweh and Jehovah going to do?"

Mortimer knocked on the partially open door to Sam's office before popping his head around the edge.

"Hey, Walter!" Staci flashed him a bright smile while her fingers tapped across her keyboard. "The boss is at a meeting right now. Do you want me to let her know you're looking for her?"

He wasn't sure if Sam's secretary knew the truth about him, Bill and Lily since the kid always used his alias. But if she was like any other broad he'd met in his life who sat behind a typewriter, she also knew when to keep her mouth shut. He trusted she would stay quiet about him dating, but if she did ask, well, there was no need to say Molly was his ex-wife.

What he was about to ask Staci made him sweat. The whole thing seemed like a terrific idea when he'd left the grocery store. "Actually, I need your help."

"My help?" The keys went silent, and she swiveled away from her computer screen, giving him her full attention.

"I, um—" He wiped his damp palms along his trousers. "I met a lady."

"Not another one of the housekeeping staff." She frowned.

"No." He grimaced at the reminder of the one night he decided to test his plumbing after his resurrection. While he had fun with the two maids, the encounter reminded him of all his past mistakes. "I've learned my lesson about dipping in the company pool."

Staci grinned. "Then it's great you met someone!"

"She gave me her number." He reached into his jacket pocket and pulled out the tiny rectangle that passed for a phone these days. "I don't have a clue about how to . . . text someone."

Staci gave him a quick tutorial, but she could have been speaking Martian for all he understood. "Try texting me a few times first. We don't want to give her a bad first impression, right?" She reached under her desk and pulled out her own phone.

Mortimer still did the slow one-finger poke, not the rapid-fire double-thumb thing Staci did, but after ten minutes and a dozen messages, he was sure he had the hang of it.

"Before you text her, what's your plan?"

"She just wants to meet for coffee."

Staci smiled. "Good starting move, but may I make a suggestion?"

He nodded.

"Don't take her to one of the chains. There's a cute little café that your lady friend will love." She named a street well off the Strip. "If you're there between the breakfast and lunch rushes, you should be able to get a table on the patio. That'll be perfect this time of year."

Mortimer shook his head. "When did asking a broad out get so damn complicated? It used to be drinks, dinner, witty banter, and maybe a little make-out session if things went well with the first three."

Staci laughed. "This is real life, not a forties movie."

"Unfortunately, I'm very aware of that, kid." Time to test drive his new skills. "Thanks for your help. I owe you one."

"Part of the job. Let me know how things work out." She winked.

Mortimer strode out of the office and quickly found an alcove out of the fear he'd forget everything Staci showed him. Nerves jumping, he punched in Molly's number and his invitation.

His heart skipped a beat when the little device buzzed a moment later with the reply.

Yes. See you in the morning!

I'd been a reporter long enough to know the five basic questions. "How do you know I'm a god?"

Ares leaned back against the couch. "I smell your power. Your physician asked for a sample of my blood to compare with yours. I understand you don't trust any deity, much less me, but why don't you trust her science?"

"Because—" Because I wanted my old life back. "Because if you and everyone else who say I'm a new god are wrong and you're all right about this ancient god coming back, a lot of people are going to die."

"And what makes you think we're wrong?"

I leaned my elbows on my knees. "The deal was I ask the questions, and you give me straight answers. None of this Socratic method bullshit."

"My apologies, m'lady." He raised his palms toward me. "The problem is that unless you accept this truth, no matter how difficult, and you are willing to fight and win this battle, all the mortals *will* die."

Wow. Nothing like putting on more pressure. "Okay, then. What do you know about the Old Ones?"

"They are the gods of the first sentient beings of this planet. Their adherents started dying off millions of years ago, and they lost their grip on this plane. As a result, we—" His hand waved in a circular motion. "All of the new pantheons came into existence, but Gaia had already banished Old Ones because they were so weak."

"What or who is Gaia exactly?"

"The first of all of us. The one who came into form when the first human considered the concept of a deity. Or the one who decided to create sentient beings from ancient primates." He shrugged. "It depends on your point of view. Gaia is the name we Olympians call her, but it is not her true name."

"When you mean 'human' you mean the first *homo sapiens*?"

"No." His wry smile sent unease down my spine. "I mean, the first human. Only mortals have the need to separate themselves into so many categories. That is why there are so many of us gods these days."

I groaned. "I need something stiffer than a soda for this conversation." I rose, stalked over to the wet bar, and examined the bottles. Yeah, rum and coke would be a good choice for dealing with the information Ares dished. Grabbing two tumblers and the liquor bottle, I set them on the coffee table before I scooped ice from the fridge's freezer into a bucket and grabbed a couple more cola cans.

Ares said nothing as I mixed the ingredients in the tumblers and handed him one. I took a large gulp of my drink before I continued with my questions. I suspected what his answer would be to the next one from my recent nightmares, but I needed the confirmation.

"How many millions of years ago did the Old Ones' followers start dying?"

"Sixty-five."

"So these Old Ones are the gods of the dinosaurs?"

"Yes."

I rubbed my forehead. My brain wanted to ache, but my transformation by the nanites was too far gone. It was more the memory of a stress migraine, than an actual one. "Why does the birth of a new god allow one of them to come back?"

"In short, what you would call basic Newtonian laws."

"For every reaction there is an equal and opposite reaction?"

He saluted me with his tumbler and took a swig.

"But according to Supay, this reaction is only triggered by a god of death. Why?"

His nostrils flared. "A question I asked my mother on yours and Phillippa's behalf." He took another drink. "I apologize for the third hand information, but my uncle refused to speak with me on the matter."

I smiled. "I'll take any tidbit I can get at this point."

"Their loss of power came about from the demise of their followers. Death is the most primal of all forces, but for every ending there is a beginning."

"Wait a minute." I set down my glass and waved my hands. "Shouldn't something be created or born or whatever before it can die?"

"You destroy sand to make glass. You kill wheat to make bread."

My hand shook as I added more rum to my tumbler. If birds came from the dinosaurs like evolutionary scientists believed . . .

I stared at Ares. "The first chicken didn't come from a chicken egg."

He shrugged. "Something like that." He held out his glass and I sloshed alcohol into it.

"So we really do create God in our image?"

He stretched out on the couch cushions and sipped his drink. "It's a symbiotic effect. Their belief in us strengthens us. It can change how we appear to them, how we act, especially if our sense of self isn't well-developed." He shrugged again. "That happens more to the younger generations of a pantheon."

"Because the belief in you came when you were born."

He nodded. "In my case, yes. And influence can fade and rise based on human whims."

"So as other deities become more popular, you lose power."

"And gain it if worship of us resumes. Or when a writer or artist brings us to the public's attention again."

I grinned. "Sounds like you owe Rick Riordan a thank you note."

Ares chuckled. "And your friend Brent Poole for his role in *The Iliad* as well."

I shook my head and laughed, too. My first cover story at *The National Scoop* was thanks to some great pics I'd snapped of him naked at the beach. Brent's animosity towards me hadn't eased after I'd started working for Caesar, even though the vampire master was Brent's great-some-thing uncle. "He had one too many gratuitous butt shots in that movie."

Ares honored his oath and didn't offer any innuendos to my comment.

My lighter mood died as fast as it arose. "So what you're really telling me is that I've become a whole new species."

He leaned forward again and stared at me intently. "That's not necessarily a bad thing, m'lady."

I gulped down the rest of my rum. "The way Supay explained it to Phil and Alex if I fuck this up, whatever it is that I'm supposed to do, we're talking about the end of the world."

"You are supposed to destroy the Old One." A grin spread across his face. "That's why you need me."

I blinked, and kind of wished I was drunk so I could claim I misheard him. "Say what?"

"What do you think the purpose of my existence is, my lady?"

"Get humans to kill each other in pointless wars?"

"To protect. By fighting to the death if necessary. I have thousands of years of experience in battle and strategy."

My eyebrow rose. "I thought your sister was the planner and you specialized in brute force execution."

"Do not underestimate me, Samantha. Athena has to cheat to defeat me when we spar."

His arrogance was wearing me out, so I switched back to the original topic. Or tried to. "What if I fuck this up? If everyone's gone, how are you going to play toy soldiers with the human race?" I said softly.

"That's why we would make a good match." He swung his legs off the cushions and set his glass on the granite coffee table. If I thought his gaze was intense before, this one was a laser drill. "You need my expertise to fight. If things go the wrong way in your battle with the Old One, you can raise the dead to assist you. You've already proven you've mastered that ability."

His use of my baby zombies against me should have pissed me off. Instead, I felt an empty pit open up in my soul. "You really don't get it, do you?" I shook my head. "There won't be anything left to resurrect."

"If you don't think you can win, forget the mortals. Come with me to Olympus." He took my free hand in both of his. No mojo from him this time. "We can spend our days—"

"Fucking and drinking until the dino god eats us?" I jerked free from his hold. The anger was back. Anger I could deal with. It was much easier than the lust and depression, mainly because I'd been pissed at my parents and the rest of the world when I was a living, breathing Normal. "Lizard Girl broke you, didn't she?"

Flames ignited in his eyes. Literal flames.

The remaining soda fizzed and hissed in their cans in response to his power. No more pretending he was human. "How dare you," he growled. The way he smoothly, unnaturally rose to his feet actually calmed me. The games were done.

I stood also. "You're afraid. I get it. I'm scared shitless, too, but I needed answers. I asked to see you because I thought we both cared about Tiffany's baby. That you'd want to see her grow up as much as I did. If I'm wrong about our mutual concern, I apologize."

The flames in his eyes flickered and dimmed. Had I actually made the Greek god of war feel guilty?

"I do care about my granddaughter. That's why I offered my assistance." He stepped closer. Blast furnace heat radiated from him. "But you need to accept that you are no longer human. I understand Tiffany and her daughter's lives are but a flicker of mine. Just as your lover's will only be a flicker of yours."

"Leave Duncan out of this," I hissed.

Ares's palm cupped my cheek. "Samantha, vampires are not immortal."

I jerked away from his touch. "I know that," I snapped. His attitude was gnawing on my last nerve. "I know they can be killed."

He shook his head. "Even if you lock up your precious St. James in a gilded cage to protect him, he will still die. His disease only slows the aging process. It does not arrest it, Samantha. In the end, you will still be alone unless you chose one of your own kind."

"Seems to me you wouldn't be chasing after anything with a vagina if that were true."

A rueful smile played across his features. "Maybe I'm tired of chasing, my lady." He bowed from his waist, a courtly gesture very out of place in the twenty-first century, before he flashed out of the penthouse.

I glanced at the clock. He had stayed for exactly three hours from the moment he swore his oath.

Once I was sure he was gone, I collapsed on the chair. For all my bravado, the same thoughts he'd given voice to had been running through my head for the last four months.

And they scared the shit out of me.

Chapter 7

Sitting in Caesar's office, Max tried to breathe normally while Bebe dialed the number for her counterpart in the Rousseau Vampire Coven. His skin under the stupid watch itched, and he wondered how much sweat was trapped between his skin and the metal and how bad it would smell because his broken arm had stunk after six weeks in its cast and would Tiffany hose him down before letting him into their bed. Any stupid thought to suppress the panic threatening to turn him into a gibbering mess on Bebe and Caesar's carpet.

"Hi, Yvonne!"

Tension pulled him tight as Bebe exchanged pleasantries with the other witch. Yvonne Head really had no reason to help him after what Sam did to her brother. Things squirmed in his belly while Bebe relayed what had happened at his office earlier this afternoon.

She frowned and said, "One moment." She stabbed the speaker button. "Okay, he's on."

"Have you asked Sam about this matter?" Yvonne's relaxed New Orleans lilt was slightly comforting.

"Frankly, I wasn't thinking straight when I left my office," Max said. "I tried calling her after I arrived here. So has Bebe. Her cell keeps going to voice-mail, and her secretary said she was in a meeting until four our time, but she hasn't seen her since."

"All right." Yvonne blew out a deep breath. "I need you to tell me exactly what this person who came to visit you said."

"That Sam had something of his father's, that he had asked for it and she hadn't given it back, and she has until midnight of tomorrow to give whatever it is back to his father." He glanced at the magickal fake Rolex superglued to wrist. "The deadline's in thirty-three hours. Oh, and that I was to call him Baron."

"What did he say he'd take if she didn't return the soul pledged to him?"

Max rubbed his chin, trying to recall the exact words. "He didn't say what he would take exactly. He just told me to show Sam this watch." The rest of Yvonne's question sank past his fear. "Wait a minute. He didn't say Sam had a soul that belonged to him."

"A soul is the *only* thing Baron Samedi would appear in person for," Yvonne replied. "She doesn't have the skill for a Soul Sphere, does she?"

"No." Bebe's curls bobbed as she shook her head though Yvonne couldn't see the motion. "At least, she hasn't developed it in the last six months." She glanced at Max, obviously wanting confirmation.

He shrugged. "She hasn't said anything to me." But then, his baby sister hadn't really talked to him since Alex and Phil's revelation in June.

"He's a loa. One of the most powerful. I don't understand why he simply didn't take what's his . . ." The sound of snapping fingers clicked through the line. "Davy. Sam binding him. The coma. It's the only thing that makes sense in connection to your wedding."

Max exchanged a look with Bebe. Her expression was as worried as he felt. Sam had accidentally put David Head—necromancer, pro basketball star and Yvonne's younger brother—into a coma after his zombie army invaded Max and Tiffany's first wedding ceremony at Mom and Dad's. The man had a seriously misguided crush on Sam's fiancé, Duncan.

Bebe cleared her throat. "What do you mean?"

"Whatever Sam did to bind Davy last April must have hidden him from the sight of the loa. Unless she's had contact with another vodoun besides me and my brother?"

Max tapped his fingers on the cherry desktop. "Not that I know of. But why would your Baron Samedi wait nearly seven months to approach me? Plus he showed up in a picture taken before the zombies invaded my parents' backyard."

"You said he contacted Sam first. I would venture that he grew tired of waiting. With All Soul's Day approaching, he needs to collect—" Yvonne's throat caught. "He needs to collect everyone who died since last year's holiday before dawn. I'm not sure about this picture you mention. I didn't see him at your wedding. He may have been there because of Davy's resurrection spell. Maybe you were supposed to die in the attack."

"Or he was there to collect one of the people from the Rousseau Coven who was killed," Bebe offered.

"Possibly. What about the three corpses Sam brought back to life?" Tentative hope threaded through Yvonne's voice.

"That was my first thought as well," Bebe said. "But I double-checked while I was waiting for Max to arrive here. All three are either Jewish or Christian."

Max closed his eyes. Shit. It was either him or David Head. And after what Head did to people she loved, he knew who Sam would pick, despite their sibling rivalry.

But what if she failed to protect him?

He couldn't imagine life or death without Tiffany. His wife wouldn't even question Sam's choice. Not after what Head did to Duncan and Kensai. She'd snarl and growl and point at her bulging abdomen, demanding Max fulfill his daddy obligations to their little girl. If other coven members were around, she'd put on her tough woman show, flash a couple of weapons, and threaten to cut off his body parts. If they were alone, she'd cry and plead and still threaten to cut off his body parts.

And dammit, he wanted to see his baby born. Hold her for the first time. Count her little pink fingers and toes.

But could he live with the guilt? Could he live with the knowledge that he basically sentenced another man to death?

"If Sam accidentally took David's soul, because let's face it, my baby sister isn't brilliant enough or talented enough to do it on purpose, what would Baron Samedi do if she put it back in David?" His toes started their nervous tapping as both witches contemplated his question.

"I don't know if she actually took it," Yvonne said. "It might still be connected to his body. I can't be totally sure but I still feel a spark of something beneath Sam's binding." Her breath whistled through the connection. "Or it could be as simple as David being sworn to the Baron's service as a necromancer, and Sam bound his powers."

Bebe leaned forward and rested her elbows on the desktop. "Either case would also explain the null reading on your brother's EEG. I'm assuming there's been no change since the last time we spoke."

"None," Yvonne said sadly. And if it weren't for her boss's wealth, the hospital would have pulled the plug on the bastard a long time ago.

Max swallowed his frustration. Neither woman seemed to want to take the bull by the horns. "Assuming you two are right, why doesn't this Baron Samedi just take back David's soul? Aren't the loa gods?"

"No." Yvonne's answer was firm. "They are intermediaries between mortals and God."

"Like angels?"

"They have far more free will than angels."

Shit. If the rest of Caesar's inner circle were right about what Sam was becoming, they were looking at a war of apocalyptic proportions. Maybe they should tell Yvonne the truth about her.

Max inclined his head toward the phone, but Bebe's sharp shake of her head deterred him. Then another tactic was necessary.

"Why can't we just ask Baron what it is he's looking for? Wouldn't that be better than guessing?"

Yvonne was silent for a moment long enough that sweat trickled down the back of his neck.

"I can try—" Yvonne started tentatively. Faint static filled the connection. "But if he's angry enough to manifest at your office, Max, I doubt if he'd cooperate with me." Fear tinged her voice.

"In other words, you're afraid to try." He spat out the words. Immediately, shame flooded him. Yvonne didn't deserve his anger.

"Max, you've seen me possessed by a ghost during a séance," Bebe said. Dread shown from her big brown eyes. "A loa riding you can be a lot worse."

That statement hit him in the gut. "I'm sorry. To both of you." His chest tightened. "I'm scared as hell, but you don't deserve me taking it out on either of you."

"I'll see what I can learn from my end," Yvonne said. "Assuming someone from the New Orleans coven is willing to talk to me."

"Would it be easier if I talked to the high priestess," Bebe offered.

"No," Yvonne said softly. "She'd deny any knowledge of such matters, and if she accidentally admitted something, she would refuse to help you."

"But why? I didn't do anything." The frustration he'd swallowed barreled back up his throat.

"No witch with a lick of sense wants to deal with any of the three Barons if they're angry. And if there's a chance that Davy dies in this mess, Laveau would take it in a heartbeat." Yvonne sounded on the verge of tears.

Max blew out a deep breath. As if he didn't feel like enough of a shit to begin with. It made sense why the heir to Marie Laveau, the famous voodoo queen of New Orleans, wouldn't endanger her people in a feud they had nothing to do with. And why she'd gamble that Sam would save him and condemn Head. Considering everything the bastard had done, the New Orleans Coven would love to rid themselves of the necromancer.

"If you can find anything that would help me, I'd be grateful, Yvonne." He glanced at Bebe. "In the meantime, we'll track down Sam."

Maybe he sounded reassuring. He didn't want to admit his worry out loud. Unless one of them was working a story, he and Sam called each other back within a few minutes, even after her death.

Things had been slow for both them since the summer. She was doing a monthly Las Vegas gossip column as a way of weaning herself from life in Los Angeles. He needed to finish the last of the five-part story on the white slavery ring before he went on paternity leave next week. And Sam was supposed to be his birthing coach backup. So there was absolutely no reason for her not to be answering her damn phone.

And the guilt washed over him again.

But if he didn't find Sam by Baron Samedi's deadline, the choice between his life and David Head's may be moot.

Mortimer leaned back in his chair and stretched. Staci had set up three computers and a coffee maker in the meeting room next door to Sam's office. He, Bill and Lily had split up the workload of trying to find any of Lily's original stand-up material.

Except Bill and Lily kept shooting each other looks over their screens.

Like it took a rocket scientist to figure out they'd banged each other last night.

Mortimer took a sip of his coffee. Cold.

Maybe he was a little jealous. Not that he had a thing for Lily. She was a hot broad, but redheads had always been bad luck for him. Not that he'd look at any other redhead, blonde or brunette either. Talking to Molly this morning had killed any urge to bang any broad but her. That she accepted a date . . .

He pushed away from the table and headed for the coffee maker. Why couldn't tomorrow morning come sooner?

"Whoever said computers were more efficient needs to be taken out in the desert and shot," Bill grumbled. He held up his empty cup as Mortimer passed.

"If I'd known I'd need my show notes a century later, I would have made different estate plans," Lily shot back.

Her anger, fear and hurt tore at Mortimer. He placed the cups on the little counter where the pot sat. He turned and rested a hand on her shoulder. "None of us expected this, Lily. This isn't the world we left when we died."

Wide baby blues stared up at him. "She's my own daughter."

"I know." He patted her shoulder, then turned to pour coffee. "Normally, we'd have assistants to help with this legwork crap."

"Why aren't those damn attorneys of Sam's doing the research?" Bill's glare had nothing to do with his words. His look clearly said, *Keep your hands off my woman.*

Mortimer resisted the urge to dump the hot cup in Bill's lap, but he made a promise to himself to be a better man. One that Molly would be proud to have escort her around town. "Because they can't. Those kids have no idea what to look for. We do. So it's up to us because we've all prepped for a show."

"I can't believe this," Lily murmured.

"What?" Mortimer set her cup in front of her before retrieving his own. He resisted the urge to pat Lily's shoulder again just to get a rise out of Bill.

"I never saw my own daughter as a greedy bitch." Lily shook her head.

"Do you know how much she got UCLA's film school to pay for my papers?"

"Mid-seven figures, I heard," Bill said.

Mortimer sat down and peered at his blank screen. "And how do you know that?" He frowned at the damn machine before he remembered to run a finger over the little plate in front of the keyboard.

"I outlived her, and I didn't have a stroke that fried my brain like you did." Bill shrugged. "It was in all the papers. I told Doris to make sure she got twice as much when I croaked." He looked at the ceiling, a wistful expression on his face. "I wonder what she'd say if she saw me—"

"No!" Lily's sharp expression matched her tone. "You heard what Sam said. No visiting our former family."

Mortimer hid his smirk behind his mug. Nothing like a green-eyed monster exploding out of Lily to confirm she and Bill were sleeping together.

Bill turned to him. "Did you know we were under a death sentence if we tell our families that we've been resurrected?"

"Yeah. Actually, it's anyone from our past." Guilt tweaked his conscience. He was playing a very dangerous game with Molly's life. If she even suspected Mortimer Stern and Walter Kinney were the same person, the vamps wouldn't have a problem icing both him and Molly. He should cancel their coffee date.

Dammit, he didn't want to though. He missed her. He still loved her. And he'd been a fool not to show her the first time around. And if she did figure out his secret, then they'd disappear.

"How'd you find out?" Lily stared at him, her blue eyes wide.

"Because I was smart enough to read the vampire rulebook," he snapped.

Her bottom lip quivered. The tough producer he'd known had only been a sucker for whatever shenanigans her kids pulled, especially Lilianne. Seeing her all emotional like this said exactly how screwed up their lives, or deaths, had become.

With effort, he said gently, "You can't tell her the truth, Red. We need to play this like Sam said."

"How can you handle this?" she whispered.

Bill snorted. "All he has left is his jailbait wife."

Mortimer squeezed his hands into fists. The motion didn't quench the urge to belt Bill in his famous schnozz. "That's no way to talk about Molly."

"Molly?" Bill shook his head and chuckled. "I'm talking about the last one. Miss Nebraska, wasn't she? Blond with tits out to—" He held out his hands to indicate her assets.

"Rhonda. And I don't have any desire to look her up." The problem was he already had researched what his widow had done out of a perverse sense of curiosity. The damn airhead managed to blow all his careful investing in less than two years after his funeral. She worked as a stripper in Los Angeles now and shacked up with his former chauffeur.

"I think I found something," Lily interrupted.

"What?" Mortimer rolled his chair closer to her to see her screen. Bill did the same.

"Ari and I had a storage unit in Reno. The bastard. He knew I'd forgotten about it because he didn't list it in the divorce assets." She clicked a couple of keys. "The contents were sold at an auction six months after he died. Bless my daughter's litigious heart. She tried to get the contents back, and the judge threw the case out."

Bill pushed back, rolled over to his computer and clicked a few keys. "Hot damn! There's still a current address listing for the buyer in Reno."

Lili looked at Mortimer. "Road trip?"

He shook his head. "We fly. Sam's attorneys need this stuff ASAP. You sure there might be something left from the unit that could help?"

She nodded vigorously, curls bobbing. "If there's anything left from our vaudeville and early Hollywood days, it would have been in those boxes."

Satisfaction filled him. A quick flight to Reno and back. He wouldn't miss tonight's show, much less tomorrow morning's date with Molly.

Unfortunately, a quick trip to Reno wasn't enough to get me out of shopping and lunch tomorrow with Ares. I glanced out the cabin window as Mai brought our private jet to a smooth stop at the Augustine private hanger.

I'd been a little surprised when she insisted she fly us herself. Maybe Kunal was afraid to be around me after the marriage proposal from one of his gods. More likely Duncan ordered her to keep an eye on me and the baby zombies.

In her excitement, Lily was the first off the jet, Bill close behind her. Morty waved me past him, and I strode down the steps.

Behind me, he said, "Ladies, first."

"I don't appreciate you staring at my ass," came Mai's cool reply.

"I'm trying to be a gentleman here."

"I have a Glock."

I bit my tongue from laughing hysterically at their byplay. Morty's reputation as a ladies' man survived well past his death. At least, neither Duncan nor I had received complaints from any of the staff, including the two maids he'd boffed.

Maybe his serial seductions should worry me more. With Bill and Lily hooking up, the poor guy must feel like the proverbial third wheel. I ran through potential partners that might make him feel a little less lonely.

Staci's mother-in-law was out, but not because she was divorced or a werecoyote. According to the grapevine, Leslie Warner was carrying on a long-distance affair with Sheriff Wolford from their hometown of Millersburg, Ohio.

The night pit chief Fern was a possibility. A relatively young vampire at one hundred-fifty, she would have a little more in common with Morty. But was it worth taking the chance that she got carried away and bit him? We had no idea what the blood of a resurrected person could do to a vamp. Or worse, Morty would insult her because she was older than him.

There was Anita in accounting. She had a touch of fairy blood in her background. She'd be good for a fuck buddy. Yeah, I'd definitely have to hook those two up when we got back to Vegas.

A goddess of death playing matchmaker. I smiled to myself. I needed to give Tiffany a call. My sister-in-law would find the whole situation hysterical.

My phone buzzed, but the sound was disjointed. I pulled out the device. No obvious problem. The screen showed an incoming call. Max. But that wasn't my brother's normal ringtone.

I thumbed the "Answer" icon. "How's the baby watch?" Static greeted me.

Another glance at the phone before I held it to my ear again. "Max?"

Nothing but more static.

"Everything okay, toots?"

I looked at Morty as we walked toward the waiting limo and shrugged. "Bad connection." I ended the call, and thumbed Max's number. No ringing, no answer, no rolling over to voicemail.

What the hell? He was staying close to home with Tiffany so near her due date. So I tried the next best thing.

Tiffany answered on the first ring of their home line. "Hey, Sam."

"Everything okay?"

"Other than I look like a beached humpback, it's fucking peachy." Crunching filled my ear.

"What are you doing?"

"Eating popcorn while binging on Buffy." More crunching. "There's not too much else I can do thanks to your fiancé."

I smiled at her attitude. She'd been bitching since the injuries she sustained at her wedding. The ones where David Head's fresh-from-the-grave zombies killed and mutilated a number of her wedding guests. She and my unborn niece were fucking lucky. "Uh-uh. You can't blame it all on Duncan. Alex is your boss now."

"Right. Like the asshole's not going to do exactly what his maker wants."

I swear I heard Tiffany's eyes rolling around in her head. "I just wanted to check on you. I got a call from Max, but there was a bunch of static on the line. When I tried to call him back, I got nothing."

The crunching stopped. "He wants to get that last piece done before he goes on family leave Friday. He probably turned his phone off when the call didn't go through so you wouldn't interrupt him. You know how he gets when you break his train of thought." Here she was, counting down to her due date, and she was trying to reassure me.

"Yeah." I climbed into the back of the limo. "I guess part of me was hoping I'd be an aunt before midnight."

"Hey, don't push it. I need all the sleep I can get before she makes her debut." The crunching started again.

"Tell Max to give me a buzz when he gets home." Next to me, Morty gave Mai the address of the collector we were meeting. Not only did she insist on flying, she demanded to escort us around Reno. Fighting with Mai wasn't worth her narcing on me to Duncan about not having adequate protection.

I thought Tiffany said good-bye before the signal went dead, but it was hard to tell amid all the eating noise. Maybe Tiffany had been infected by one of my nanites accidentally.

The thought disappeared as soon as the neuron finished firing. No, Bebe had been keeping a very close eye on the pregnancy after the beating Tiffany suffered at her first wedding. We'd all been terrified she might lose the baby despite the witches' healing skills.

Lily reached over and put her hand on my knee. "Everything all right at home?"

"Yeah, Tiffany's fine. Probably interference from the airport electronics." Except my sixth sense said something else was going on, and I'd learned to trust that instinct. The last time I hadn't paid close attention, a fairy assassin tried to kill Anne and me in Ohio over the summer.

A glance at the time said my brother might still be at the office. I scrolled through my contact list and thumbed the main number for the *Times*. When the receptionist answered, I said, "This is Sam Ridgeway, Max Howell's sister. Is he still there?"

"No, ma'am. He left a little after noon. Right after a friend of yours stopped by."

"A friend of mine?" The only mutual friend of ours outside of the *Scoop* had been murdered by the same mad scientists who'd experimented on me. "Did you get a name?"

"No, but Max had an awfully nice Rolex after your friend left."

A Rolex? While Max wasn't poor by any means, Tiffany was the one with the trust fund. "You sure it wasn't a delivery from his wife?"

"No, Ms. Ridgeway. The man definitely said he was your friend."

"Can you describe him?"

"Ummm . . . .no, I can't. That's funny." Paper shuffled in the background, then came the sound of keys clicking on a keyboard. "I'm sure he gave me his name, but the guest register is blank.

"Did Max say where he was going when he left?"

"No, ma'am. He just said he had a personal errand to run."

The queasy feeling grew in my stomach while I politely said goodbye. Automatically, I hit Alex's number.

"How's my favorite yellow journalist?"

If I wasn't in love with his maker, Alex Stanton could make my panties melt, for which Phil would definitely shove an entire case of grenades down my throat for even thinking that about her boyfriend.

"I've got a problem, and you can't tell Tiffany."

Immediately, he turned chief enforcer serious. "What's going on that Mai can't handle?"

"Mai's with me. It's Max I'm worried about." I quickly ran through the problem with my phone as well as my conversations with Tiffany and the *Times*'s receptionist.

"It could just be bad timing," Alex offered.

"After everything that's happened with your coven over the last three years, do you really believe that?"

"It's your coven, too." He chuckled. "And no. I was hoping to keep you from going off half-cocked until I had a chance to check into the matter."

"Please make sure he's okay." I tapped the "End Call" icon after his affirmation. The hairs on the back of my neck rose at the feeling of someone staring at me.

Mai's eyes met mine for an instant before her attention returned to the freeway. "Do we need to head to Los Angeles?"

"Let's get through this meeting first." I thumbed the texting icon on my phone. "Besides, it's probably nothing."

The fact that Mai remained silent instead of scoffing at my growing unease said more than I cared. Instead of pushing her, I typed out my text to Max.

Where the hell r u? Call me now!

Chapter 8

Max jumped when Caesar and Bebe's house phone rang. He resisted the urge to snatch up the old-fashioned receiver and waited for her to answer. Instead, he crossed his fingers. *Please let Yvonne have some good news.*

The witch sat aside the spell book she'd been paging through and picked up the receiver. Her initial smile when she checked the caller ID immediately turned into a frown. She glanced at him. "He's right here." A pause. "He's been trying to call her since noon." Another pause, and she huffed in exasperation. "Let me put you on speaker."

"Max, don't fucking disappear like that!" Alex's irritation emphasized his Texas drawl. "When you give Sam a heart attack, she gives me a crapload of shit in return."

Max exchanged looks with Bebe. Even she appeared puzzled.

"What the hell are you talking about?" he asked.

"Who's this visitor at the paper today who gave you a Rolex? Because if I have to cover your ass with your wife as well as your sister, I'm going to be mighty ticked."

Had the coven resorted to bugging him? "How did you—"

"Because your sister was a gahdamned reporter, too, numbnuts!" Alex roared through the speaker. In a calmer voice, he added, "There's no record of your visitor at the *Times*, and the receptionist couldn't describe him, which means he was probably a supernatural. Which in turn, makes me as the Augustine chief enforcer worried as hell."

"For the record," Max snapped. "I've been trying to call Sam all day. Even if she wasn't picking up the call, the phone wouldn't go to voice mail."

"That's what she said was happening to her phone when she called you." Alex sounded as confused as Max felt. "Which means you still should have called me when weird shit happens."

"You're right." Max glanced at Bebe. "My visitor was Baron Samedi."

A string of curses flew out of the receiver. Alex paused long enough to say, "Didn't we have enough of that voodoo shit at your first wedding?"

Max rubbed his chin stubble. Even blonds got five o'clock shadow. It just wasn't as noticeable. And if he continued thinking about mundane things, it would keep the panic in his gut at bay. "He says Sam has something of his father's. Bebe's already called Yvonne Head. She thinks it has something to do with the binding Sam put on Head's brother. Sam has until midnight tomorrow."

"And?" Alex prompted.

"He's the loa that guards the door between the living and dead," Max said. Bebe may not let him look at her books. It didn't mean he couldn't hit the internet with his phone. "If she doesn't give whatever it is back, I'm guessing he'll take my soul."

"You're guessing?" Alex's incredulousness carried across the connection. "Did he say that?"

"No," Max admitted. "But isn't that how these hostage things work?"

"Hostage? Who the hell is a hostage?"

Bebe quickly explained about the Rolex and her efforts in getting it off him. Just thinking about the damn thing made his skin itch. He scratched at his left wrist, only for the witch to reach across the desk and slap his hand.

"All right," Alex finally said. "Lemme call Sam back, and we'll see about getting this straightened out."

"Alex, please—"

"I know, I know. Don't tell Tiffany."

While Mai pulled the limo to a smooth stop, I examined the place through the vehicle's tinted windows. The layout wasn't anything like I expected for some big-time collector. Behind the sun-whitened stucco building, labeled "Office" in blood-red paint, sat four equally sun-whitened stucco buildings. Dust-covered windows stared at us as we climbed out of the vehicle.

Despite the setting sun, the heat from the baked concrete penetrated the soles of my sensible two-inch heels. I headed for the door, baby zombies and Mai in tow. When I pushed open the door to the office, the smell of fresh-baked brownies greeted me.

A thirty-something man leaned back in a chair. His feet on the desk were covered by blinding white athletic shoes. A Montreal Canadiens jersey and jeans dulled the glow from the footwear leather. A backwards baseball cap completed the ensemble. His short dark beard caught the crumbs from the brownie he munched on while his sleepy brown eyes swept over us.

"Hi." I turned on my most charming smile. "I'm Sam Ridgeway. I have an appointment with Robert Kirby."

The man slowly nodded before he stuffed more brownie into his mouth. I took a deep breath. There was definitely a certain ingredient in the chocolatey goodness, one of the few things still illegal in Nevada.

"It's about the items he found in the Lily Bell-Aristotle Milonas storage unit."

He nodded again.

My temper started to fray. I was already stressed between the stupid marriage proposals, my pouting fiancé, and the lawsuit. Not to mention, I hadn't had this much trouble talking to a Native American water spirit last summer, and he had the excuse of not knowing much English.

Etiquette will open doors for a lady that cannot be forced by brute strength, Samantha. I hated that both my mother and my fiancé were right.

I tried smiling again. "Look, could you please get Mr. Kirby?"

He chewed and swallowed the last of his brownie before he said, "I'm Kirby."

"Aren't you a little young for a vaudeville fan?"

One of his dark brown eyebrows rose and disappeared under the rim of his baseball cap.

Lily elbowed me aside. "Mr. Kirby, this is very important to me. I've been sued by a member of Lily Bell's family."

He ignored her statement. "Plastic surgery?" His perusal of her was a little more appreciative.

Lily's mouth scrunched in confusion, a signature expression from her sitcom. "I beg your pardon?"

He rubbed his beard, sending brownie crumbs cascading over the giant "C" on his chest. "Did you pay to look like Lily Bell?"

Lily shook her head. "No. Just lucky with the genes. And I know a good make-up artist."

He continued to stare at her. "Why do you need the stuff I bought at the auction?"

I opened my mouth, but Morty yanked me away from Lily and Kirby. I didn't need telepathy to know the slight inclination of his head said to let Lily handle this.

The comedienne sucked in a deep breath. "Like I said, a member of her family has sued me, saying I'm desecrating her memory. The problem is I'm staying faithful to her original act, which is what the family member objects to."

Kirby grinned. "You mean the fact that Lily was raunchier than Betty White?"

"Betty White learned at Lily Bell's knee." She grinned back.

"I like a woman who knows her entertainment history." He leaned forward. "But there's no recordings of Lily Bell in those days."

"There was," she said.

Panic exploded in my stomach. Now was not the time to game this guy. I started to say something, but Morty ground his heel into my little toe and broke it. I bit my tongue to keep from crying out, or whacking him upside the head. Which would probably crush his skull. My fingernails dug into my palms while the nanites fixed my abused appendage.

"My grandfather used to be in film," she continued. "He had a couple of reels of her act when she did the New York supper club circuit. He showed them to me when I was a little girl." She smiled wistfully. "So many times I had them memorized and I could do the bits along with her."

No longer pretending to be sleepy, Kirby's brown eyes glittered. "Now, those I'd be interested in making an offer on."

A sad look filled her face. "I wish I had them, too, but—" She shrugged. "Cellulose nitrate film stored in an attic. By the time I found them after his death, they were a total loss."

Kirby slapped his forehead. "Oh, man, what a waste!"

I brushed Lily's surface thoughts. Cottony clean. She was telling the truth. The photographer in me wanted to cry. So many early movies were lost forever because of the tendency of that type of film to rapidly degrade if it wasn't kept refrigerated.

Lily's voice hitched. "L-like I said, I had seen those films so many times I had her two sets memorized." She reached out and grasped Kirby's hands. "I'm hoping, praying, that some of m—" She caught herself. "Lily's notes were in that storage unit. I'm not asking to keep anything. I just need something to prove to the court I'm honoring her work."

He winked at her. "Let me show you something." He released Lily, rose, and snatched one set of keys off a series of hooks embedded in the wall above the desk. After he circled around the metal monstrosity, he held out his elbow, which Lily took with a giggle.

Waves of ammonia-scented jealousy rolled off Bill as we trooped out the door after them. Kirby carefully locked the office before leading us to the nearest building.

This one had more than a simple key lock. The man had a thumbprint and a retinal scanner installed as well.

"Isn't that overkill for the junk you find in storage units?" I muttered.

He glared at me. "One woman's junk is another man's treasure."

Instead of the garage or warehouse I expected, we entered what looked like a laboratory clean room. A shiver ran through me at the antiseptic smell. The nightmares of my imprisonment and torture at Mallory Labs may have been fewer and farther between lately, but I had a feeling they'd be returning tonight.

"If you don't mind, put on the anti-static booties and the rubber gloves." Kirby pointed to a series of boxes on shelves along the wall. "They're non-latex in case any of you are allergic."

I grabbed a pair of the footies. "We don't warrant a clean suit?"

He eyed the extra-large pair of booties I'd selected. "No, Bigfoot. And if you didn't already have your hair in a ponytail though, I'd make you wear a hairnet."

Mai sidled up to me and grabbed a pair of gloves. "Sam, shut up, and let her handle this," she whispered. "This is her career on the line, not yours."

Nothing like your babysitter pointing out you're an idiot. The problem was Mai was right. My ego wanted to be in charge, making things worse in the process. Lily had run her own film and television studio back in her day, the first woman to do so in the history of Hollywood. She knew how to finagle deals with the major power brokers of the old system.

I had always admired her business brilliance. I could learn so much from her. Yet, guilt at accidentally bringing her back to life led to a gigantic protective streak.

Once Kirby was satisfied we were adequately covered, he punched a code into the opposing door. Pneumatics hissed, and the door swung open. He led us into another room. My skin immediately puckered at the frigid air. The low ceiling threatened to induce claustrophobia.

"How much does it take to cool this place?" Bill asked.

Kirby named a figure, and Morty whistled between his teeth. "That's a pretty penny."

"Yeah, but it's worth it to preserve history." He glanced back at us as he escorted Lily past the huge filing cabinets lining the walls. "By the way, I caught your acts in Vegas a couple of weeks ago. Incredible job, man."

The compliment made Morty beam. "Thank you, Mr. Kirby."

"Call me Bob." He stopped before the third door. This one had a voice-print lock. Even the vampires' security measures paled in comparison.

I grinned at my own joke, which resulted in everyone giving me odd looks.

As we followed Kirby into his sanctum, I brushed Mai's arm. *Did I accidentally transmit again?*

"No," she whispered. "You just look creepy as hell when you smile for no reason. As in eating babies creepy."

Guess I was one death goddess who needed to keep a neutral expression at all times. With my luck, everyone would accuse me of eating babies once my niece was born.

The air in this room wasn't as cold as the last. A couple of long tables dominated the middle of the area while a multitude of industrial steel shelves lined the walls. Kirby headed to his right where a cardboard sign proclaimed "Bell/Milonas Estate" in bold red letters.

"Here's paperwork and small items." He looked at Lily. "Furniture and house stuff is in the next building. Any reason you need to see those?"

My fingers curled, and my nails dug into my palms. He was testing her, but she shook her mop of red curls. "Only out of curiosity."

Kirby nodded, satisfied with Lily's answer. "I've only done an initial sort through the contents. Wedding memorabilia is the top shelf. Personal correspondence is the second shelf. Business related items are on the bottom two." He tapped the third shelf. "I suggest we start with this one since it has the obvious vaudeville items."

We each grabbed a relatively new banker's box, spread out, and set them on the tables behind us. As I flipped off the lid, I caught a whiff of chemicals. "What happened to the original boxes?"

"Silverfish ate 'em." An evil grin lit Kirby's face. "I wouldn't sniff inside there. I had to fumigate the contents."

"Great," I muttered. Nothing like creepy, crawly bugs to worry about, even if neither the silverfish or the insecticide would do a thing to me, and I wore latex gloves. Yellowing paper greeted me. At least, the gloves gave me a better grip.

There were play bills from the Catskills. Tickets to a boat ride at Niagara Falls. Programs from Broadway shows, listing Lily as part of the dance chorus.

I smiled when I saw a couple of one-page contracts. They were so easy to read compared to the ones Colin and I poured through for my trio's Vegas show. Lily's pay gave me a start, a miniscule amount as opposed to Ari's, even considering it was the middle of the Depression.

Carefully laying the paperwork aside, I continued digging. A packet of photos, their negatives crumbling with age. Lily's grandchildren would probably love to see these. I know how much I loved listening to my grandmother's stories of West Virginia back in the day. A pity that Lilianne had turned into a money-grubbing bitch.

What looked like a couple of diaries came into view. I carefully paged through the one with a red leather cover.

And quickly laid it aside. There were things about my heroine's past

I didn't need to know, much less wanted to know. Not that I faulted Lily for acting like a regular twenty-year-old, but the mom she played on TV was the closest I had to a normal middle-class upbringing.

My own mother was too busy trying to climb the Beverly Hills social register to pay much attention to me. She only trotted me out when it suited her purposes. That didn't last long since I knew her game from an early age and deliberately sabotaged her efforts.

I reached for the next diary, this one in royal blue leather. Is that why Lilianne had such a love/hate relationship with her mother? Was she trying to shape Lily's image into the mother she wanted, instead of the painful reality?

Flipping open the first page, I prayed this volume didn't have any sexual exploits. Familiarity rattled my brain. There on the paper in Lily's neat script was a variation of one of the jokes she'd told last night on stage. "I found it!"

Lily's head rose. Recognition flared in her eyes. "That's my—" She coughed to cover her slip. "I heard she kept notes in her diary. I didn't think they still existed."

"Here." I handed her the diary. From the way her hand shook, we'd hit the jackpot.

"Th-this is it." The paper rattled when her index finger rapidly flipped through it. "I can't believe it. I thought—"

I felt so bad for her. She was freaking out and couldn't say anything in front a Normal that would potentially incriminate her.

Incriminate me.

At least she had listened to my pre-breakfast lecture about not revealing the truth about herself.

Kirby leaned over her shoulder, mouthing the words he read. He scratched his beard. "Didn't realize that was in there." He nudged Lily's arm with his elbow. "Personally, I like your version of the routine better."

I sucked in a deep breath. "Mr. Kirby, would you be willing to sign an affidavit concerning the diary and how it came into your possession? And could our attorney have it until the trial is over? I'd be happy to pay you."

He watched me for a long moment. I was sure he was about to say no when he said, "Who's the family member suing you guys?"

I flicked my attention to Lily, and she gave me the briefest of nods. "Her daughter Lilianne Milonas Costas."

"That bitch?" An evil grin spread across his face. "Sweetheart, I'll let you have whatever you need. And if you need a character witness to show what a two-faced skank she is, your attorney just needs to tell me when and where."

Chapter 9

Sitting in a kitchen chair, Max jumped when his phone buzzed. Bebe glared at him and smacked his left hand before she returned to her task. She'd been trying to remove the watch with different potions for the last three hours. Her work gave them both something to do while waiting for either Sam or Yvonne to return their calls.

He glared right back and reached for his phone. Unfortunately, the caller ID said "Tiffany," not "Sam." He grimaced at the time displayed on the device. His wife would be expecting him home soon.

Breathing through his mouth while talking to Tiffany wasn't practical. He leaned as far away from the noxious green gel Bebe was currently spreading on the cursed watch and his wrist before he thumbed the "Answer" icon.

"Hey, babe! What's up?"

"Hey, sweetie!" A thick slurping sound came from the receiver, followed by a belch.

Max wanted to cradle his head in his hands, but he didn't have any palms available. Instead, he squeezed his eyes shut. "Please tell me you didn't go to Starbucks."

Bebe rolled her eyes, dipped her small paint brush into the gel, and continued coating his skin.

"Lighten up. It's a caffeine-free Frappuccino. With your daughter's latest gymnastics, I'm not about to give her any coffee. Did you get your story done?"

"Ummm . . ." He glanced at Bebe who shrugged. "Not yet. There was an emergency meeting at the paper this morning."

"Lemme guess. Donald Trump's hair filed for emancipation."

"No."

He must have sounded too serious because she gasped. "Lay-offs? Sweetie, you know we'll be okay. My trust fund—"

"No, babe. Nothing like that." He needed to come up with an excuse, but dammit, he'd never lied to Tiffany. Ever. There wasn't a doubt in his mind that she would literally kill him if he ever did. "There's a problem with one of my sources. I'm trying to straighten it out before the paper goes to print tonight."

"Oh." She was silent for a long moment. Had his lie already been discovered? Under Alex's tutelage, she'd learned to hack pretty much any computer on the planet. Was she looking at his account at work even as they spoke? "I guess that means you won't be home for dinner, huh?"

"I'll be pretty late so don't wait for me to eat." He almost suggested she order from her favorite Mexican place, but stopped himself in time. Cajoling her would be a sure tip-off something was wrong.

"I was just, sorta, hoping we'd have dinner together tonight."

He detected a slight sniff. Great. His kickass, kill-anything-that-moves wife was beset with pregnancy hormones, and he couldn't go home and hold her. At least, not yet.

"So was I. Let me get this story done, and I'll be home and cuddle all you want for the next twelve weeks."

Bebe looked up from her work, eyes wide in disbelief.

Max ignored the doctor. He was the only one who ever saw Tiffany's softer side, and he wanted to keep that to himself.

Another sniff over the receiver. "Okay. By the way, Sam's been trying to reach you."

He chuckled. "Yeah, I've heard. She panicked and called Alex, who called me. I think my baby sister accidentally zapped her personal cell phone again and doesn't want to admit it."

Tiffany sighed. "Won't be the last either until she gets a grip on her powers. Duncan probably got on her case about wasting money."

He chuckled. "Hey, I'm staying out of any vampire/goddess financial issues."

She laughed. "Even I'm not that crazy."

Tiffany didn't sound on the edge of tears anymore. Maybe it was safe to sign off. "Let me get this thing in front of me done, and I'll be home as soon as I can." Which wasn't a lie. Exactly. "I love you, babe."

She giggled. "I know." Their ritual sign-off from a movie made before either of them were born was reassuring. His phoned beeped, signaling Tiffany had ended the call.

"Is she okay?" Bebe asked. She tried inserting a nail file between the watch and his skin. No luck.

"Yeah." He winced at a particular painful poke of the sharp steel. "But I won't be."

Steady brown eyes regarded him. "You know we'll do everything to protect you from Baron Samedi."

A wry grin tilted Max's mouth. "I know. It's what the enforcer on maternity leave will do when she finds out I lied to her that really worries me."

Mortimer checked his phone for the umpteenth time. Still no additional text from Molly, but what exactly was he expecting? For her to change her mind about coming to the show tonight?

Bill peeked over their seats at the ladies, who sat at the table in the back of the jet. Mortimer turned and checked as well. Lily poured over her old diary while Sam tapped notes into her own phone. It looked like they had more than enough material from Lily's journal to fight Lilianne's lawsuit.

"Hot date tonight?" Bill nudged Mortimer with his elbow.

"No." He pressed the button that turned off the phone's screen and slid it into his jacket pocket.

Bill gave him a knowing smile. "Then why do you keep checking for messages?" The Nose was too smart for his own good. And he'd bring the subject up in front of Sam, which was the last thing Mortimer needed. Time to fess up.

"I'm meeting a lady for coffee tomorrow."

Bill's right eyebrow rose. "You're that worried she's going to bail on you?"

"A little, yeah."

Bill shook his head. "You got it bad, my friend."

That comment snapped Mortimer's last nerve. "Not all of us have a fellow zombie to play hanky-panky with. Unless you're planning to share."

Bill's cheeks and nose flared brilliant red, and Mortimer immediately regretted his words. He checked the ladies again, but they were thoroughly engrossed in the diary's contents.

"Sorry, Bill. I was outta line."

"Damn straight, you were." His expression softened a bit. "We didn't mean to make you feel like a third wheel. Things sort of . . . happened between Red and me." His gaze dropped to his lap.

Mortimer guessed what Bill was feeling. Lily's widower George had passed a couple of years after her. It wasn't like she was married anymore, but his and Bill's widows were both still alive. Not that he gave a shit about Rhonda anymore. Bill, on the other hand, had loved his Doris with all his heart despite what the bottom feeders said about him. You just didn't stay with a broad for nearly seventy-five years if you didn't.

Mortimer leaned closer to his friend. "You do know you can't contact Doris, right?"

Bill met his eyes again. "You do know there's a death sentence on us if we contact anyone from our pasts?"

Mortimer nodded. "Yeah, because we had funerals. I told you I read the damn vampire rules. Sam checked. They aren't going to hold this stupid lawsuit against us. We didn't initiate it, and Lilianne doesn't have a clue she's suing her mother. If you visit Doris though, you're doing the initiating."

Bill nodded. "I know. It's more wishful thinking than anything else." He glanced back at the ladies before returning his attention to their conversation. "I'm more worried about Lily contacting her kids. Seeing Lilianne in person shook her. Shook her bad, Morty."

"You don't think she'd do something that stupid?" he whispered.

"Yeah, I am." Bill stared at the glass in his hand. "And I'm more afraid of that than me giving in to seeing Doris." Guilt that had nothing to do with Red weighted his voice, and he took a gulp of his drink.

Mortimer looked hard at his old friend. Something in his tone didn't sit right. "Bill, she's nearly a century old."

Another gulp of vodka from the alcohol-only smell. "She'll be one hundred and one on November 1st. If I went to the rest home, she wouldn't know me with the Alzheimer's, but I'd like to see her one last time."

Mortimer wished he had a stogie to light. Could he really tell Bill not to be stupid when he planned to meet Molly for coffee tomorrow?

He checked Sam again. Nope, she was still engrossed in Lily's old diary. "Look, you know what the penalty is if you do," he whispered.

Bill's chin jutted as far as his nose. "How would they find out?"

"They read minds," Mortimer hissed.

Bill smirked. "Not all the time. Sometimes, they rely on gossip just like us old-fashioned humans."

His friend's smart-ass comment sealed the deal. He couldn't ever tell anyone about Molly, not even Bill and Lily. "Just be careful if you decide to be stupid."

He pressed the button and reclined his chair. If he went through with his coffee date tomorrow, he couldn't stay in Vegas. All he needed was a plan on how to lay his hands on a huge wad of cash. Then he and Molly could head for Mexico and disappear.

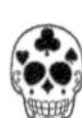

With my phone acting stupid, I used the jet's air-to-ground service to relay our find to Colin. He sounded practically giddy about Kirby's offer to authenticate the diary and his character reference, or assassination in this case, for Lilianne Costas.

Lily joined the men near the cabin's wet bar, her scent a mix of banana happiness at the excitement of old memories and stale cracker/rancid butter sorrow at having to take on her daughter in court. Part of me wanted to slam Lilianne into a wall for dragging Lily through all this bullshit. But I couldn't tell the bitch she was hurting her very own mother.

Uncertainty at my next call sent a nervous trill through my cast-iron zombie goddess stomach. I punched the number on the airphone anyway. I didn't like the way Duncan and I had left things last night, and I knew I'd used the lawsuit as a way of ignoring our issues today.

One ring. Two rings. A soft click, then a feminine voice said, "Karnak Casino and Hotel. Duncan St. James's office."

The bastard had declined my call to his cell phone, and it had forwarded it to his personal assistant.

"Uh, hey, Trudy. It's Sam Ridgeway. Is Duncan in a meeting?" He'd better be talking to Caesar or one of the other supernatural leaders.

There was no missing the hesitation in her voice. She was pretty damn young for a vampire, having been Turned in the '70's. I couldn't blame her for not wanting to cross an older member of the coven, especially someone as highly ranked as Duncan.

"He's . . . unavailable at the moment, Ms. Ridgeway."

Yep, he was dodging my call.

It took a hell of a lot for me to swallow my pride and make any kind of conciliatory gesture. After all this time—

Reality punched me hard. We'd only met nine months ago. A few days before I died and got turned into a freak.

Yet, Max and Tiffany met only couple of days after I died, had fallen madly in lust, and were expecting their first baby. Not to mention getting married along the way. The thing I hated—they were making their situation work.

So what was the difference between us? Other than the whole live people versus creatures of the night thing.

Trudy cleared her throat, interrupting my wallowing. "Would you like me to take a message, Ms. Ridgeway?"

"Um, please tell him our Reno trip was successful, and I'll see him at home tonight."

From her sigh of relief, I'd put enough positivity into my attitude. "Absolutely, Ms. Ridgeway. Have a safe trip home!"

Therein lay the problem. I stared at the gold band capped with a solitaire diamond on my left hand. After nearly four months, living with Duncan in Las Vegas still didn't feel like home. And I didn't know if it ever would.

Chapter 10

Max sat in his Volvo in his Tarzana home's driveway as the engine ticked from cooling. The only light that glowed was the antique lamp Grandma Neel had sent as a wedding present. It sat on a stand in the center of the living room picture window. It meant Tiffany was lounging in their bed, watching TV and waiting on him.

And leaving crumbs of God knew what on the sheets.

He mentally slapped himself for going there. His wife was carrying his first child. It was a miracle Tiffany hadn't miscarried after getting knocked around by zombies during their first attempt at a wedding. Her enforced maternity leave due to some complications hadn't helped her normal enraged-wolverine mood.

Neither would him being this late.

By the time Bebe was done experimenting, Caesar, Alex, and half the Augustine Coven enforcers knew about his little encounter with Baron Samedi. They still hadn't heard from Yvonne, and Bebe had started calling her contacts with other witch covens. When no immediate answers came, Caesar ordered Max to go home.

And to top it off, he still hadn't finished his story for the paper.

Metal clinked against the handle as he pushed the car door. Bebe had managed to lay a glamour over the watch, so Tiffany wouldn't see it and ask questions. It was still firmly attached to his wrist though. He prayed he wouldn't do anything stupid to shatter the illusion. Otherwise, his wife wouldn't stop until she beat the truth out of him.

Just act cool. Cuddle. Finish the story after she falls asleep.

His arm tingled from the witch wards reacting to the watch when he entered the front door. The sensation was worse than the smell of fresh garlic in the planters around the house. He punched in the security code and reset the conventional alarms before he sauntered back to the bedroom.

Only dark hair poked above the covers. He peeled back the comforter to find Tiffany nibbling on hazelnut pirouettes with her tablet in her free hand and watching—

He closed his eyes and shook his head. "Honey, I love you, but are you sure watching *Saw* movies is good for the baby?"

She tapped the pause icon with the end of her cookie before she popped it into her mouth. "You won't let me watch them after she's born," she mumbled as she chewed.

He tried to ignore the spray of crumbs. "I said please don't watch them while she's awake."

She finished chewing and swallowed. "Did you get the crap about your source straightened out?"

Max managed to nod. "Yeah, but I still have a little work to finish up."

"Did you talk to Sam?" She pulled another pirouette out of the canister and handed the treat to him.

"No." He crossed to his side of the bed and curled around Tiffany. "Apparently, she's on a plane with her baby zombies and won't be back until later tonight. I left a message with her assistant."

He took a bite of cookie. Contemplating not getting a hold of his sister before midnight tomorrow left a queasy feeling in his stomach. The overly sweet filling in the cookie didn't help. Maybe he should have told Staci it was an emergency.

Neither of them said anything as they munched on their pirouettes. There was a ton of things that still needed to be done before the baby arrived, but he wanted to enjoy this moment.

In case, it was his last.

Max gently plucked the tablet from her hand, sat up and laid it on his nightstand. He turned back just as Tiffany tried to hand him the cookie canister. It hit his left wrist. A metallic ring filled their cozy space.

"What the hell?" Tiffany knocked the canister against his wrist twice more. She couldn't miss how the aluminum didn't actually touch his skin, much less the sound. She leaned over and sniffed his arm.

When she rose, her dark brown eyes were narrowed. "Maxwell Theodore Howell, what the fuck is going on?"

Chapter 11

I finished my second call with my attorney as Mai dropped the men off at The Vegas Grand for the first show of the evening. Without a word, she swung the SUV toward the Karnak.

Beside me, Lily was quiet as well, staring out the passenger window. The glow of LED lights were rapidly replacing the Strip's traditional neon bulbs, but that wasn't why Lily's face scrunched with a mix of anger and resignation. It didn't take me three guesses about the cause.

"Colin was pretty damn positive the evidence we found will boost your defense," I said.

"I know." She swiped at an escaping tear. "It's . . . I . . . being on stage . . ."

"You found your passion again," I said softly.

"I even have a new routine almost ready for the New Year's Eve show."

In a way, I was a little envious. I'd been searching for my passion for nearly twenty-seven years, and only found a talent for pissing off people. Telling Lily that wasn't going to help her.

I reached for her hand and squeezed it. "Finish it. Have it ready on time. I'm sure we'll get this resolved before then." *Even if I have to mess with Lilianne's memory to do it.*

My body stiffened, and I released her hand. Where had that thought come from?

I was usually on the "don't mindfuck people" bandwagon. Had Ares's little talk this afternoon gotten to me more than I realized? The damn nanites didn't make me better than anyone else.

Just different.

Right?

"Sam, you okay?"

I glanced up at Mai. Concern filled her brown eyes. Her words pulled Lily out of her funk to look at me, too.

"Yeah. Just realized it's been a while since I've eaten." On cue, my stomach growled.

Mai reached for something in the front seat. Cardboard and plastic rattled. "Here." She passed two granola bars over her shoulder. "This should tide you over for the last couple of blocks."

I took the bars, grateful that she accepted my excuse. "Thanks."

She was already on the phone, calling to order ahead for me. I'd have a six-course meal waiting in the penthouse when I arrived.

I pulled out my phone to check my calendar and e-mail while I munched on oats and nuts. Tomorrow, I only had the shopping trip with Ares. Maybe I should stop by and talk to Colin directly about the case while I was in Los Angeles. But when I clicked on my e-mail, nothing happened.

I checked the signal. The full five bars shone. Incoming texts were blank as well. The oats went to war with the nuts over who exited first.

Actually, I hadn't heard from Alex or Max either. I tried my brother's cell first. Nothing, just like in Reno. I tried his home number. Again, nothing. I tried to ignore the gyrating granola chunks in my gut and punched the number for Alex's cell.

The same flaky screech I'd gotten when I tried Max a few hours ago clawed at my ear drum. What the hell was going on? Every time I'd blown the circuits of my old phones, they'd crashed immediately. There wasn't any of this gradual "I can't call anyone" shit.

I hit the speed dial for Mai's phone. Immediate old-fashioned ringing came from the front seat. She was the only person I knew, besides Caesar and Duncan, who didn't bother to program ring tones for various people.

She glanced at her phone in its cradle on the dash, then back at me in the rear of the SUV, annoyance squinching a line in her immaculate forehead. "What are you doing? I'm right here."

"I know," I shot back. "Just testing my phone. I can't seem to place a call outside of Las Vegas."

"Did you blow the electronic—"

"No," I snapped. "This time isn't my fault."

"Sam . . ." Lily wrapped her arm around me, like she had in the hospital months ago when I was having trouble with out-of-control feeding rampages thanks to the zombie attacks. She'd been strictly professional with me since then. Was that what she needed? A surrogate daughter to keep her mind off of Lilianne?

"I'm fine," I muttered. Funny how someone else's mom wanted me when my own could barely stand me.

"Do you want to use my phone?" Lily asked.

I sighed. "No, I'll get another one from Staci."

But then, I'd have to hear another lecture from Duncan about my spending. Dammit! None of this was my fault. I was stumbling through this new world I'd been dropped into like a blind person who didn't know any of the rules.

After Mai dropped us at the private entrance, I was so stuck in my thoughts I rode the elevator up to the penthouse instead of stopping by my office. Since I was already up here, I decided to take a shower. After digging through Kirby's boxes, I needed one despite his obvious efforts at keeping his warehouses as immaculate as possible.

Except the elevator doors opened to Duncan wearing a hole in the living room carpet by pacing. The scent of sandalwood coupled with brimstone overwhelmed me. What was pissing him off this time? Had Mai already narced on me about my misbehaving phone?

The second he caught sight of me, the emerald glow of his eyes shifted to neon green. "Did you think I would not smell *his* odor all over *our* home?"

If Duncan hadn't agreed to managing Las Vegas after Kensai and Jamal's deaths, long before Ares decided to take up residence on Earth, it would be easy to assume it was only jealousy causing his tantrum.

But *our* home? It didn't feel like *our* home, but I didn't want to argue with him. Not after the day I had, which started with him not coming to bed. "It was the safest place I could think of for me to question Ares."

"Question him about what?"

Why the hell was I getting the third degree? "Is this about the damn potted rose he sent me? Because I didn't solicit anything from anyone."

"Yet, you felt comfortable enough inviting someone you know is attracted to you into our penthouse."

"You're acting like a jealous freak, you know that?"

"Then why did you not tell me of his visit before he came?" The temperature of Duncan's tone dropped to arctic levels.

"Because *you* didn't bother to come home last night." His mouth opened and a slash of my hand halted the excuse I knew was coming. "And don't bother using me not calling you before hand as an excuse because you shunted me to your fucking secretary when I *did* call. Just like I knew you would."

"You did not call until you were on your way back from Reno."

I threw up my hands. "Where the hell is all of this coming from? I already had Phil threaten me if I touched her father, and I haven't done anything. We talked. That's it."

"Let me guess—" He sneered. He actually sneered at me. "Your discussion was far beyond us mere mortals."

My vision grew blurry, but I'd be damned if I would cry in front of him over something this stupid. "I'm here with you. If you can't get that, I can't help you."

The muscle in his jaw twitched. "For how long?"

I cocked my head. "You seriously didn't just say that."

"Then why are you entertaining men alone?"

"In case you haven't noticed, women can own property and vote these days. It means I can talk to whoever I damn well please without your permission!" The floor beneath my feet shivered, and the crack in the drywall from this morning grew longer.

Duncan didn't seem to notice either thing though. "I cannot converse with you when you are acting this way." He strode past me, heading for the stairwell door once again.

I bit my tongue to keep from asking how I was acting. I knew all too well his opinions on women's behavior. If I didn't agree with whatever stupid thing entered his head, I was being an illogical female. He didn't treat Phil, Bebe or Anne like this, but me or Tiffany? Oh, hell, yeah. He simply couldn't transform his sixteenth century thinking into the twenty-first century version when it came to women he considered family. It was a wonder his sister Margaret hadn't staked him when she had the chance.

The slam behind him elicited a trickle of dust from the fissure in the kitchenette ceiling.

I waited a minute. Two. Three. With a sinking sensation in my gut, I realized he wasn't coming back.

Fine. He didn't want to be here. Neither did I.

I stalked to our bedroom and over to the closet. The angry tears started to fall as I yanked out my carry-on and stuffed the basic necessities into it. I debated taking a car from the casino vehicle pool or calling Mai to fly me to Los Angeles.

And immediately realized what a dumbass I was. *I'm a fucking goddess. I can teleport anywhere I want.*

Or could I? I'd never tried before. No one was currently in the living room. I closed my eyes and concentrated on that space. I counted to three and opened my eyes.

I was still in our bedroom.

Since I'd grown up watching old sitcoms, maybe using one of my namesake's measures would work. I tried wiggling my nose. Nothing happened.

Okay, instead of imitating witch magic, maybe I needed something more powerful like a genie. I crossed my arms and sharply nodded.

A wave of vertigo smacked me and I stumbled. Flailing my arms to regain my balance, I looked around.

I stood in the middle of the penthouse living room.

Hot damn!

Concentrating again, I repeated my actions. I popped the several yards back to the bedroom without taking a step. The vertigo wasn't as bad this time.

I had no doubt teleporting to Los Angeles would be just as easy. The next question was where to go. It wasn't like I had a whole lot of friends who wouldn't narc to Duncan. I couldn't put Max and Tiffany in the middle of our fight, not with Tiffany so close to her due date. I sure as hell wasn't about to go to my parents for a round of I-told-you-so's by my mother.

And going to my ex-fiancé Jake's was definitely out of the question. I'd been stupid and done that after mine and Duncan's last major fight. Doing so again would nuke whatever chance Duncan and I had of working this shit out.

Maybe there was one person who would let me couch surf for a night while I tried to figure out if my relationship with Duncan was worth continuing.

I slung my bags over my shoulder and concentrated hard. The processed air of the penthouse gave way to smog mixed with ocean tang. While the sun had set, it was still bright enough the streetlights hadn't winked on yet.

The neighborhood around me was older, comfortable. A nice mix of apartment buildings and shops. Not super expensive. Nowhere near decrepit enough to attract the investors who'd want to gentrify the surrounding blocks.

Luckily, it was late enough in the evening no one noticed me literally popping into existence. I definitely needed to be more careful about checking an area before I materialized.

I marched over to the apartment building in front of me and punched the call button.

"Yes?"

"Hey, Agnes. It's Sam. Can I ask a favor?"

"Come up."

I expected a little more of a battle from my *Scoop* colleague, given her normal paranoid tendencies, before I was allowed entrance, but I'd take the opening while I could. The main door hummed and clicked. I yanked it open before she could change her mind.

While I could have teleported straight into her apartment, I figured, well, manners. No need to alienate the handful of friends I had left.

I jogged up to Agnes's floor and knocked politely on the door. Wallowing in my own shit, I wasn't prepared for who opened it.

"Emerson?"

The man who stood in front of me could have been my boss Ralph, a hundred pounds and washboard abs ago. But the touch of gray at his temples said he wasn't Waldo. Which meant he was the third triplet. I'd heard Aphrodite cursed him and Ares had mitigated the curse as best he could.

I'd simply never seen Emerson when he wasn't a bulldog slobbering on my jeans.

"Hey, Sam. Come on in." He stepped back and motioned.

Then I really noticed his unbuttoned shirt, the candles, and the wine.

"Oh, shit! I am so sorry." I took a step backwards. "I didn't mean to interrupt—"

"No. Sam." Agnes rushed out of her bedroom, clothes obviously donned in haste, and her messy hair—

"Did you get highlights?"

She blushed and ran a hand over her normally gray and ragged locks. "Last month. What's wrong?"

Once again, I'd stuck my size ten foot somewhere it didn't belong. Agnes was getting her normal back together, obviously due to a certain werebulldog. "I'm sorry I interrupted," I repeated. "You should have told me to fuck off."

I whirled and stalked back toward the stairs.

"Sam!"

Agnes grabbed my arm, stopping me at the landing. "What happened?"

That was when I burst into ugly-cry tears.

At his signature music, Mortimer jogged onto the stage. The audience's enthusiasm soothed the anxiety that had been nibbling on him all day. Maybe it was a good thing Molly had turned down his offer for show tickets. He didn't think he could get through his monologue if she had.

A sharp wolf whistle cut through the applause when he exited after introducing the next act. One he recognized coming from the direction of the front tables. But he couldn't make out any audience details with the spotlight in his eyes.

No. He wanted to see Molly so bad he was hearing things.

Once he was behind the curtain, he grabbed Marshall's arm. "Who's at the VIP table tonight?"

"A friend and some of her clients." Marshall looked distinctly uncomfortable. "I hope you don't mind. She was Mortimer Stern's second wife."

"Really?" He didn't have to feign his shock.

"Yeah. She stopped coming when I hired you, even though I told her a million times you're nothing like her asshole of an ex."

Mortimer swallowed hard. This wasn't going to be pretty but he had to know. "What do you mean I'm nothing like her ex?"

"Look, man." Marshall peered around them. None of the performers or stage hands were paying any attention to them, but Marshall lowered his voice anyway. "I don't like to speak ill of the dead, but the real Mortimer Stern put my friend through the ringer. Always criticizing her and accusing her of sleeping around when he was the one that had a string of mistresses. It's the reason she never remarried after their split. To top it off, he dumped her before she was thirty, saying she was too old." He shook his head. "If he were still alive, I'd kick him in the cajones myself."

Mortimer grimaced. He had done everything Molly accused him of. Shame filtered all the way to his toes. Maybe it was a good thing he didn't believe in Hell. He would have definitely deserved it for the atrocious ways he'd treated the one person who had actually loved him, warts and all.

Marshall clapped his shoulder. "Sorry to dump on you, Walter. Since she knows about you, why don't I bring Molly and her clients backstage to meet you? Like I said, I've been pushing how you're much better than the real thing."

"I don't know about that . . ." All his desire for Molly and their coffee meeting tomorrow felt like molten lead eating through his stomach. How could she even stand to be around him? And after everything he had done to her when they were married, he'd never be able to tell her the truth about his second life.

This had to be the real reason for the vampires' rules about no contact with living family and friends. Who wanted to hear about what a shit you were in your previous life?

"If you don't want them backstage, then go out to their table after the show. Do it as a favor for me," Marshall said. "It'll help Molly land the deal she's working on."

Dammit. If he could help her, he'd schmooze. It wouldn't make up for all the shitty things he'd done before he died, but it would be a start. "All right. I'll come out after the show."

Chapter 12

Agnes wrapped her arm around me and practically dragged me into her apartment. She was damn strong for a Normal. Within seconds, she had me on her couch with a full box of tissues shoved on my lap. Emerson stowed my bag in a corner of the living room before he poured a third glass of wine and pressed it into my hands.

"I'm sorry." I hiccupped. "I didn't know where else to go that wouldn't cause more problems."

"Do you want to tell us what happened?" Agnes asked.

"Nothing. Everything." I waved the wine glass, sloshing red liquid into the air.

Horrified at the mess I was about to make, I concentrated on the wine. Black diamond energy swirled around the liquid, which coalesced into a blob in mid-fall before it reversed course and dribbled back into my glass.

Emerson chuckled. "Neat trick. Wish I could do that."

Depression hit me even harder. "I didn't know I could until just now." I set the glass on the antique steamer trunk Agnes used as a coffee table and leaned back into the couch. "No wonder Duncan's afraid of me."

"Afraid of you?" Agnes patted my hand. "What happened, Sam?"

I rolled my head to the side to face her. "Have you heard through the grapevine what the nanites are turning me into?"

She shared a concerned look with Emerson. "Mr. Augustine told Ralph, Emerson and me, but only because we are your friends. He's worried about you."

"And because Ares and Aphrodite had a major fight in Reno's, and they let something slip in front of Agnes and me. Aphrodite accused him of chasing you." Emerson shook his head. "For being the goddess of love, she's a real bitch."

I raised my head to look at him where he sat cross-legged on the carpet. "You're kidding me."

"About her being a bitch?" He chuckled. "She's the reason I ended up like this." A wave of his hand indicated his human form.

"No, I mean, were they really arguing about me in public? Is that what caused the riots in July?"

"Yep." He grinned. "Don't worry. No one there that night had a clue of what they were shouting over." His grin faded. "Is that what the fight with Duncan was about? Ares?"

"Yes, but he's making assumptions because Ares proposed to me."

"Can't imagine how *that* could possibly be misconstrued," he said, sarcasm thick in his voice.

I glared at him. "I think I like you better as a dog."

His grin popped back into place. "I can still slobber on your jeans if you want."

"You're not helping, Emerson." Agnes pointed at her bedroom. "Out. Now."

"I was just joking," he muttered under his breath, but he climbed to his feet and left, closing the door behind him.

"You know he can still hear what we're saying," I said.

Agnes rolled her eyes. "As long as he keeps his mouth shut while we talk—" Her voice rose in volume. "I won't take him to the vet for neutering tomorrow!"

I snickered. "You know, you're beginning to sound like me."

She smiled. I realized it was the first time I'd ever seen her smile. She had a very pretty smile.

Her smile broadened. "Thank you."

I slapped my hands over my face. "Crap. Was I transmitting again?"

She laughed. "It was just your emotions, and not any more than a Normal."

I dropped my hands to my lap. My next question would need a delicate touch, but there was no tactful way to ask it.

"Go ahead and ask, Sam." Once again, she laughed at my expression. "I can feel your curiosity."

"You seem to have a better grip on reality lately. Is it Emerson? 'Cause if it is, I should have gotten you laid years ago." I expected more laughter, but her expression turned thoughtful.

Her fingers toyed with the belt of her bathrobe. "Our relationship may be part of it, but the changes started before Aphrodite cursed him. I think it's because of you."

I did a slow blink. "What do you mean, it's because of me?"

She stared at the carpet. "Certain sections of my brain were . . . destroyed when the . . . when I was attacked."

For Agnes to talk about the mind-rape she suffered at the hands of rogue vampires said how important this was to her. The incident had happened years before I started working for the *Scoop*. Even with the brain damage, she was still the best researcher I'd ever met. So for one of the rare times in my life, I held my silence and let her take her time in explaining.

She sucked in a deep breath. "Dr. Xavier and Dr. Zachary said the dead neurons are coming back to life. It started slowly at first, but there were a couple of major leaps. Both of them were documented right after you stopped by the office to say hello." She looked at me, a mix of concern and hope on her face.

I was afraid to ask the next question, but I had to know. "When did it first start? Do they have proof?"

Agnes nodded. "They've been doing monthly CAT scans. The first noticeable difference was during my check-up the first week of March." A shy smile appeared on her face. "Right after Josh Williams's murder."

Crap. I leaned back and gazed at the ceiling. Agnes had ghost-sat Josh for me while I'd been checking out some leads in his very suspicious death. She couldn't see the dead actor's shade the way Emerson or I could, but she still had enough of her empathic skills at the time she could communicate with him.

"Let me guess. The next big jump was in April."

"Yes," she murmured.

"Then June?"

"Uh-huh."

"So every time I had a new ability manifest—"

"Yep."

"But I wasn't around you at the end of June."

"You called me during your road trip to Ohio, and then came in to clean out your desk at the *Scoop* the second of July."

"Shit. I'm so sorry, Agnes—"

She grabbed my hand again. "Don't be sorry. You resurrected my dead brain tissue. I'm not a neurotic basket case like I was before you died. I have control of my gift back. I'm not having nightmares."

I stared at her. "At all?"

She shrugged. "Not as often, and not as bad. I don't have to take Xanax anymore, and you have no idea what a relief that is."

My right eyebrow rose. "What about your office and your tinfoil hats?" There was a reason the staff at my old job nicknamed her Agnes of God though the foil of her headgear and the lining in the closet she used was actually silver.

"I have your old desk, and my reliance on foil is . . ."

"Agnes . . ."

"Okay, I still use the closet as a safe room once in a while." She groaned. "You have no idea how loud Bill projects his feelings."

Bill Morton and I had been competing for the assistant editor position at *The National Scoop* before I died. The bastard had gotten the job by default. That felt like decades ago instead of months. So much had happened since I pursued a story that Emerson's brother, our editor-in-chief, had warned me off of.

Agnes cleared her throat. "And you're sidetracking me so you can avoid your real problem. What did you say to Ares?"

I threw my hands in the air. "I told him no!"

Emerson's muffled voice came through the closed bedroom door. "Then why were you secretly meeting with him?"

"Honey," Agnes yelled. "Stay out of this." She turned back to me. "Sorry, but he has a good point. Were you secretly meeting with Ares?"

"It wasn't a secret," I grumbled. "I had to talk to Phil first in order to set up a meeting with her dad."

"But you didn't tell Duncan," she prodded.

I crossed my arms and huffed. "Whose side are you on here?"

Agnes eyed me over the top of her black, emo spectacle frames. "I seem to recall you venting at the office back in April because Duncan planned to move you both to Las Vegas without discussing the matter with you. It works both ways, Sam."

"I liked it better when you were more worried about which politician was possessed by a conspiracy of birds." I stuck out my tongue at her.

A wry smile tilted her lips. "And you only stick out your tongue at people when you know they're right and you're wrong."

And she *was* right, as much as I hated to admit it. "Are you saying I need to leave?"

"No," she said at the same time a muffled "Yes" filtered past the bedroom door. She rolled her eyes. "I understand needing some space to work things out, and you're more than welcome to stay here, but you need to let Duncan know where you are."

"Okay," I said as my phone started playing "Lawyers in Love." I glanced at Agnes. "I need to take this."

She smiled, shook her head, and reached for her glass of wine.

I punched the answer icon. "Hey Colin—" High-pitched feedback squealed through my eardrum and into my brain. Past my own pain, I heard Emerson curse a blue streak.

"What the hell was that?" Colin asked.

"Problems with my cell phone. Talk fast before I lose you."

"I've got an emergency hearing scheduled for tomorrow morning at nine. Can you be there?"

"Yes." I stopped, remembering where I was. "Do I need to bring Lily?"

"No. Let's not tempt fate. I don't want to take the chance she slips in front of her—"

Another high-pitched squeal interrupted my lawyer. I stretched and worked my jaw to relieve the pain.

"—daughter," Colin finished. He told me at which courtroom to meet him. "You really need to get that phone fixed."

"I'll stop and get a new one after this hearing. See ya in the morning." I ended the call before the damn device destroyed Emerson's hearing for good. Weres had some natural speed-healing ability, but nothing close to mine.

He came out of the bedroom, rubbing his ears. "Please borrow my phone or Agnes's if you need to make anymore calls tonight. I don't think I can handle another one on your phone."

"I don't think I can either," I mumbled.

Agnes rose and retrieved her phone from its charger on the bar that divided the living room from the kitchen. She didn't say a word when she handed the device to me, but her expression spoke volumes.

I sighed and punched in Duncan's cell number. This time, my call went straight to voice-mail. Relief swept through me. I had to give him a little credit for not forwarding me to his secretary, but I didn't have to talk to him either.

"Hey, it's me. I'm spending the night in Los Angeles. Colin's scheduled a hearing on Lily's case for first thing tomorrow morning." I sucked in a deep breath. "And since you didn't give me a chance to explain, I told Ares I'd help him shop for the baby tomorrow afternoon in return for some advice on dealing with this deity battle I'm allegedly supposed to fight. He went to the mat for me to question Hades."

My heart ached at the thought that things had gotten this bad between me and Duncan that we were only talking through voice-mail. I hoped he took my explanation with some grace.

"Whether we like it or not, he's going to be involved in our niece's life. We both need to find a way to adjust."

A lump in my throat grew, and I had to get the rest out before it completely paralyzed my vocal cords. "I love you, and I'll see you tomorrow afternoon when I . . . get home." There. A little compromise on the move to Vegas.

I just hoped I still had a relationship to go home to.

Mortimer gritted his teeth while he peeked around the corner and into the showroom. The sensation felt a little odd, considering he'd had a partial denture when he died. One more thing to thank Sam for, even if she hadn't fixed his teeth intentionally.

That was the least of his problems. Perspiration had soaked his pits once he'd found out Molly sat in the audience after all. Only decades of professionalism helped him get through the two-hour show. Thank God, he hadn't known she was out there during his opening monologue.

And that he had a spare shirt and jacket backstage.

The overhead lights glowed, and the waitstaff cleared glasses from the tables in preparation for the second show. He dodged people with full trays on his way over to the table where Molly sat with Marshall. They were accompanied by a couple that looked to be closer to his real age than what his new appearance indicated.

Marshall made introductions. Surprisingly, Molly didn't say anything about already meeting Mortimer, but he recognized the slight smile that meant she was highly amused by the entire situation.

Her clients, the Jenkins, complimented his performance tonight, and then talked about watching the original "Uncle Morty" on TV when they were children. Hearing himself being discussed as a historical personage felt even odder than his teeth. Of course, he couldn't take credit. And they remembered shows he didn't recall performing.

After a bit of small talk, they said their good-byes and headed for their hotel room, but not before assuring Molly they'd be by her office to sign papers first thing in the morning. Marshall departed, claiming he needed to check on some props backstage.

Mortimer watched his ex-wife, waiting for her to cancel their morning coffee date. When she didn't say anything, he offered, "I didn't think you were coming to the show tonight."

"I wasn't." She looked as nervous as he felt. "The Jenkins were supposed to leave this morning, but they decided to have a second look at one of the houses."

"Congratulations on the sale," he replied, and he meant it. Instead of wasting the divorce settlement like his first wife, Molly had created a business and jobs, something she could be proud of.

She knocked on the fake wood veneer tabletop. "They haven't signed yet."

"They will. They trust you not to steer them wrong."

"Is that what you plan to do? Steer me wrong?"

He nearly choked on his spit. When had Molly become so assertive?

"I was hoping to make it through our first coffee date before anyone did any steering."

She leaned on her elbow, her cheek resting on her palm. "You're not used to dating older women, are you?"

"Older women?" He blinked slowly.

She chuckled. "You're ten years younger than me. I asked Marshall."

"Um, well . . ." How did he gracefully handle this? He'd never dated an older woman in his life. What was the new term kids used? "I thought cougars were the 'in' thing."

She leaned back and crossed her arms. "Oh, I'm a cougar, am I?"

Damn, he'd insulted her. Well, he'd promised himself he'd be honest with her from now on. "I'm sorry. I'm a little out of practice with the whole flirting and dating scene. I just wanted to get to know you over coffee tomorrow. Not when I'm dressed and acting like your ex. If you don't want to come after my word vomit, I understand."

He started to rise, but her soft hand over his stopped him. "If you didn't want to talk to me tonight, then why did you come over to our table?"

Mortimer began to run the tip of his tongue across his lower lip, but stopped himself. It was an old habit that could give him away, one he'd been trying to break for the last six months.

Instead, he drew in a deep breath. "Marshall told me you are a friend of his. He asked me to do a favor and help you schmooze your clients."

"Did I look like I needed help?"

He smiled. "No, you didn't, which makes me wonder why Marshall was pushing so hard for us to meet."

She laughed, a genuine one. The type he hadn't heard from her in a very long time. "Marshall and Daphne have been trying to fix me up for years. And this thing—" She flicked an index finger to indicate the two of them. "— is Marshall playing amateur therapist."

"Therapist?"

"Trying to make me face my issues since my ex is dead," she said.

Mortimer leaned back in his chair. He should play stupid, he wanted to play stupid, but he just couldn't do that to her. "Yeah, he told me about some of the crap your ex pulled. That's part of the reason I wanted to give you an out."

"By rescinding your invitation?"

He nodded.

She folded her arms again. "Well, I decline."

He started to say it was all right, but the twinkle in her eyes gave her away. Was she really teasing him?

"You decline the invitation, or you decline my recension?"

"I decline your recension."

"Yo, Mr. K!"

Someone grabbed his shoulder. He looked up to see one of the stage hands with a frown on his face.

"I've been trying to get your attention, man. The door needs to start letting the paying customers in."

"Of course," Mortimer murmured. He climbed to his feet and held out his hand for Molly. She graciously took it and rose as well. "Until tomorrow."

"Is that offer to watch your show still open?"

"Didn't you just sit through it?"

She paused, as if arguing with herself. "I was thinking we could have a drink afterward. I promise not to bring up my ex."

A trill of excitement ran through his blood. "Sure."

Her brilliant, and very real, smile lit up the room. "I'll see you in a couple of hours."

"Max—" Tiffany's warning growl was scarier than the alpha's of the Los Angeles werewolf pack. He also knew it was the last warning he'd receive from his wife.

"I didn't want you to worry," he began.

"Too late." She shifted in bed.

He automatically covered his boys. "Bebe's working on it!"

Tiffany froze. "Bebe's working on what exactly?"

There was no hiding now. He laid out the incident with Baron Samedi and everything Bebe had done so far to remove the enchanted watch.

Her original homicidal inclination didn't melt. "Why haven't you told Sam about any of this?"

"I've been trying to call her all day," he protested.

Her *harrumph* emphasized her disbelief in his efforts. He winced as she yanked her own recharging phone out of the wall socket by its cord. She jabbed at the plastic as if she were staking rogue vampires. Her phone emitted a high-pitched squeal before the light on the panel died.

"What the fuck?" She threw the offending device across the room. It narrowly missed the Ming dynasty vase the Chinese ambassador had given him.

Tiffany held out her hand for his phone. He handed it to her, praying she wouldn't chuck it into the antique mirror behind the vase.

Again, she punched Sam's number. His phone gave a faint *peep* before it too died. Tiffany's expression shifted from pissed to cold enforcer mode.

"You said Bebe and Caesar's house phone was doing the same thing?"

He nodded.

She flipped off the covers and waddled to the closet. "Three phones aren't a coincidence. Someone's sabotaging coven communications." She yanked out a maternity t-shirt, a pair of his sweats, and a set of no-heel, slip on boots, two sizes larger than usual. "Get the car warmed up, honey. We're heading back to Caesar's."

Chapter 13

— • ⚊ • ⚊ • —

The steel gates in front of Caesar Augustine's Brentwood mansion swung open as Max guided his car onto the drive. From the odd twitching of Tiffany's face, one of the vampire guards had confirmed their identity telepathically.

He swung the vehicle around to the garage. Several vehicles were parked, but the only ones he recognized were Alex's pick-up and Phillippa's Mustang. Something big was happening, and Max had the sick feeling he was at the center of it.

Tiffany was out of the car before he threw the gear into "Park". The rubber soles of her new boots slapped on the concrete as she waddled as fast as the baby allowed towards the side entrance into the garage. He ran after her, and they both nearly crashed into Miko when she charged out of the house.

"Everyone's in the master's office," the enforcer said as she dodged around them.

"Wait! Where are you going?" Tiffany demanded, shuffling into the kitchen.

"I've got to make a pick-up for Master Augustine," Miko called over her shoulder. "See you in a bit, cuz!" She slammed the door shut behind her. A few seconds later, the garage door rumbled to life before an engine revved and tires squealed.

"This is so not good," Tiffany muttered.

"C'mon." Max rested a hand against the small of her back. "Let's find out how bad this is." They stepped from the kitchen into the main hallway of the mansion.

Vampires and Normal Family members raced past them, laden with cardboard cartons with the bright insignia of a telecom company stenciled on the sides. They dodged the staff and walked into an animated conversation between Caesar, John Lannigan and Ziva Epstein in the main living room.

Normally, a vampire, a witch, and a werewolf would be the start of a bad joke, but if John and Ziva, Los Angeles's other two supernatural leaders, were here, things were much worse than he thought.

Bebe and Phillippa were in a corner with grimoires piled around them. Alex commanded the couch, cases from the same telecom company surrounding him. Another vampire cracked open the boxes and plugged in portable power units before handing the phones to Alex. From the way his fingers flew over the keys of his laptop, he must be verifying phone numbers and assigning them.

The house phone rang and Bebe snatched the receiver beside her. "Yvonne?" Her expression shifted from hopeful to horrified. "Hold on! Let me put you on speaker."

Her eyes met Caesar's. "It's Jean-Pierre."

There was a click and a rash of static. The voice of the vampire master of the Southeastern U.S. Coven burst through the receiver on the end table. "What the hell are you doing, Augustine?"

"Doing?" Caesar's aristocratic eyebrows drew together. "Explain yourself, Rousseau."

"My phone communications are collapsing, and my eclectic was found catatonic three hours ago! If you want a challenge, I will give you a challenge! I will rip your territory from your bloody grasp for what you did to my Yvonne!"

Tiffany grabbed Max's arm and pulled him to where she could whisper in his ear. "Now we know why she didn't call you back this afternoon."

Mortimer had never been fond of dungarees when he was alive, but both Sam and Lily said his ass looked good in them, and they were what men his fake age wore. The damned things felt like they were squeezing his package when he walked into the hotel's main bar two hours later.

His gaze went immediately to Molly seated in a corner table, away from the rowdier traffic. She still wore her sea green suit, but her jacket was draped over the back of her chair. Her white lacey blouse lent a gorgeous silhouette while still being classy. And her legs were crossed, displaying the fine arch of her ankle.

The entire package was stunning. His cock twitched like a school boy's, who had finally noticed girls for the first time.

Maybe this really *was* his first time. At least, his first time with a real lady.

Damn, why hadn't he appreciated Molly in his previous life?

He waved to the hostess, who nodded in acknowledgement, and he approached Molly's table. Her smile was as beautiful as ever.

He touched the back of the chair next to hers. "May I?"

"Of course." She didn't lean away as he half-expected. "The second show was very good."

He sat carefully, part of him still expecting the arthritis to kick in even after six pain-free months. "Better than the first?"

Her laugh was self-deprecating. "Honestly, between seeing you and the business part, I wasn't paying as much attention as I should have."

"You definitely know how to flatter a guy."

Her cheeks pinked. "I'm sorry. When you're onstage—" She waved a hand. "Sorry. Less than two minutes, and I'm already breaking my promise."

"It's okay. He's a part of your history."

"Instead of my ancient history, let's focus on yours, Walter Kinney." The way Molly said his alias sounded like she was reminding herself of who she was really with. "How'd a sweet guy like you end up in Las Vegas?"

Could she be any more cliché? But she was trying, and that was more important than all his old success and money.

He flagged the waitress. "Gin and tonic, and a—" He turned to Molly and stopped himself from blurting her usual.

From the odd look on her face, she noticed his order was her ex-husband's. "R-r-rum and coke."

He really needed to be more careful around Molly. She knew him better than Rhonda ever did.

When the waitress sauntered away, he forced a smile. "What would you like to know?"

"Where were you born?"

He couldn't claim his real hometown. Blood and screams from the night of his resurrection flashed through his mind. "Promise you won't hold it against me?"

"Promise." She even crossed her heart.

Telling her as much truth as he could seemed the best proposition. "Beverly Hills."

"Ah, a silver spoon."

"Not exactly, but we were comfortable. My dad had a software business. He sold it before the dot-com collapse." Sam wouldn't mind if he borrowed her life story, would she?

"Did you work for your dad?"

Thankfully, the waitress brought their drinks. The interruption gave him a chance to consider how to spin this.

He took a sip before he answered. "Sales. I wasn't bad at it, but it wasn't where my heart was, so Dad selling the company gave me a chance to do what I really wanted."

"And what was that?" She rested her chin on her fist, her whole being focused on him. He'd missed that with Rhonda. The former Miss Nebraska had only cared about her appearance and his money, and he only cared about how good she looked on his arm.

"Stand-up."

She laughed. "And how'd your parents react to that?"

"How do you think?"

They laughed together. Damn, it felt good sitting here with her.

"I did the clubs, but never made more than drinking money. Not until a friend suggested that with the right clothes and props, I could . . ." He was back in dangerous territory.

She shook her head. "I guess there's just no avoiding that subject." She took a large swallow of her rum and coke. "Any serious relationships?"

This could be even worse if he got careless. "Divorced. I thought I was in love, but she was in love with Dad's money. It didn't last long."

"Her or the money?"

He chuckled. "Both. Last I heard, she'd burned through the settlement, and she's now living with a former porn star turned limo driver."

"Oooo, ouch." She winced in sympathy.

"C'mon, look at this mug." He indicated his face. "I should have known better."

"I think you're selling yourself short." She reached over and covered his hand with her soft palm.

"Well, there are other compensations if you put a bag over my head." He waggled his eyebrows.

Another wince crossed her face, and he realized he'd stepped over the line. "Sorry. I keep forgetting."

"It's not you. It's me."

"Yeah, but I shouldn't . . ." His mouth dried out when she licked her lips and leaned closer.

"I know it's terrible of me, but I've been wondering if you look like him in other departments, too." Her gaze flicked toward his crotch.

For the first time in his life or death, Mortimer Stern had no idea how to react to a woman coming on to him.

Some insecure little part of me waited through the entire night for Duncan to call me back, even if it was through Agnes's phone. His caller ID would have recorded her number. But the little device didn't make a peep all night.

I gave up at five a.m. and grabbed a shower before her alarm went off. The cold water helped shake off the disappointment. And I wasn't about to be the rude guest who uses up their host's hot water.

As much as I'd rather curl up on Agnes's couch, eat ice cream, and watch Michael Bay flicks, I dabbed on some makeup and donned the conservative suit I'd brought with me. I figured something so dull and utilitarian would keep Ares at bay, but it would work double duty as a court outfit. Besides, the shopping expedition would be in public, so he shouldn't flaunt his powers or try anything stupid with me.

I hoped.

Emerson sauntered out of their bedroom as I exited the bathroom. "You finished?"

I nodded and stepped aside.

He grinned. "I try to get up before sunrise. It saves an embarrassing trip to the park." He entered the bathroom and closed the door behind him.

I couldn't blame the guy one bit. Thanks to the stupid nanites, the eminent sunrise tingled along my skin. I'd hate to turn into a four-legged creature at that sensation, and then have to depend on the staff at the Karnak to take me outside to do my business.

Making coffee in Agnes's neat little kitchen didn't keep me busy enough to ignore the bathroom doorknob twisting. Emerson left the door ajar. Soft grunts followed.

It must totally suck not have any control over his changes like other weres did, but then he'd never been in human form in his entire life until Aphrodite cursed him last summer. I had to give Ares a little credit for mitigating the bitch's punishment. Even half a life with Agnes was better than no life.

A black nose nudged the bathroom door open, and Emerson trotted out on all four legs to where I waited by the coffee maker. He looked up at me with his previous grin still on his bulldog face.

"Brew's almost done."

He wagged his tail and followed with a soft *woof*. Of course, he knew I hadn't slept last night. Not that I read Emerson's mind. He was simply easier to understand than most Normals.

"I promise I'll talk to Duncan when I get home."

Another whisper-bark followed. I would have sworn he said, "Good."

Chapter 14

With the entire coven on high alert hours later, Max made himself busy, brewing coffee and warming blood. His worthlessness in a crisis was beginning to gnaw on him.

Sure, he'd made jokes about being the male damsel in distress, especially considering what his sister and his wife could do. But being used as a pawn—

Well, it just pissed him off.

He rinsed and slammed mugs into the dishwasher.

"Hey, Max." Miko strode into the kitchen.

"What?" he snapped.

"Whoa." She held up both hands. "Just a greeting while I grab some more caffeine."

"Sorry," he muttered and turned back to the sink. "I just restocked the fridge. Grab the cans out of the freezer. They're colder."

She yanked open the freezer door. "Flirting with the possibility of exploding cola? Living dangerously, I see."

"Really?"

Miko stopped in mid-swig and lowered her cola can. "I didn't mean anything—"

He braced his palms on the lip of the sink. "No. I'm the one who needs to apologize."

"No, you don't." She clasped his shoulder. "I can't imagine what it's like having this loa threaten you."

"It'd be easier if I knew where my little sister is," he grumbled. "And shouldn't Mai and Duncan be here by now?"

Miko frowned. "No, Duncan's got to deal with Vegas crew first. Then they're flying to San Francisco to pick up Stan. Bebe wants some fae input on your situation." She squeezed his shoulder before releasing it.

"Sam will show up. Obviously, Baron Samedi is too much of a shit to take her on directly."

He shook his head. "I can't believe Sam took off without telling anyone where she was going. And I know damn well she wouldn't go anywhere without her phone. Especially since she's my-my birthing partner b-backup." The idea of never seeing his daughter, much less not be there when she was born, punched him in the gut.

Miko released him, crossed to the doorway to the rest of the house, and poked her head through. When she returned, she lowered her voice. "Alex and Tiffany can't get a handle on the virus that's messing with our servers. Sam could have left a message for one of us, and we never got it."

"All of them are affected now?"

She nodded. "And I'm sure Sam's phone is just as screwed up as all of ours were."

Something about Miko's manner said the situation was worse than Caesar had said. Not that Max expected the coven master to confide in him. He reached for the dishtowel to dry his hands. "What's really going on?"

She hugged herself. "It's not just the phone servers anymore. The malware is in the entire coven network now."

He blew out a deep breath. Someone wanted the vampires deaf, blind and speechless in the worst way. "Any word on how Yvonne's doing?"

"No. Bebe's step-grandfather is flying out to Miami." She took another drink of soda before she continued. "Apparently, the resident witch coven refuses to get involved no matter how much Jean-Pierre threatened them."

"At least he's no longer blaming Caesar for this mess."

"True." A thoughtful expression crossed Miko's face. "I'd like to ask a personal question, and please believe me, I'm not pointing fingers."

He sighed, anticipating her query. "No, it's not like Sam to disappear with no word. Believe me, I'm the one who used to sneak out of the house at night. If it weren't for Anne, I'd probably would've gotten myself killed years ago."

"Do you think cold feet could have prompted her to disappear now that she and Duncan are engaged—"

He bristled at her implication. "No. She's not with Ares. My sister may be a lot of things, but she's not the type to cheat. In fact, she's brutally honest when she dumps a guy. If you don't believe me, ask Jake."

"Ask me what?" The daytime enforcer, and Sam's former fiancé, stalked into the kitchen and headed straight for the coffee pot.

"Any luck finding our missing gods?" Miko asked.

"That sounds like a change of subject." He poured caffeine into a clean mug. "And no, Sam isn't at any of her usual haunts. Neither is Ares." Dark circles stood out under his eyes.

"When was the last time you got some sleep?" Max asked.

"Thirty-six hours ago," Jake grumbled. He opened the fridge door and stared at the contents.

"The hazelnut creamer is in the last shelf of the door," Max offered.

"Thanks." Jake pulled out the bottle and proceeded to pour what Max estimated to be a quarter cup of the sludge into his mug. "At least, we wrapped the stunts for Jimmy's latest movie last night before all this shit hit the fan." He gulped some of his concoction before he said, "So what does Miko not believe?"

Rose spread up her tan cheekbones, but she straightened. "I asked about the possibility Sam may be with Ares."

Jake's second mouthful sprayed across the kitchen tile before laughter pealed from him. "No." He sliced a hand through the air. "An affair with Ares? Definitely not."

"What makes you so sure?" Miko asked.

Jake cocked an eyebrow. "Have you seen the way she looks at Duncan? I have no doubt she's off somewhere pouting over the fight Duncan won't admit they had, but screwing Ares?" He shook his head. "That's not her style."

"Not to mention, she cares too much about Phil's feelings to pull something like that," Max added.

Jake lifted his cup. "I second that."

Miko pursed her lips. "Then where the hell is she?"

Mortimer woke with a start. Faint gray light edged past the heavy hotel suite drapes. The soft orange glow of the clock illuminated the form curled next to him. He stroked Molly's soft waves, amazed that she lay beside him.

Her eyelids fluttered. A sleepy smile spread across her features. "Morning."

"Good morning to you, too." He kissed her forehead.

"My lips aren't up there." She cupped the back of his head and launched a tonsil-searing kiss.

He couldn't believe how lucky he was. Second chances were a screw-up's pipe dream. Yet, here she was. And he was getting hard again from her mouth on his.

She pulled away, reluctance reflected in the orange light. "I can't," she groaned. I have to meet the Jenkins at my office."

He nuzzled the sensitive spot behind her ear. "So are we still on for coffee afterwards?"

"I can think of other things we could do besides coffee." She reached between his legs and stroked his cock.

"Lady, if you want to make that meeting, you need to stop doing that."

She laughed. "Make me."

He didn't bother trying to stop her. Not when things led to their natural conclusion.

Nearly a half-hour later, Mortimer withdrew and collapsed next to her. A chuckle tickled the back of his throat. "Next time, you're riding me, cowgirl."

Molly's soft curves pulled away from him. Her muscles drew rigid lines underneath her skin as she sat up abruptly. "What did you say?"

His mouth opened, but nothing came out. Which was probably a good thing while he rewound what had just happened.

"I'm sorry. I didn't think you were . . ." *God, please help me say the right thing.* "Um, that traditional about positions," he finished lamely.

"Only one person has ever called me 'cowgirl.'" She was out of bed and grabbing her panties before the faux pas registered.

Oh, shit. With all his blood somewhere else besides his brain, he'd slipped up big time by using her old nickname.

"Molly, babe, I'm sorry. I didn't mean to upset—"

"Shut up!" Her eyes glistened with extra moisture. She turned and searched for the rest of her clothing. "I should have known this was nothing but a con job." She clutched the wad of material in front of her bosom. "How did you find out what he called me?"

How to cover? "You did. Last night." He tried to smile. "It fits you. I didn't mean to upset you."

"I didn't say a damn word about that," she hissed.

"Maybe you shouldn't have had that third rum and coke—"

Bitter laughter poured from her. "You've got Mortimer down too well, Kinney. It was always someone else's fault with him, too."

"That's not what I—"

Instead of listening, she turned and marched toward the suite's living room.

"You can't go out there naked," he spluttered and jumped out of bed, pulling the sheet with him. She ignored him and kept going.

"Wait! I'll tell you the truth, but can we please do this dressed first?" He wrapped the sheet around his waist.

She stopped short of the door to the suite's living area and pivoted to face him. "No. Either tell me now or we're done."

He may be damned, either by the vampires or by hell itself, but he couldn't let her walk out for a second time. "My name's not Walter Kinney."

Her lips pursed, but she didn't move.

He let out a deep breath. "I'm sorry, babe. I'm your ex-husband. I'm Mortimer Stern."

Chapter 15

I teleported into a dark corner of the court's garage. Cars breezed by, drivers desperately searching for a free space before their hearing or trial started. For once, I was very thankful for my new gifts. The fees for the parking garage were bad enough to take out a second mortgage.

If I owned a house, that was.

I double-checked my scribbled note for which floor I needed as I headed for the elevator. Anxiety rattled along my nerves, jarring my normally excellent memory. This wasn't my first time in court, and it wasn't that I didn't trust Colin's talents as an attorney, but it was the first time someone else's fate rested in my hands. I started praying, and stopped myself just as abruptly. The last thing I needed was the wrong deity showing up in the middle of my legal mess.

Dozens of people dressed in drab suits just like me rushed back and forth in the hallways. Despite the constant flow of humans, Colin wasn't hard to find. I followed my nose.

He waited for me in a little alcove across from the court room he'd mentioned, checking his watch. The heavy scent of sandalwood overpowered his aftershave, which meant he was a tad bit nervous about the hearing.

The wash of humanity avoided the alcove unconsciously. Something in their hindbrains recognized a predator even with their preoccupation over whatever trouble brought them into the legal system.

With worse predators than one newly Turned vampire in my opinion.

The only person not avoiding Colin was the young lady by his side. Her scent was crisp Melrose apple, and her Roman nose and dark olive complexion meant she was one of Caesar's great-who-knew-how-many-nieces.

Except I knew her from a totally different context.

"I'm Veronica Monroe." She smiled and held out her hand. "You may not remember me, but we've—"

"Met before. Yeah, I remember." I shook her hand anyway. "I still have a copy of the restraining order."

"Restraining order?" Colin looked askance at me.

Veronica laughed. "Our entertainment division also represents my cousin Brent. He . . . objected to some pictures Ms. Ridgeway took without his knowledge."

I folded my arms over my chest. "So, are you going to hold my last career against me?"

"As long as you don't eat my brain, we're copacetic, Ridgeway," she shot back.

I grinned and relaxed my stance. "Good enough for me."

Colin must have decided our past wasn't worth asking about. Or he'd simply read Veronica's mind. "Let us do the talking unless you're asked a specific question," he interjected. "Judge Harewood is a stickler for protocol and decorum in his court."

"She'll be fine," Veronica said. "If anyone could have found those journals, it would be—" She smirked. "—an investigative reporter."

Apparently, her memory was just as good as mine. That had been my correction when she called my old profession by a very uncomplimentary name during the hearing over my alleged violation of Brent Poole's privacy.

"Well, you're the only one besides Jack's attorney who has managed to nail me with a restraining order." I smirked right back at her. "I hope you're still as good after all this time."

"Sam," Colin hissed under his breath.

"I'm sure Ronnie here can take a little teasing," I said. But even she had an expression of concern.

"Her eyes aren't glowing silver." Colin looked around, positively frantic.

"Really? They are?" I reached into my purse, grabbed my compact, and flipped it open. My irises were a little shiny, but as I watched, whatever the two attorneys had seen totally faded.

I frowned before I put the compact away. "That's weird. I'm not pissed or horny or—"

My stomach chose that moment to gurgle.

"—hungry," I finished lamely.

Colin ran a hand over his face before he said, "Please tell me you ate before you came here."

"I did."

His right eyebrow rose.

"I swear I did." In fact, I'd spent what used to be my old grocery bill at Burger King's. Thank BK's corporate execs for their two-for-one deal on bacon croissant sandwiches.

Colin rolled his eyes. "Let's go over everything one more time before we go in there."

Max held on tight when Jake whipped his Jeep into the parking garage for the office building housing *The National Scoop*. It had been ages since Max had dropped by to talk shop with his old boss.

Just one more thing in a list of "should haves" in his rapidly dwindling time.

Neither of them said anything as they climbed out of the vehicle. The garage shouldn't be this full this early in the morning. Not unless a major story was breaking, and Max hadn't heard a damn thing through anyone at the *Times*.

As they rode the elevator, Jake finally said, "Is there anyone here she's close to?"

"Besides Ralph?" Max shook his head. "Can't think of anyone."

The doors parted. Shouting, banging, and phones ringing whirled together into a scene of controlled chaos.

The editor's door was wide open, which meant Ralph O'Malley wasn't in his office. Max recognized a particularly loud bellow, and pivoted to follow it. Ralph and his assistant editor Bill were yelling overtop each other. Both men were gesticulating wildly.

The only one who noticed Max and Jake approaching was Emerson. The bulldog barked, and everyone in the vicinity immediately shut up.

Ralph charged toward them, his skin cherry red amid his gray receding and thinning hair. "You two know anything about what's happened to our computers?"

"Corporate-wide cyber attack," Jake responded crisply. "It's not just your magazine."

Ralph's bushy brows drew together to form one giant caterpillar. "Is that why you two are here?"

"Sort of," Max said. "Have you seen Sam in the last day?"

"No! Why the hell would she be—"

Bark! Emerson took off as fast as his stubby legs could carry him. He disappeared around a cubicle. A second later, more barking echoed across the bullpen. The werebulldog raced back around the cubicle and toward them, Agnes Durley on his heels.

Even stranger was Agnes of God without her foil cap for once.

"Emerson said you needed something?" She peered through her glasses at the men.

With all the funky looks both Bill and the rest of the staff gave their little group, Ralph pointed. "In my office. Now."

They marched to his office as ordered. Ralph plopped himself in the same squeaky chair that had been ancient when Max worked at the *Scoop* in high school. Jake closed the door and leaned against it, and Agnes took one guest chair, so Max took the other one.

Emerson parked himself between Agnes and Max and barked again.

"When did you and Emerson last see Sam?" Max asked more for Agnes's benefit than anyone else's. At least, he assumed that's what the werebulldog was trying to tell her.

Agnes poked at the nosepiece of her glasses. Not only wasn't she wearing the foil hat, her hair had been . . . highlighted?

If he wasn't so damn worried about his own soul and his sister's life, ur, well-being, he might have asked the reporter.

"She spent the night on our couch after she and Duncan got into a fight," Agnes said.

"Is she still at your place?" Jake said.

She shook her head. "No, she left this morning for a court hearing. Colin called her last night." Agnes's gaze locked onto Max. "What's going on?"

To anyone else, what he was about to say would make him certifiable. "She has something belonging to a loa, and he wants it back."

Her eyes narrowed. "Which loa?"

Max sucked in a deep breath. "Baron Samedi."

Agnes jumped to her feet and turned to Ralph. "That could explain the problems Sam had with her phone. Since I can't do anything here until the servers are cleared and rebooted, I'm going with them to look for Sam at the courthouse."

Emerson barked.

She looked down at him. "You're going to have to wear the vest. You hate wearing the vest."

He barked again.

She gave a short, sharp nod. "All right. We're both going with you. Sam wasn't going to pick up a new phone until after the hearing, and I have no idea what courtroom she's in. You'll need our help to find her."

Jake was halfway out the door before Ralph roared, "Go!"

Max shook his head and trooped out after Agnes. At the elevator, he muttered, "I can't believe I waited for him to dismiss me."

Emerson barked. No one needed a translation for that one.

Mortimer's heart sank into his gut at Molly's wild-eyed stare.

"Y-you're stark raving looney tunes." She edged through the doorway and further into the suite's living room. "My ex-husband is dead. I was at the funeral."

If he made another move toward her, he was sure she would bolt. "I *was* dead. Let me explain. Please. Then if you think I'm crazy, I'll stay in the bedroom while you get dressed and leave. Please."

She stared at him for a moment that seemed like an eternity. "Why would you even say something like that?"

"Because once upon a time, you said I couldn't tell the truth even if my dick depended on it." He held out one hand. The other gripped the sheet, though the Egyptian cotton didn't give him as much dignity as he would have liked. "I got another chance at life. Another chance with you. I shouldn't have lied, but I know how insane the truth sounds."

"Even Mortimer didn't come up with something so fantastic, so-so asinine!" She took a step backward. "I watched them fill in the grave. Do you really think I'm that gullible? Naïve? STUPID?"

At the crescendo of her voice, his eardrums should have shattered. How did he make her understand? If she went out that door and one of the vamps read her thoughts, she'd be dead before she made it to the lobby.

"I remember the night you said I couldn't tell the truth if my dick depended on it. It was the night you came home from the hospital after your dad died. He'd had a heart attack. You caught me in bed with Rhonda." He sucked in a harsh breath. "You were right about me and my dick, but I can tell the truth if *your* life depends on it. And it does."

"So this is a scam?" She shook her head. "You think I have money?"

"This isn't about money, Molly." He ran his free hand through his hair and sat on the corner of the bed, trying to look non-threatening. "I'm sorry. I wasn't supposed to contact anybody from my former life. But when I saw you—"

"What do you want from me?" She shook her head again, as if to clear the confusion.

He didn't blame her for not accepting his asinine story. His rebirth haunted his nightmares. "Like I said. I wanted a second chance. With you. I know how bad I fucked up the first time around. I knew the moment I let you walk out on those damn scarlet designer shoes I bought you."

She put her hand over her mouth. Maybe he was getting through to her because he never mentioned those shoes during the divorce negotiations. And he'd bet from the look on her face, she hadn't mentioned the one thing she'd taken when she left their house that night and her parting words to him to anyone else either.

Mortimer sucked in a deep breath. "Molly, I really need you to listen to me. The man who did this to me, who brought me back to life, is in custody. But the folks who stopped him own this hotel. They control more than you realize."

He swallowed hard. "They let me live and work here as Walter Kinney provided I don't let any former associates know about what's been done to me. There's some very bad people out there who'd love to dissect me. And they'd do worse to you if they found out what you know."

This was the most godawful thing he'd ever done, but if he didn't warn her, then he was a far worse person than the asshole he'd been the first time he was alive. "The people that are helping me? They have their own secrets. I was already told if I stepped out of line, they'd kill me and anyone else I revealed the truth to."

She shook her head. "Do you really expect me to believe all of this shit you're spewing?"

"No. In fact, it would be best if you thought I was a kook, but the problem is you will be thinking about this as you leave." He wiped a palm over his face. "And they have people here who can read minds."

Molly laughed, but the sound had a hysterical edge. "Oh, that is just the cherry on top of your bullshit story."

"Let me get you out of the Karnak—"

"Sure, and then you disappear with a sad 'I can never see you again' story." She scowled and crossed her arms over her fabulous tits, panties still wadded in one hand. He thought of the most disgusting thing he could in order to keep his johnson in check. Unfortunately, it involved the night he was reborn. His empty stomach grumbled its displeasure at the memory.

Mortimer held up his hands. "Actually, I plan to go with you. You've got your meeting this morning. Then we can get breakfast somewhere out of the way, and talk about this."

"Or are you planning to go with me so I don't call the police and then I'm found dead out in the desert?"

"If you feel safer calling the cops, all I ask is you wait until we're off the Karnak's property." At her unsure expression, he added, "Please."

Her arms dropped, and she stared at the underwear in her hand for a moment before her head rose. "All right, but you're buying breakfast."

Chapter 16

I tried not to chew on my lower lip as Judge Harewood reviewed the copies of Lily's diaries Colin had presented him. The judge was younger than I expected. Maybe a year or three older than my attorney. Piercing brown eyes darted back and forth as he read. Occasionally, he stroked his beard that was the same black streaked with gray as his short-cropped hair.

He set the papers aside and stared down at Lilianne's attorney. "Do you have anything to add, Mr. Constantine?"

The man subtly straightened. "Only that the alleged diary is an obvious forgery, Your Honor."

The judge's eyes narrowed. "Are you saying Mr. Kirby lied on his affidavit?"

"Mr. Kirby has gone out of his way to deny Mrs. Costas her family heritage. I find it convenient that he miraculously produced these alleged diaries, which are items of historical significance, and provided them to a tabloid reporter in an effort to smear the reputation of my client's mother." Constantine even added a sniff at the end of his speech.

The impulse to refute his lie was ground out by Colin's heel on my toe.

You could have asked nicely, I shot at him.

He ignored me and kept his attention fixed on the judge.

Harewood leaned back in his chair. His fingertips formed a steeple below his chin, a pose reminiscent of Caesar right before he delivered an ass-reaming. "Which tabloid?"

"*The National Scoop*." The opposing attorney's voice held a hint of glee.

The judge turned to me. "Ms. Ridgeway, do you work for the *Scoop*?"

"No, sir."

"Have you ever worked for the *Scoop*?"

"Yes, sir."

"Your dates of employment?"

"From my graduation from UCLA until July 1st of this year, sir. I'm currently freelancing as a guest-columnist." The court recorder tapped away on her little device.

"And you manage Maryann Tolley?" he said, using Lily's new identity Mai had set up for my baby zombie.

"Yes, sir." I could feel a rush of relief from Colin that I was only answering the question asked and not embellishing.

"How long have you been managing—"

"You Honor, I must protest you questioning a witness," Constantine interjected.

The look Judge Harewood gave the attorney should have incinerated him on the spot. "This is a hearing on a TRO, not to mention *my* courtroom, Mr. Constantine. I can ask whatever questions I wish. And if you interrupt me again, I will hold you in contempt."

He didn't wait for an acknowledgment from Lilianne's attorney, much less ask for one. A power play I'd witnessed Caesar use in the past. And I began to wonder if there was a reason Judge Harewood used a windowless courtroom.

"Ms. Ridgeway, how long have you been managing Ms. Tolley?"

"Since April, sir."

"When did you discover the existence of the diaries?"

"Yesterday, sir."

He turned his glare back to Constantine. "Anything else you wish to add, counselor? Like maybe an explanation of why Mr. Kirby had to take out a restraining order on your client?"

"No, sir," the attorney mumbled.

"The Motion for a Temporary Restraining Order is denied." Judge Harewood leaned forward and pinned Lilianne with his glare. "Mrs. Costas, if I find out you have harassed Ms. Ridgeway or Ms. Tolley again, there's going to be hell to pay. Got me?"

"Yes, sir," she ground out.

"Plaintiff has until Monday to amend their complaint." The judge eyed Lilianne again. "I would consider your position very carefully before you lie to me again." He rose and disappeared through the door to his chambers.

Lilianne started toward me, but Constantine grabbed her arm. After some furious whispering, which really wasn't as quiet as they thought because Colin and I could hear every word, they marched out of the courtroom.

"That went better than I thought," I murmured.

"It helped you and your clients found those diaries," Ronnie said. She hadn't done much during the hearing. In fact, she had acted more like a senior attorney letting a junior spread his wings.

"Because she *is* the senior attorney," Colin said.

"Shit. I—"

"Transmitted," Ronnie said. "Yep. You need to watch that. And keep your emotions under control in public. You can't have people see your eyes glowing."

"I didn't glow during the hearing, did I?"

"No, but you know the rules about revealing yourself to the general populace." Her demeanor was as stern as Mai's when the same subject came up.

"I think I can keep myself in check while shopping for baby stuff this morning."

"Are you taking Tiffany on an expedition?" Colin stuck the last of his paperwork in his briefcase and snapped it shut.

"No, I promised to take one of the grandparents," I muttered.

"Not your mother, is it?" Colin looked at me in mock horror as we left the courtroom.

I grinned. "No, it's worse. Tiffany's foster grandpa."

"Oh." The way he said the single syllable made it clear he didn't think it was a good idea.

"What's that supposed to mean?" I said.

He stopped and turned to Veronica. "Can you give us a minute alone?"

She cocked her head. "Really? You think I'm that stupid? Who do you think had to analyze liability when the potted roses attacked that poor housekeeper? Memory alteration doesn't take care of all the pesky little facts and hospital bills."

"I was going to advise Sam as a friend, not her attorney," Colin muttered.

Ronnie turned to me. "Here's the short version, Ridgeway. Men are fucking insecure. It doesn't matter how old they are. If you think St. James is bad, you should see Uncle Caesar in one of his snit fits over Dr. Zachary."

I faced Colin. "You were going to say the same thing in ten times as many words, weren't you?"

He sighed. "I would have been gentler."

Ronnie smirked and rolled her eyes.

I wasn't sure if I wanted to smack her or take her out for drinks. "I'll tell you two the same thing I told Duncan. He's the one who made Phil his co-guardian over Tiffany, which means he's the one who brought Ares into the family. The only reason Ares is interested in me is because I have a vagina and I'm a god like him—"

"Whoa!" Ronnie held up her hand. "Roll that last sentence back. I thought you were a zombie."

"Not as up on the coven gossip as you thought, hmmm?" I scowled at the bitch. "Yeah, your client's a god. Got a problem with that?"

She considered the matter for a moment, then shook her head. "Nope. Glad to hear you won't be eating my brain any time soon."

The brains jokes were starting to get very old, so I ignored hers.

"Anyway, back to the Ares problem." I looked at each of them in turn. "I hate to tell you this, but I am more powerful than Ares, which was another reason he wanted his hooks in me before I realized it." I smiled. "And unfortunately for him, I already know. We've come to a truce, and this baby shopping expedition is a test. If he can't pass, I kick his ass back to Olympus."

And that was everything I'd wanted to tell Duncan last night, except he decided to play the holier-than-thou card. Or maybe he knew all of this, and that's why he was avoiding me.

I didn't like the idea of my fiancé being scared of me. It didn't bode well for our wedding, much less our marriage.

Colin and Ronnie glanced at each other. They turned to me in unison and nodded.

"We'll stay out of it," Colin said.

"You're right. None of our business," Ronnie added.

"Thanks." I inclined my head. "And Ronnie, thanks for making sure the maid and her family were taken care of. I didn't know the flowers had been delivered until after she'd been attacked."

"You're welcome." She nudged Colin. "You ready to go?"

"Can I please have a minute?" Colin cut her off when she opened her mouth. "It's about my wife, and it is none of your business."

She shrugged. "I'll be down in the car then. See you later, Sam."

I waited until she was well out of earshot. "What's up?"

He gestured to one of the private rooms attorneys used to consult with their clients. I followed him inside.

He closed the door behind us. "Do you know what's going on in the coven?"

"You've got to be a little more specific."

"Anne's been gone the last couple of nights. She insisted I have a new phone when she came home this morning." He shook his head. "But she won't tell me what's going on, so I totally understand about the whole over-protective, significant-other-being-an-enforcer problem. I was hoping you might know something."

"Duncan," I muttered. That mother-fucking asshole! "No, I don't know, but a lot of things in Vegas make more sense now." I pulled my defunct phone out of my suit pocket and held it up. "Let me guess? Virus hit the phone system?"

"I believe that's part of it." He set his briefcase on the table and folded his arms across his chest. "But there's more to it than just phone problems, or Anne wouldn't be involved."

Even after nearly seventy years as a vampire, his wife hadn't given up her Amish upbringing. Oh, she'd use a smart phone, a computer, or a gun when pushed, and she was almost as good as Phil, who was born and raised an Amazon, when it came to hand-to-hand fighting.

But playing with the coven's servers and networking? No.

"I'll swing by Phil's later." I grinned. "And if she doesn't know or refuses to talk, my sister-in-law will find out for us out of spite."

Colin laughed and shook his head. "Remind me not to get on your bad side."

"Actually, you need to remind my fiancé not to do that," I said sourly. "But thanks for saving mine and Lily's asses today."

Colin's smile turned wry. "Do you need my phone to tell her everything's okay?"

"Nah." I gestured with my broken phone. "The next thing on today's to-do list is pick up a new phone before I head over to the Beverly Center. I'll call her once it's activated." I dropped the device back in my suit pocket.

He opened the door to the little room and we both merged with the human traffic heading for the elevators. "Did you need a lift?"

"No, thanks." I waved. "I'll let you know the scoop once I find out."

He saluted and joined the crowd waiting for the next car. I parted from the people traffic and glanced out the window. It was too nice a day not to enjoy the California sunshine, but I didn't feel like waiting with the rest of the herd.

I entered the ladies room and headed for the last stall. Luckily, no one followed me into the restroom, and no one was washing their hands.

I popped back into reality in the same dark corner of the parking garage. The place was packed with cars, and the stench of exhaust fumes mixed with the sauna-like heat from the concrete baking in the sun. I headed for the pedestrian exit and the electronics store two blocks from the courthouse.

Twenty minutes later, my new smart phone and I teleported into the coffee shop bathroom in the Beverly Center. A grande triple espresso mocha later, I was leaving a message for Lily when Ares swaggered into the coffee shop.

Yep, definitely sex on a stick. I gritted my teeth and stood. I just needed to get through baby shopping and lunch to prove to Duncan there was nothing to worry about.

Right?

Max braced himself on the Jeep's dashboard as Jake whipped his vehicle around a street corner with one hand and punched a call into his mounted phone at the same time. The phone rang once.

"Did you find her?" Anne said. None of the normal niceties with the overly polite vampire.

"We're on our way to the downtown courthouse," Jake reported. "Sam spent the night with Agnes and Emerson from the *Scoop*, but she had a hearing. They're with us. Did Colin say what courtroom he would be in this morning?"

"Oh, God," Anne wailed. "I didn't even think to ask him about his schedule this morning. I just handed him a new phone when I dropped by our place for a change of clothes."

"That's all we needed to know, Anne. Thanks!" Jake tapped the receiver hooked over his ear. He took another turn faster than the speed limit. Emerson barked from the back.

"I'll make the calls if it'll keep you on the road," Max said. He scrolled through his contacts and tapped the icon for Colin's phone. After four rings, the signal rolled over to the attorney's voicemail.

Max tried again and counted the rings. On the fourth one came "You have reached Colin Fitzgerald. I'm unable to answer—"

He muttered an obscenity under his breath. "He's not picking up."

"He's required to silence his phone during court," Jake said.

"Or he could be in the elevator," Agnes added.

"Arf!" Emerson said.

Max wasn't sure if they were agreeing with the other two or if he offered a third excuse.

Tires squealed when Jake cut off another motorist and tore into the parking garage. Max wasn't sure if it was the Jeep or the other driver's vehicle.

The seatbelt dug into his chest when Jake slammed on his brakes. "You three spread out. You can search the public scheduling database for Sam or Colin. I'll swing through the garage."

Max bailed out of the vehicle. Agnes and Emerson followed. Tires squealed again when Jake accelerated deeper into the concrete maze.

They ran toward the main elevators into the building, and Max jabbed the button. Red numbers ticked above the doors until they hit "P1". The doors parted, and people spilled out.

Including a familiar auburn head that was already turning in his direction.

"Colin!"

"Max?" The attorney separated from the crowd who were heading for their cars. "What's going on?"

"Where's Sam?"

"She was headed for the ladies' room last I saw her. What's going on?" Colin repeated.

Max could feel his stomach plummet. He was too late once again.

Agnes jammed her elbow between the closing doors. "Come on, Max. We can catch her. What floor, Mr. Fitzgerald?"

Colin gave them the floor number.

Max glanced at the bank of elevators. "You two go, Agnes. I'll wait here in case she comes down in one of the other cars."

Emerson barked and trotted into the elevator. Agnes dove in behind him, and the doors snapped shut just as the emergency bell sounded. The noise cut off as the car began its upward climb.

"What's going on?" Colin said, and Max realized it was the third time the vampire had asked. "You smell like ozone."

Max held up his left wrist. "A loa named Baron Samedi is after Sam, and I'm the bait."

"Since when is a Rolex bait?" Colin frowned. "Wait, is this what the coven emergency regarding the phones is about?"

Max lowered his arm. "The enforcers don't have proof the two incidents are connected, but—"

"It's too much of a coincidence not to be," Colin finished.

"Yeah, we'd have Sam by now if you and your wife had better communication skills."

"Excuse me?" Colin bared his fangs. "I asked what the hell was going on this morning when she nearly dropped a new phone in my coffee . . ." He pulled a smart phone out of his inside jacket pocket. "Sam said she needed to pick up a new one, then she was meeting Ares at the Beverly Center to do some baby shopping—" He winced. "Sorry. I probably wasn't supposed to tell you that part. Act surprised by whatever they get you."

"Ares? Seriously?" There was a time Max would have pinned his baby sister to the floor and noogied her for acting stupid. Now, he wouldn't dare do it with Sam any more than he would the Greek god of war. "Is she deliberately trying to force Duncan to call off the engagement?"

"And you're giving me shit about my marriage?" Colin shook his head, and the faint golden glow of his eyes receded. "No, she's not trying to piss off Duncan, but if we need to get to her first—"

He thumbed a number into his phone. "Hi, honey." A pause. "I understand you're busy, but I thought you might like to know where Sam is . . ."

Chapter 17

Relief flooded Mortimer once Molly agreed to get dressed. She shot occasional looks at him while they waited for the elevator, but she no longer had the panicked expression. Or the furious one.

Since it was well past daybreak, the security staff shift change should have occurred. Fewer vamps on duty meant he had a reasonable chance of getting Molly out of the hotel without their minds being read.

"Crap," he muttered. "I have to sign out a car from the vehicle pool."

"Did you already forget I drove us over here from The Vegas Grand?" she said dryly.

He chuckled. "You always were the smartest person in our marriage."

"Stop." She closed her eyes briefly. "I really need you to stop saying that."

"Sorry," he muttered. It finally dawned on him that even if he convinced her of the truth, she may not want him back. The realization felt like a punch in the gut.

The elevator chimed, and the doors parted. He followed Molly inside and reached for the "Lobby" button.

"Hold the elevator!"

The crisp British accent sent a wave of molten lava through Mortimer's virtually abused intestines. *No, no, no. Please don't let it be him.*

Before Mortimer could stop her, Molly jabbed the "Open" button, and the closing doors parted again. The tall, imposing manager of the Karnak stepped into the car with his head of security. Even if Duncan St. James never showed his fangs or wasn't even a vampire, he'd make people nervous. He was just one of those types of alpha males. The doors closed, and the shift of Mortimer's stomach said the elevator was headed down.

At least, that's what he hoped his stomach was telling him.

Think about pink elephants, Mortimer told himself. It didn't work.

Images of Molly and what they'd done last night danced through his head instead.

Duncan St. James was only a couple of inches taller than Mortimer, but he always felt like the vampire was his father glaring at him. Maybe it was the green eyes. It didn't matter that the first time he met St. James, the British vampire had been naked and tortured. The vampire still made him jittery.

"Walter, do you know by chance where Samantha is this morning?"

Of course. Since a stranger was with him, St. James would use his new identity.

Mortimer shook his head. "I haven't seen her since she and Ms. Osaka—" He nodded in Mai's direction. "—dropped us off at The Vegas Grand for last night's show."

He'd been so worried about one of the vampires reading his and Molly's minds the import of St. James's question slowly dawned on him. "You can't find her?"

"Not at the moment," St. James said, his voice tight. "Our communications system was compromised last night as well. The IT department says it is a particularly virulent virus. Please stop by Staci's office when you have a chance and pick up your new phone."

For the vampires' anal security measures to be that fouled up, things must be pretty bad.

"Is there anything I can do to help?"

A faint smile touched St. James's mouth. "Not at the moment, thank you. I appreciate the offer."

Mortimer's attention flicked to Mai. She stared at the floor, her lips pressed in a straight line. From her posture, she was taking the fact Sam was missing personally.

He was torn between getting Molly to safety and helping with the search for Sam. What he owed Sam for his new lease on life won out. "Have you checked with her girlfriends in L.A.?"

At St. James's scowl, Mortimer held up his hands. "Look, I know it's not my business, but everyone here knows you two have been having some issues lately. Check with her girlfriends."

Those intense green eyes bore into his. "And how would you know this?"

Mortimer grimaced. "Unfortunately, experience."

Beside him, Molly laughed before she said, "He's right. If you two had a fight, she'll be at a girlfriend's place, eating ice cream and bitching about you."

Mortimer's stomach imploded when St. James's attention landed on Molly.

And especially when the vampire turned all his British charm on her. "I beg your pardon, madam. We have not been properly introduced."

"Molly Weiss." She held out her hand. "Weiss Real Estate."

St. James took her hand and smiled. "Duncan St. James. Karnak Hotel and Casino."

Behind the vampire, Mai stared at Mortimer, her expression pure suspicion. All she'd have to do was check his old online bio, and he and Molly would quite literally be dead.

He did his best to keep his face impassive, but he could feel sweat gathering along his hairline.

The elevator bell dinged, and the doors parted.

St. James released Molly's hand. "A pleasure, Ms. Weiss." He strode out of the car.

Mai pointed two fingers at her eyes, then her index finger at Mortimer. *Shit! She knows!*

Or at the minimum, Mai suspected something. He'd been so worried about the vamps he hadn't considered the Normal staff.

He followed Molly out of the elevator. When they were at the main entrance, he grabbed her elbow. "If Sam's missing and the phones are screwed up, I need to run back upstairs, get my new one, and check in with her secretary. Why don't you head to your office for your meeting? I'll grab a cab."

Mistrust clouded her features. "What's going on? Or is this your even worse attempt to ditch me than your cockamamie story?"

He tried to smile, but it failed. "I need to make some phone calls. The boss's girlfriend Sam? She's my manager."

"She knows about—" Molly waved at him.

"Yeah. I'll explain everything when I get to your office. I promise. Go." He glanced around the lobby but no one was paying any attention to them. "Now."

Worry replaced the suspicion on her face. "I expect a full explanation later." She kissed his cheek. While they had spent the night together, the gesture was more than he expected after her freak-out earlier.

"I will." He pressed his hand against the small of her back to urge her out the door.

Once she was gone, Mortimer headed back to the elevators. If Molly knew what he was about to do, she'd scream bloody murder, but if Sam was missing, it would be the only way to keep Mai from putting bullets through both his and Molly's foreheads.

In Macy's, I tried not to laugh when Ares held up a dress with a bright pink tutu.

"This is not a warrior's garb," he muttered.

"Is this your first child?"

I turned to find a middle-aged sales lady with a bright smile on her face. And by bright, I mean her lipstick was neon orange. It clashed with her black-dyed hair that only emphasized her wrinkles.

"No. We're not a couple," I said.

"We could be," Ares proclaimed.

I glared at him. "We. Are. Not. A. Couple." I turned back to the blinding lipstick lady and pointed at myself. "Aunt." I pointed at Ares. "Grandpa."

Her attention shifted to him, and she batted her eyelashes. "Really? You don't look old enough to be a grandfather."

Before Ares could answer, I said, "Actually, he'll be a great-grandpa. My asshole brother knocked up his teenage granddaughter."

The sales lady's mouth hung open at my oversharing. I wasn't about to correct myself over Tiffany turning twenty a few weeks after she'd discovered her pregnancy. It took the sales lady a couple of tries to plaster her smile back on her face. "Is it a boy or a girl?"

"With our luck, it'll be a hermaphrodite," I said.

"That only happened once in our family," Ares grumbled.

For a second, I thought the sales lady was going to hyperventilate.

She recovered her smile once again. "Well, um, we have some cute unisex onesies over here. Would cartoon animals work?"

"Do you have any with 'World's Greatest Aunt'?" I asked brightly.

"I saw one once that was ebony with a human skull on it," Ares interjected. "It said, 'Protected by Biker Grandpa.' Do you have any of those?"

I cocked my head. "Since when do you ride motorcycles?"

"Since the Industrial Age." Ares shrugged. "My flesh-eating horses and chariot made of bones don't have the same impact they used to."

"Um, maybe you should try the Harley Davidson store in town?" the sales lady squeaked.

I wrapped my arm around her shaking shoulders. "Why don't you go back to the register and let us look? I promise you'll get the commission."

"A-all right." She took off as fast as her sensible heels would carry her.

"Are you going to lecture me about my conduct with mortals?" Ares asked once she was out of sight.

I started sorting through the rack of newborn outfits. "Hell, no! You haven't done anything I haven't done."

"What do you mean?" he said.

I looked up. "Wait. You mean you weren't deliberately fucking with the sales lady?"

He frowned. "No."

I grinned. "Tiffany and I need to take you shopping with us on a regular basis."

Before he could turn the conversation smarmy, my new phone rang. I pulled it out and looked at the caller ID. Anne. OMG! If this was another question about baby shower etiquette, I'd seriously consider shoving the phone up her ass. When would she ever get over her stupid Amish guilt when it came to using Google?

"Hello, Anne."

"Where are you?"

"I'm—" If she found out I was baby shopping with someone else, it would hurt her feelings. "—at Macy's. What's up?"

"Where in Macy's?"

She didn't ask which Macy's in the Los Angeles area. Granted, everyone else I knew would assume I was at the Beverly Center, but not Anne, being the sideways Amish freak she was. Who else runs around L.A. like she's Batman, then toss Bible quotes at the pimps and drug dealers she beats the hell out of? "Are you tracking me?"

"If I was, I would have chained you and tossed you in a car by now. Where are you?"

"Look, bitch, if you had a fight with Colin, don't be taking it out—"

"Sam, shut up! Just . . . shut up and listen. Max is in trouble. I've got Miko on her way to the Beverly Center to pick you up."

My blood froze. "Where's Max?"

"Colin is bringing him back to the mansion."

"What happened to Max?" Ares asked at the same time.

"Tell Miko to turn around. We're on our way, and we'll be there before she can get to the Beverly Center." I punched the icon to end the call. "I'm not trying to renege on our deal—"

Ares handed my purse back to me. "If my granddaughter's husband is in trouble, then we go to his aid." He wrapped his arm around my shoulder and Macy's baby department winked out of existence.

He didn't even try to cop a feel.

Chapter 18

Mortimer knocked on Staci's partially open door. When she looked up, he said, "Mr. St. James said I needed to see you about a phone."

"Yes." She swiveled on her chair and pulled a box from a larger carton. "It's already charged and your contacts loaded from the last good backup the IT department was able to retrieve. And give me your old phone."

"Not that I want it, but why?" He tried to act nonchalant, but Molly's number and text were on the old phone.

"Did Mr. St. James tell you what happened?"

"About the virus, and about Sam?"

Staci nodded. "The virus is why we need the old phones back. Otherwise, the virus will re-infect the servers." A frown curved her mouth. "It's not like Sam to take off without letting someone know."

"Yeah, I agree." He handed his old phone to her and accepted the box. There was no way of getting out of it without arousing suspicions. "By the way, thanks for your help with my lady friend." Not that he wanted to mention it, but he needed a reason to stay in the office.

Staci glanced at her computer screen. "Aren't you going to meet her this morning at the café I suggested?"

He chuckled. "She showed up at last night's early show."

"And?" Staci waggled her eyebrows.

"She sat through both of them, and we had drinks afterwards."

A sly smile spread across the assistant's face. "You dog."

"Back to our boss," Mortimer said, and Staci immediately sobered. "Do you have her contacts list?"

"Not on my computer. Why?"

"If she and St. James had a fight, which of her girlfriends would she stay with overnight?"

Staci rolled her eyes. "That English bastard! He left out that little bit of information when he asked me about her location." She stood and pushed back her chair. "Let me pull the most likely possibilities."

The instant she disappeared into Sam's office, Mortimer circled Staci's desk. He'd noticed months ago she kept petty cash in the bottom drawer for Sam's huge appetite for when the boss needed to go out of the hotel on business.

And if Sam was in Los Angeles, she'd have cash on her already. He wouldn't feel too guilty about stealing her lunch money this one time.

Bingo. He snatched a couple of bundles of bills and stuffed them into back pockets of his dungarees. The casual jacket he wore would cover the bulges.

The office phone started ringing, and he jerked. Lucky for him, Staci picked up the line in Sam's office. Mortimer moved back to the other side of the desk. He opened the box with his new phone.

When he'd gotten his first modern phone, Sam had said it had something called a global positioning system that could locate him anywhere in the world if he got into trouble. He frowned. The intrusions people could do in the twenty-first century made Hoover's FBI and McCarthy's Red Scare look like child's play.

He needed to dump the new phone, but not in Staci's office. No, leaving it in his room would be a better idea. If the vampires thought he'd left it behind by accident, he and Molly would have a couple of extra hours to disappear.

Staci strode back into her office. "You were right. That call was one of the Los Angeles enforcers. Sam spent the night with her friend Agnes." She shook her head, and a subvocal growl rumbled deep in her chest. "If Mr. St. James had simply admitted they'd had a fight—"

For the first time, Mortimer actually felt sorry for the Brit. "He's probably didn't think it was that big of deal."

Staci cocked her head, and her eyes took on a yellowish sheen.

Oops. Mortimer held up his hands, fingers spread. "I'm not saying he's right. I'm just pointing out why he was acting like an idiot. Last thing I'd ever do is piss off Sam. I mean, the woman's death incarnate."

Staci crossed her arms. "Then maybe you should explain it to him in terms his pathetic male brain can understand."

Mortimer dropped his hands, and he took a step back. "Uh-uh. There's no way I'm getting in the middle of a love spat between a vampire and a death goddess. I'm resurrected, not stupid. And I already told St. James that exact thing on the elevator not five minutes ago."

"Fine," Staci muttered. "I'll talk to Kunal and see what we can do to fix the situation before Mr. St. James leaves."

Mortimer slipped his new phone in his jacket pocket. "You'd better hurry. I think he and Mai were headed for Los Angeles. Something about last night's computer hack."

Staci's posture relaxed a fraction. "Go have some fun with your lady friend while you can."

His heart sank. The kid was probably worried about her job if St. James and Sam split up, especially since Staci and her husband had just had a baby. And here he was stealing money the kid was responsible for.

Mai's gesture earlier that she was watching him roared back to the forefront of his mind. The vamps would know Staci was telling the truth when she said she didn't take the money. On the other hand, Molly was dead if he didn't get her out of Las Vegas in the next couple of hours.

On impulse, he circled the desk and hugged Staci. "It'll be okay. Sam and St. James will work things out. You'll see."

The kid patted his back. "Sorry. Old reactions from when my parents got drunk and fought."

He released her. "The boss is safe. That's the important thing. The rest will sort itself out." He chucked Staci's chin. "I've got some errands to run now that the crisis is over."

"I hope it involves a nooner with your lady friend." Staci's exaggerated wink lightened both their moods.

"A gentleman does not kiss and tell," he said in mock seriousness. Damn, he was going to miss her. Staci was the daughter he'd always imagined that he would have had.

If he'd made time for fatherhood like Molly had wanted. One more fuck up in his life that would never be rectified.

He pivoted and marched out of the office before Staci noticed his emotional shift. With his luck and her canine senses, she'd smell it on him if he didn't get out of there quick.

Heading back to the elevator banks, he made mental notes of what to take with him, and how to get to Molly's office without tipping off the Karnak's security. He silently prayed his plan would work because he couldn't bear losing Molly for a second time.

A shriek greeted Ares and me when we popped into existence in the middle of Caesar and Bebe's living room. It was followed by a *pop*. A *pop* I knew all too well before the equally familiar sensation of something slamming into my chest.

"What the fuck?" I looked down. Blood welled across my only decent dress shirt. Then the pain started.

My attention fixed on the enforcer who had shot me. A werewolf from the sour canine smell emanating from her. A very scared werewolf from the ashy scent that mixed with her doggy odor.

"What's going on—" Anne stopped abruptly in the entrance to the mansion's main hall. She took in the scene and immediately got between me and the were. "Cara, go outside."

"But—"

"Now," Anne snapped.

Whatever the were was about to protest, she took another look at me and decided against it. "Yes, ma'am." She gave me and Ares a wide berth as she headed for the foyer.

The petite vampire faced me once the front door slammed behind Cara. "Sam, are you all right?"

I concentrated a moment on the bullet, mainly because I didn't feel like sticking my fingers in my own lung to fish out the annoying hunk of metal. The bit of silver and steel popped out of the hole it made when it entered my body and into my hand. I held out the bullet between my index finger and thumb millimeters from the tip of Anne's nose. To her credit, she didn't flinch.

"That bitch owes me a new shirt and the dry cleaning bill for my suit." I flicked the bullet into the trash can next to the loveseat. The metal pinged the side as it went in. The nanites had already closed the entry wound, and breathing became a little easier. "You wanna tell me why I'm being shot at when I just told you on the phone we were coming?"

Anne sighed and crossed her arms. "Because you teleport faster than thought. You've got to give me a chance to warn everyone you're coming before you arrive. Especially when the coven's in the middle of an emergency situation."

"Speaking of which, where's my brother?"

Anne's arms dropped to her sides. "He's in the conservatory with Bebe."

We followed her out of the living room and down the main hall. To my surprise, Ares still hadn't said a word.

"What exactly is going on?" I asked Anne.

She glanced at me over her shoulder. "It's best if Max and Bebe explain everything to you."

I didn't like the worried look on her face. What kind of trouble had my brother gotten himself into?

Caesar and a lot of the coven's enforcers were in the room Bebe used for her witchy stuff, but my attention arrowed on Max and Tiffany sitting at the large table by the floor-to-ceiling bookcase that covered the back wall.

I rushed across the room. "Dammit, Max! I've been trying to call you for the last day!"

Typical me. Anytime I was upset, the emotion came out as anger, no matter what the situation was.

A wry smile crossed his lips. "Thanks for caring, baby sis."

"What the hell is going on?"

He held up his left wrist. "I got a little present from a friend of yours yesterday."

"A Rolex? Who gave you a Rolex?" I tilted my head and touched the watch.

He disappeared. Simply flashed out of the room.

"Max!" Tiffany screamed at the same time I did.

Shocked silence filled the conservatory. Static electricity raised the hairs all over my body the instant before the magick backlash slammed me into the wall.

Chapter 19

I was still seeing stars when arms grasped mine and pulled me to my feet.

"Sam? You okay?" Alex's voice barely made it past the ringing in my ears.

"Yeah." I started to shake my head to clear it, but thought better of the idea when a wave of dizziness threatened to topple me back on my ass. "What the hell was that?"

"An interaction between your magic and voudon." Bebe flashed a penlight in my eyeballs.

I grabbed her hands and shoved them away from my face. "I'm fine, Doc. The nanites are doing their job." Even as I spoke, the ringing in my head subsided. Liquid tickled the spot under my nose. I swiped a sleeve across my upper lip. More blood ruined another spot on my white blouse.

Ares released my right arm. "Which of your personnel do you still need, Augustine?"

I never thought I'd see Caesar with a startled expression. I really wished I had my good 35mm digital camera with me. I could make some serious moola with such a portrait.

"Um, Mai is on her way with Duncan," the coven master said. "They're flying to San Francisco to pick up Stan Gryffudd."

"Very well." Ares curtly nodded. "I shall retrieve your people and return shortly." He winked out of room.

Phillippa sidled up to me and Alex. "Who was that man, and what did he do with my father?"

I swallowed the first smartass comment that popped in my head. Now wasn't the time. Not when Tiffany was struggling to keep her own tears in check. I shrugged off Alex's hold on my arm and crossed over to my sister-in-law and knelt beside her.

"Start from the last time I talked to you, Tiffany." I took her hands in mine. "Tell me what happened. Don't leave anything out."

With a choked sob, she started spilling everything from yesterday and last night. When she pointed to a woodcut picture in one of Bebe's books, my blood chilled. Baron Samedi was the mysterious stranger in Max and Tiffany's wedding album.

Mortimer passed his transit card through the turnstile and boarded the monorail that ran through the major casino/hotels along the Strip. With his baseball cap, sunglasses, and carry-on bag, he looked like any other tourist. It wasn't much of a disguise, and it wouldn't help when Karnak security got their mitts on the monorail's surveillance footage. But blending into the crowd would buy him a little more time to get Molly out of the U.S.

He got off at the Convention Center stop and worked his way through the Marriott to the cab stand. So far, so good. Vampires wouldn't be out in the bright Vegas sunshine. He hadn't spotted any weres or witches. And he'd made a point of listening to Sam when it came to identifying supernaturals.

However, that didn't preclude any Normal Family members following him. But people had departed and boarded the monorail, and the group of ten people, who had boarded behind him at the Karnak, had headed straight for the Convention Center when they exited with him.

Damn, he hadn't been this nervous since—

Since the first time he'd cheated on Molly.

The attendant waved him forward. He slid into the backseat of the taxi and gave the driver the address for Molly's office.

Mortimer stared at the passing traffic. He still hadn't learned a damn thing, had he? All he cared about was how he felt. What he wanted. He hadn't given a shit about Molly's safety.

Until it was too late.

There may be no way for him to save her. And if she died, it would be all his fault.

Chapter 20

I was beginning to worry when Ares finally popped back into the conservatory about fifteen minutes later with Duncan, Mai and Stan. From the way Duncan's eyes glowed, he was as pissed now as he had been last night.

He glared at Caesar. "I do not understand why you found it necessary to send *him*—" He jabbed a finger in Ares's direction. "—to abduct us."

Caesar's eyes didn't glow gold like they normally did when he was irritated. Instead, his eyes turned blood red. If the color wasn't an indication Duncan had gone too far, the fact that every other person in the room cleared space between the two men definitely was.

Even Ares and Phillippa.

"Maybe if you'd get your head out of your ass for two seconds, you'd notice *our* niece's husband has been kidnapped," Caesar snapped. Which was impressive because he sounded totally threatening and not lispy at all with his fangs fully extended.

I stood and marched over to Caesar and Duncan. "If you two need to prove whose dick is bigger, Alex will get the measuring tape."

"Oh, god, please leave me out of this," Augustine's chief enforcer mumbled behind me.

Tiffany waddled over to stand beside me. "Yeah, if you two aren't going to help, Sam and I will take care of this."

Duncan's face reddened, no mean feat for a vampire. "You are on maternity leave."

Tiffany crossed her arms. "You aren't my boss any more."

Anne joined us. "And with Kensai gone, Alex needed her computer expertise."

The hairs on the back of my neck rose. I glanced at Caesar, but his eyes had their normal brown color again. My attention shifted to the left.

Stan cocked his head and stared at me. And frankly, I didn't like his suspicious look one little bit.

"What is it?" Bebe asked. Her expression was equally suspicious.

"I'm not sure," he murmured. He took a step toward me.

I took a step back and raised my hands. "Wait a minute—"

"Hold still." The giant half-fae took another step.

My fingers and scalp tingled. I could feel my own power behind my eyeballs react to his magick. I couldn't help it. Maybe Caesar and the rest of Augustine Coven trusted him, but the price on my head could buy Stan back into the good graces of the Unseelie queen.

Or even a place at the Seelie Court if he wanted it.

"Sam, please." Duncan's familiar touch on my shoulder kept me from launching a psy-bolt at the other enforcer. "Let Stan do his job."

Well, at least my fiancé wasn't acting like a jerk any more.

I dipped my head in acquiescence, but tension still tightened every muscle in my body.

Stan circled us both, his head cocked like a bloodhound trying to pick up a scent. "Your purse."

I handed it to him. He dumped the contents out on Bebe's table and handed my purse to Duncan. Thankfully, it wasn't that time of the month, so no tampons decorated the dark wood. Even though Bebe said I was sterile thanks to the nanites and/or my death, Aunt Flo still came like clockwork.

On the other hand, the three Little Debbie cakes, two protein bars, and movie-sized box of Swedish Fish were almost as embarrassing.

Stan ran his palm a couple of inches over my wallet, brush, etc. His eyes were half-closed, his huge body swaying. When his hand darted out and snatched my old phone, I jumped.

"Well, isn't that clever," he muttered. He whirled to face me. "Where'd you get this?"

"What?" I stared at him.

He turned to Alex. "Is this from Augustine supplies?"

"No," Alex and I said at the same time.

"I bought it at a store on the Strip a couple of weeks ago," I added.

"It has a virus," Stan said. "Fae magick. Dormant until activated by the proximity of active witch magick."

Bebe frowned. "You mean I accidentally triggered the spell? But the interaction—"

Stan grimaced. "Think of an electric eye opening a door. No actual contact between the two systems."

I shook my head. "She couldn't have." I turned to the witch. "I haven't seen you since I bought the phone—" Maybe I hadn't been around Bebe, but I had been in the same room with another witch. "Shit!" My hands rose and covered my mouth.

"What?" Stan asked.

I lowered my hands and swallowed hard. "Quinn. The chief enforcer for Golden Eagle Coven. He came to the Karnak at Mai's request after Staci smelled ozone on a package I received. He couldn't have tripped the virus on purpose."

Stan shook his head. "No. Not unless he knew about it. And I can't see anyone from the Las Vegas coven dealing with any of the fae. They hate Harry and me as it is."

So I wasn't the only one who was suspicious of the two half-fae enforcers.

"What about me?" I asked. "Could I have done it? We all know I'm not the most adept at controlling my abilities."

Again, Stan shook his head. "This was specifically tuned to witches. Like a radio-controlled bomb. Your frequency wouldn't have set it off. Clever." But he didn't sound all that congratulatory to his kin.

Then a horrible thought occurred. I jabbed a finger in the direction of the chair my brother had been sitting in when he'd disappeared. "But what if Max's watch was keyed to my frequency?" I filled him, Duncan and Mai on what had happened before they arrived.

Stan nodded. "That makes sense if he disappeared as soon as you touched the watch."

"What doesn't make sense is why slip me a phone booby-trap that's not activated by me unless . . ." I looked at Bebe. My gray matter finally linked everything together. "Split the Vampire Nation, so they are paying more attention to the witches than who's really after us. Baron Samedi has to be in league with the fae."

"Not the Seelie," Tiffany said. "Duke Millanthropas wants peace. He had a suspicion of what you were becoming before Alex, Phil and Grandpa Ares confirmed it."

Anne inserted herself into the conversation. "The Unseelie Queen can't have been happy about my husband killing her top assassin last summer. Perhaps she blames Sam anyway."

Stan shook his head. "But still, why go through all the trouble of negotiating with either one of the queens when all Baron Samedi had to do was ask Sam for whatever it is he wants?"

Shit. This all went back to last April. "Oh, fuck me. He did ask. On the day of Max and Tiffany's second wedding. Except I didn't know who he was, much less what he was talking about. He must think I'm playing some kind of game, so he's playing one in return."

Duncan spun me to face him. "Bloody hell, woman! Why didn't you tell us?"

"Because I thought I hallucinated the whole thing!" I threw up my hands. "It took me forever to find a parking space that day. I was crossing the street when the world turned wonky."

His emerald eyes glowed. "What do you mean 'turned wonky'?"

"I mean—" I took a deep breath to try to calm myself. "When I stepped out of the crosswalk while crossing the street, the whole world turned into some kind of sepia-toned dystopia. All the people and cars were gone. And the buildings looked like they'd been abandoned for decades."

"Oh, Goddess," Bebe murmured. "You were in Otherwhere." Stan had the same stricken look on his face as our resident witch did.

"In what?" I asked, totally confused.

"What they call Otherwhere," Ares said. "It is the space between places. When you entered the middle of a crossroads, Samedi pulled you in to speak with you privately. Only our kind and the fae can walk those paths, and only if we're strong enough the predators avoid us."

"Predators?" My voice squeaked. "What kind of predators?"

He grinned, the kind of grin that promised blood and pain. "The kind that eat souls."

Chapter 21

The cab pulled up in front of Weiss Realty. Spotting Molly's convertible relieved Mortimer to no end. She was still here. Good. He climbed out and paid the driver.

A little bell jingled when he entered her office. The interior definitely showed Molly's taste. Warm tans with touches of medium and dark blues. Two hallways framed the front desk.

The twenty-something blond receptionist looked up from her monitor. "Welcome to Weiss Realty! How can I help you?"

"I'm—" Why did he feel like he was in quicksand and sinking fast? "—Walter Kinney," he finished, using his alias.

The alias he was really beginning to despise.

"So you're Molly's mysterious Walter." The receptionist grinned. She glanced behind her before she turned back and lowered her voice. "We're so glad you've gotten her out of her rut."

"Rut?"

"Yeah, she doesn't date much." The girl's pleasant expression shifted to viciousness. "However, if you do anything to hurt her, every realtor in America will make your life a living hell."

Mortimer regarded the receptionist. It was like being threatened by a teacup Chihuahua. "What are you going to do? Put 'For Sale' signs in my yard?"

"It means we'll find you, no matter where you run. No place is safe from us."

What the hell? Now, his mere presence pissed off the opposite gender? Molly had every reason to be infuriated with him, but first Mai, now this little girl threatened him.

At the sharp click of heels on tile, the receptionist's expression transformed back to pleasant. Molly rounded the corner on the left, accompanied by the elderly couple from last night.

"Again, I'm very sorry about my tardiness. Thank you so much for waiting." Her full attention was on her clients, the Jenkins, and she didn't see him. Why didn't he relish her unwavering attention on him when he had it?

Mrs. Jenkins did spot him, and she nudged her husband in the ribs. "I think now we know why she was late."

Molly whirled to see him. She frowned. Only her eyes gave away her pain. She glanced at his carry-on, and her frown deepened.

Mrs. Jenkins giggled and leaned closer to Molly. "Is his johnson as big as the original's?"

Molly's cheeks blazed bright red. She opened her mouth, but nothing came out.

"You're embarrassing the kids, Phyllis," Mr. Jenkins chided.

Mortimer grinned. "Actually, mine's bigger."

The Jenkins found his claim hilarious. Molly, on the other hand, would have shot him if she had a gun in reach from the murderous look on her face.

Once Mr. Jenkins's laughter died to the occasional chuckle, he said, "I'll have the bank fax you the confirmation of the funds in our account, Ms. Weiss." His wife was still laughing hard as he guided her through the main door.

The receptionist swiveled toward Molly and smiled brightly. "Your ten o'clock is here, Ms. Weiss."

Molly glared at Mortimer. "I may need to cancel that one."

He smiled, or he tried to. "Can I be your—" The off-color joke he was about to make wouldn't do a thing to save Molly's life, and that needed to be his priority now. "—lunch appointment? Please?"

The left side of her mouth twitched, but he couldn't tell if she were on the verge of a smile.

Or the verge of decking him.

Finally, she nodded curtly and motioned for him to follow her. Mortimer started after her when the hairs on the back of his neck rose. He glanced over his shoulder.

The receptionist had rolled on her chair to the edge of the wall, and peered around it. She was shooting him the same vicious look as before.

They entered Molly's office, and she closed the door. Instead of sitting at her desk or taking a seat on one of the visitor chairs, she crossed her arms and tapped her foot. "On the drive here, I began to realize what a fool I was to believe your cock-and-bull story."

He raised his hands and spread his fingers. "Just let me explain."

"You have one minute."

"Oh geez! Where do I begin?" He dropped his carry-on on the nearest chair. "I know how crazy this is going to sound, but please, let me finish before you say anything."

"Fifty-five seconds." She wasn't joking.

He sucked in a deep breath. "Last spring, a voodoo guy tried to kill Sam, the lady that's now my business manager, by raising the dead in the Hollywood Cemetery, including me. Sam's a little different. If something alive drinks her blood, it kills 'em. If something dead drinks her blood, it brings 'em back to life. I was a zombie controlled by this friggin' asshole—"

"Wait." Molly blinked and her hand sliced horizontally through the air. "Who's the asshole? Sam or the voodoo guy?"

"The voodoo guy." Morty drew another breath. "Please understand. I wasn't in my right mind being an animated corpse at the time. I slashed Sam's throat. Blood went everywhere. It smelled and tasted so good I started licking every drop."

Molly's eyes widened. "Wait a minute. Did you kill this woman?"

He shook his head. "No. That's part of Sam's physiology. She heals damn fast. Next thing I knew, I was me again." He tapped his fingertips against his chest. "I remembered my entire life, but I was half the age I was when I croaked."

Molly's toe was no longer bouncing, and her arms dropped to her sides. "If this woman can do all the things you say, why isn't the government studying her? Dammit, her genes could be the answer to cancer!"

"No, they aren't, Molly. The reason Sam is that way is because she was kidnapped and illegally experimented on. There were a lot of side effects. Some really ugly shit that I wouldn't wish on my worst enemy."

She gripped the back of the other visitor chair and slowly sank down. "I don't understand. If your Sam was kidnapped, how'd she get away? Why didn't she call the authorities?"

Morty shifted the carry-on to the floor and sat beside her, though he didn't dare touch her. They were well past her minute, but she was still listening. "She didn't because she was rescued." He stared at the ceiling for a moment before he met Molly's gaze again. "By a vampire."

She started laughing. "Okay, you had me until—"

"You've already met him, cowgirl. The Brit on the elevator this morning as you were leaving the hotel."

"St. James? The manager of the Karnak?"

He nodded. "That's why I was hustling you out. Vampires can read minds."

"So Sam became a vampire? Is that why she's dating St. James? He turned her into one?"

Mortimer shook his head. "Depending on who you talk to, she's either Frankenstein's monster or a zombie." He figured it was best not to mention the third alternative circulating through the coven. That would definitely send Molly over the edge. "That was part of the experiments. The people who kidnapped her were trying to figure out immortality without the sunlight problem St. James has."

She shivered. "Then who was the woman with him on the elevator?"

"Mai's the head of security at the Karnak. She's Normal, like you, and one sharp cookie for a broad."

Molly straightened her spine. "Excuse me?"

"Sorry," he muttered. "The ladies I work with are trying to beat the twentieth century out of me."

"So what's the problem with the security chief?"

"She knows about us spending the night together."

"And?"

He closed his eyes. God, he'd so fucked up. "She'll investigate you. Find out everything about your past. And she'll know that we used to be married."

"So what?"

He opened his eyes. "Because of the circumstances of my resurrection, I agreed to the vampires' rules. The biggest of which is you don't contact anyone from your previous life." Tears welled in his eyes, something that hadn't happened since the day his mother died. "When I found out you were living here, I wanted to make things right with you. Do things right. And I'm so sorry for being such a selfish bastard."

"Mortimer," she whispered. "What will happen when the vampires find out about me? About us?"

"We're both dead."

I stared at Ares. "Would Baron Samedi take Max to this Otherwhere?"

The god shook his head. "Your brother would attract too much attention if Samedi did so. If I were him, I would keep Max in a place of my power. Another god would have difficulty breaching such."

I cocked my head. "So I need a way to lure Samedi out?"

He nodded and stroked his beard. "There may be a way."

"What is it?" Tiffany demanded.

"Let me make some inquiries, Cherry Blossom. I do not wish to raise false hope." He hugged my sister-in-law and released her before he popped out of the conservatory again.

"Does anyone here really believe he has a plan?" I muttered.

"Father's taken with Tiffany," Phil said. "And Max by extension. He's not as dumb as he likes to pretend to be, so, yes, he has a plan."

"I think it is more that he wishes to impress Samantha. After all, Max is her brother," Duncan muttered.

Phil and I glared at him. He glared right back.

I jabbed a finger in the general direction of Caesar's backyard. "Outside. Now."

I expected one of his long-suffering sighs. Instead, he pivoted and marched out of the conservatory. I followed. Surprisingly, he didn't head for the garage as I half-expected. He strode toward the French doors leading to the patio.

Outside, the wind had picked up. Waves rippled across the surface of the pool, and the awning flapped. Clouds scudded across the bright blue sky. Duncan found the deepest shadow under the covered section of the patio. Once I closed the French doors behind us, we simply stared at each other. He didn't try to touch my mind. Neither did I try to touch his.

"I don't know why you insist—" he started.

"Shut up!" I sliced my hand downward. "Just . . . be quiet and listen." I sucked in a deep breath. "Look, I know you're used to being the top of the food chain. I know you have a hard time looking at women as something other than property."

He opened his mouth, and I held up my index finger. "Still talking here. But the worst thing is when you asked me to marry you, I assumed you trusted me."

Tears welled in my eyes. "It's pretty obvious you don't. But this isn't about me choosing between you and Ares. You're asking me to choose between you and Max. And I'm sorry, but I'm choosing Max. It's my fault he was taken. Just like you would have chosen Tiffany if she'd been the one captured by Samedi."

Duncan raked his hands through his midnight locks. "I would have found a way to do both."

"Except you're not giving me a choice here." I twisted the engagement ring around my finger before I yanked the gold and diamond band off and held it out to Duncan. "Let's get Max home, then we'll talk about the future. And whether or not you trust me."

When he wouldn't take the ring, I concentrated. The bit of jewelry floated through the air and settled in Duncan's jacket pocket. I pivoted on my damn sensible heels and stalked back into the mansion because I didn't want him to see my heart break.

Chapter 22

Mortimer sighed. It was dark outside. Except for a couple of bathroom breaks and a single interruption from one of the junior realtors, Molly grilled him about the supernatural world like an experienced CIA interrogator.

"I don't get why you want to know all this shit."

"If they're going to kill me just for talking to you at the supermarket, I might as well know everything." She grimaced.

He took her hands in his. "Now, do you see why I need to get you out of the country?"

She shook her head. "Morty, don't you see? It doesn't matter where we go if there are monsters all over the world. They'll track us down anyway."

He held out his hands. "Please, cowgirl. I have to try to save you."

She shook her head again. "You're still a selfish shit, Mortimer Stern." She nibbled on a thumbnail. "What if we split the difference? We'll go down to Mexico like you want."

"Thank you—"

She placed her other hand over his lips. "For three days. If nothing happens in those three days, we are coming home."

"But—"

"No 'buts,' Mortimer." She cupped his cheek. "When we get back to Las Vegas, introduce me to Sam. It sounds to me like she'd understand our situation."

"Okay, but can we please leave now?" He was supposed to be onstage in three hours. The longer they waited before they fled, the more likely they'd be found.

"I need to run home and pick up a few things."

"As long as we go now," he pleaded.

"For the love of—" She stomped around her desk. "You need to use your head, Morty. Let me send a couple of e-mails. Otherwise, your new buddies will try to claim you abducted me to spur on a police search."

"We're going to need a new car," he said loudly to be heard over her rapid-fire banging of the computer's keys. "They'll run your registration."

"I can take care of that." She jabbed the switch to shut down her computer. "Aren't you more worried about our phones being tapped?"

He smiled. "That's why mine's sitting on my nightstand back at the Karnak."

She froze. "You really think they'd stoop to—"

He glanced out the window. "Actually, I'm more worried about getting out of Las Vegas tonight before we run into a vampire."

"Then get your bag, and let's go." She grabbed his arm and dragged him out of the now quiet office.

Twenty minutes later, Molly pressed the button for her garage door. The double-wide vinyl slid up to reveal a thirty-year-old Buick in the second parking space. She pulled into the empty side.

She nodded toward the burgundy sedan. "My father's car. I got it when Mom died, but it's still registered in her name. Will that do?"

Mortimer grinned at her. "That'll do, cowgirl. That'll do."

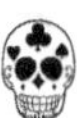

I walked back into the conservatory. Duncan didn't follow.

A minute after I returned, Mai got a constipated look on her face. The one that was her telepathy face, meaning one of the vampires was issuing orders.

I hoped for her sake, her sex face was better.

She looked at Caesar who nodded. She marched out of the room. A couple of minutes later, I felt the subtle vibration of the garage door opening.

Other than Alex and Stan mumbling to each other about the fae phone virus, no one said much as we waited for Ares to return. At least, not until Tiffany announced the baby needed chocolate pudding and stalked through the door.

Everyone else decided food was a good idea. They shuffled out of the conservatory. With nothing else to do and my stomach grumbling, I started to follow. Caesar touched my arm and inclined his head toward his office.

Crap. I'd learned over the last eight months, he wasn't just Duncan's boss. He had kind of a big brother relationship with my fiancé as well. Was I about to get a lecture? Because if he even thought about delivering one, I was going to—

"Are you all right, Sam?" he asked softly as he closed his office door behind us. He took a seat on the couch and gestured for me to join him.

Oka-a-y. If he wasn't sitting behind his desk, this wasn't going to be an official dressing down.

I perched on the edge of the leather cushions. "You didn't have to send Duncan away on my account."

Caesar took my left hand and rubbed his thumb where my missing engagement ring should have been sitting. "You have something you need to resolve before you two can deal with your relationship. I gave him a task to occupy his time as well. Once he's done, he will wait for you back in Las Vegas." He squeezed my hand. "Don't give up on him just yet, Sam."

Okay, *definitely* not what I was expecting.

"What am I supposed to do? He doesn't trust me." I waved my free hand. "I'm more likely to sleep with Alex before Ares."

Caesar rubbed his forehead. "That comes under TMI, and I wouldn't say that anywhere near Phillippa."

"You know what I mean. I'll admit Ares has been trying to start something, but I've said no at every turn. I have even less in common with him than I do Duncan."

Caesar released me hand, steepled his fingers, and rested his chin on the tips. "And what exactly do you have in common with Duncan?"

"Besides the fact we were both born Normal?"

A slight smile tilted the corners of Caesar's lips. "Yes, besides that."

"I . . ." I couldn't think of a damn thing. Hell, I had more in common with Tiffany than Duncan, and Max had already claimed her.

And *that* was a disturbing thought for the sheer reason it had popped in my head.

Caesar's smile grew. "You two have more in common than Bebe and I did."

I grimaced and leaned back against the arm of the couch. "Says the guy whose proposals have been turned down how many times?"

He chuckled. "Point scored. All I'm saying is if what Alex and Bebe are saying is true, you're going to need him."

"Why?"

"The same reason I need Bebe. To hang onto your humanity."

<h1 style="text-align:center">Chapter 23</h1>

The Buick handled like a dream between Mortimer's hands. Molly sat beside him, contentedly slurping on her chocolate milkshake from their supper stop at a fast-food drive-thru. Now that they were finally on the road south, he was beginning to relax.

She licked her lips. "If these vampires have infiltrated the government as much as you said, wouldn't they have access to the records for border crossings?"

"Yeah, they do, but since Homeland Security focuses more on flights than car traffic, the coven's access is limited and dated."

She was quiet for a bit. It wasn't until her first snore he realized she'd fallen asleep. He carefully took the empty cup from her lax hands and set it in the paper bag with the rest of their trash.

He couldn't remember the last time he'd taken a road trip, just him and his lady. A strange feeling spread through him, and it took a moment to identify it.

Happiness.

The Buick purred through the moonlit desert night.

Bill straightened his tie in the backstage mirror. Lily leaned over and pecked him on the cheek.

"Hey, lady!" He laughed. "You're going to get lipstick on my shirt."

She grabbed a tissue from the dispenser and swiped at the red smear. "There's places I can kiss you where the audience won't see."

He groaned. "Look, I know you're happy you can go on tonight, but you need to relax." She'd been ecstatic since Sam had called this morning and said the restraining order had been denied. She'd been incorrigible since the show's producer had confirmed it.

"Or we can relax together." Her mischievous grin informed him it was going to be a very long night.

"Marshall is not going to be happy if you don't go on after all that lawsuit crap."

"Hey, Jerry! Maryann!"

At their fake names, Bill looked up and spotted their producer. Speak of the devil. Marshall Wagoner puffed to a stop next to them. "Have you two seen Walter?"

"Not since the end of last night's second performance." Bill frowned. "What's wrong?"

"*No one* has seen him since last night. That's the problem. One of the cocktail waitresses served him and my friend Molly after the second show. She said they left together. And that's it."

"Molly?" Bill asked with a sinking feeling. "Molly who?"

Marshall's frown deepened. "Molly Weiss. She's a real estate agent here in Vegas and came in with a couple of clients, who were big fans of Mortimer Stern. I introduced them last night between shows. I've called the Karnak, and I've called Molly's house, her office, every number I have for either of them. I can't even get a hold of Sam right now!"

During Marshall's word vomit, Bill exchanged looks with Lily. Her expression mirrored his worry and fear. After all the crap with Lily's daughter, why on earth would Morty hang out with his ex-wife? He knew the stakes better than they did. Hell, he'd been the one lecturing them the last couple of days.

Marshall sucked in a deep breath. "What I'm trying to say, Jerry, can you take over tonight?"

Bill held up a hand. "Wait, I don't want to be stepping on toes. What about Harv?"

"He may play a mean Ed Sullivan, but he can't get here in the next ten minutes," Marshall said. "I just need you for the first show."

"Don't worry," Bill said. "I'll take care of this."

As soon as their producer disappeared in the milling crowd of performers getting ready, he turned to Lily.

Her expression was grave. "After all the shit he gave me, you don't think he would have run off with Wife Number Two, do you?"

Bill stared in the direction Marshall had gone. "I hope to god they did run off."

"What? Why?"

Bill met Lily's gaze again. "Because if they didn't, it means the vampires already found out about Molly and decided to take care of the situation themselves."

Ares popped into the kitchen right behind our resident witch just as Bebe pivoted to set the tomatoes she'd sliced on the island countertop. She shrieked, and the plate, tomato slices, and knife went airborne.

I would have thought solids would be easier to catch than liquids after my stunt with the red wine at Agnes's place last night. I mentally wrestled everything back to the granite counter. However, one slice slipped by and landed with a splat on the floor.

I guess that was better than the knife accidently skewering Bebe's foot.

Everyone stared at me, except Ares. He had a pleased expression. "Your control has improved."

"Not enough," I muttered as I tore off a couple of paper towels. I cleaned up the red slime off the imported Italian tile.

"Quit blabbing about Sam doing her Carrie routine," Tiffany snapped. "What did you find out?"

Ares frowned. "Samedi does have your husband, but I—" Anger and shame created a weird mix in his expression. "I cannot retrieve him for you, Cherry Blossom." He looked at me. "Only Sam can go. I can take you to the edge of this place."

A chorus of protests rose in the kitchen from everyone but one. I looked at the silent and very concerned Stan.

"You know what he's talking about, don't you?"

The huge half-fae's attention flicked to Ares and then back to me. "I've heard stories. There is a place in Otherwhere where only death can walk."

"Which is why I can't take her straight to Max." The war god shook his head sadly when he looked at me. "I can do nothing more to aid you, Samantha. I cannot tell you who may be your foe besides Baron Samedi, but you will have one friend. One of my half-sisters has promised her aid. However, we must leave now. You have to retrieve Max before midnight."

I tried to shove my own panic into a very dark hole. I still didn't know what it was Samedi thought I took from him and his father though I had a sneaking suspicion it had something to do with David Head raising the dead of Hollywood last spring. It didn't help when Tiffany waddled over to face me.

"All I'm going to tell you is you'd better get my husband back." Her voice was deadly calm. "Or I'll make it my mission in life to find a way to kill you permanently."

<h1 style="text-align:center">Chapter 24</h1>

Ares materialized us on the corner of Wilshire, a block from the Beverly Center. The mall was closed, dark except for the occasional neon sign.

I whirled on him, my fist raised to belt him. "What the hell are you trying to pull? You said you'd take me to Max."

"I told you I can't take you to him directly. There're places even I cannot go." His expression was grim. Any flirtation lost. "When I contacted my sister, she said Baron Samedi has called a grievance against you."

I lowered my hand. "What do you mean? Like a union grievance?"

He tilted his head as if judging whether I'd lose it. "You could say that. The gods of death hold a special status. They rarely involve themselves in other gods' conflicts." He sucked in a deep breath. "And they police themselves."

"What you're saying is I'm about to go before a jury of my peers when I don't even know the rules." Fear chased a million thoughts through my head. At least this morning, I had Colin and Ronnie by my side when facing the judge. "Max and I are screwed."

"Possibly." He shrugged. "You'll have to prove your innocence in order to save your brother."

"And how am I supposed to do that?"

He placed his palms on my shoulders. "You'll find a way. And you won't be alone. My sister will be your ally."

"You still haven't told me which sister," I said sourly.

"Persephone."

Of course. Which other sister could possibly be helping me in this conclave of the dead except the wife of Hades?

I wrapped my arms around myself. I so didn't want to deal with this. If this did involve David Head, well, he had already paid for so many of my mistakes in addition to his own. At least he was still alive, even if he was in a coma. Max wouldn't be that lucky if I didn't figure out how to fix this. "How long before she gets here?"

"She's waiting for you."

I pirouetted in an effort to spot her. There wasn't enough folks on the sidewalks this late at night to mask her, and the cars all sped by.

Ares grabbed me and twisted until I faced the intersection. "The crossroad, Samantha."

All I could see was north and south-bound traffic whipping by while the people in the east-west lanes waited impatiently for their turn. "I don't see her."

"It's a crossroad," he said slowly, as if speaking to a child.

Which only added to my general pissiness. "Yes, I know," I said equally slowly. "Crossroad. Intersection. It doesn't matter what you call it. I still don't see her."

Ares sighed, a loud, gusty sound, before he shoved me into the street, right in front of an oncoming SUV. I screamed . . .

. . . and the world tilted and blurred. Nausea rose, and my stomach threatened to heave. Then my left foot landed on something solid, and everything righted itself.

Like the last time this happened to me, the cars and pedestrians disappeared. But instead of the buildings appearing desolate and deserted, jagged sections of basalt replaced them. The streets were tiled with uneven sections of the same black stone. It was night instead of sepia-toned murky sunlight from the last time this had happened, but I could see everything clearly.

And once again, a figure stood in the middle of the empty intersection. She reminded me of Anne. Waif-like with long brown hair, but this woman's dark eyes carried far more years. She was dressed in a black Greek chiton with her feet bare.

She smiled. "Hello, Samantha Marie Ridgeway. I am Persephone."

Chapter 25

"Um, hi." I waggled my fingers. "Nice to meet you." I tried to surreptitiously look around, but Ares was nowhere in sight.

She walked over and looped her left arm around my right. "We have a little ways to go, so I can tutor you as to what you can expect as we walk."

When I didn't move, she laughed a light, tinkling lady-like one that actually sounded sincere. "Ares did warn me you were a stickler." She inhaled before she started, "I vow upon the River Styx that I will guide you to the Conclave of Death, I will answer all your questions truthfully and honestly as long as I know the answer, I will inform you if I don't know the answer to your question, and I will return you to this spot in order for you to reenter the mortal realms." She smiled, a brilliant, sweet one. "Does that satisfy you, Samantha Marie Ridgeway?"

I relaxed an iota. "Yes, thank you. And please call me Sam." I was starting to like Phil's aunt.

We took a couple of steps in the direction she indicated when I heard the growl above us. Something perched on one of the basalt pillars. The only thing I could make out in the dark were its eyes, and only because they glowed fiery orange.

"What's that?" I whispered.

"One of the denizens of this realm," Persephone answered. She took a step forward, raised her right arm, and shouted, "Be gone!"

Whatever it was, it turned tail and disappeared behind the pillar. And I mean tail, because I caught a glimpse of a slender cat-like appendage with a tuft of feathers at the tip.

Faint sound of claws on rock surrounded us before they faded into the distance.

"Were we in danger?"

Again, Persephone laughed. "Us? No. They aren't stupid enough to fight gods head-on."

I glanced at her as she tugged me down what had been Wilshire Boulevard. "Which means they're not averse to attacking us from behind."

Another brilliant smile. "I see why both Ares and Phillippa are enamored with you."

I jerked to a halt, yanking Persephone back. "What do you mean Phil is enamored with me?"

"Not in a romantic sense. She admires your fortitude in the face of your difficulties." Persephone resumed walking, pulling me along. "Now, in Ares's case—"

"I'm well aware of what he wants," I grumbled.

She sighed. "And that describes every male in our family. Except my Aidoneus, of course."

It was rather sweet she used his ancient given name instead of the Greek word for hell. But given that I really needed her help, I wasn't about to correct her on her husband's extra-curricular adventures. Instead, I focused on my immediate surroundings.

A faint silvery sheen gave the place some visibility, but there were no stars in the sky. No moons either. Not even the vague impression of clouds. There was a slight incline as we trod along the stony version of Wilshire.

"What is this place?"

"It has many names in the mortal plan. The Void. Between. Otherwhere." She shrugged.

That did not help at all, though I remembered Bebe and Stan mentioning the last term when I described my previous encounter with Baron Samedi. "But what is it?"

Persephone hesitated a moment, but I got the impression she was searching for the right words rather than considering a lie to spin. "Think of it as the place between life and death."

I shuddered. "Like Purgatory or Limbo?"

Another sweet laugh. "No, those are actual territories used by the dead. Think of it more as a neutral place. Like your United Nations building."

Other than the thing with the feathery tail, this place didn't seem bad though it had a creepy air. "Ares said he couldn't come here. Why—"

She patted my arm. "This place is far more dangerous for those like our brothers than it is for us. Unless a living thing is powerful enough to keep free of the denizens here, then they are quickly killed . . ."

"And eaten," I finished for her.

Persephone nodded. "Even the sidhe use the pathways through Otherwhere sparingly, and only because the Morrigan gave them the tools to do so during the wars with the Formor."

In that moment, I wished I hadn't done quite so much research into the death gods of various cultures. The stories about the Celt's Morrigan were pretty brutal.

"However, they merely sensed my presence," Persephone continued. "They won't bother you."

"Me?" I squeaked. "Why not me?"

"They only consume the living, Sam," she said softly. "I never died in the conventional sense. Not like you or my Aidoneus."

My thought process clogged at that little reminder. I didn't know what to ask, and Max depended on me to get him out of this mess I'd accidentally dumped him into.

"First of all," Persephone continued. "Don't let any of the others intimidate you. They're so used to their worshippers falling over in fear they sometimes forget what it's like to have an equal."

I snorted. "Like I have worshippers."

"You will." She smiled up at him. "You've already started converting mortals."

"No, I'm not," I protested. "That's so wrong on so many levels."

She laughed at my outrage. "Sam, you can't tell a mortal what to believe. Their belief shapes us as much as our powers do."

"But I'm not recruiting people!"

"What about your family? Your friends?"

I searched the landscape, trying to find answers to Persephone's questions. The stony cliffs were receding. Black sand was interspersed between the growing gaps of the paving stones. The area no longer looked like a warped Paleolithic version of Los Angeles.

"They don't worship me," I muttered.

"No, but they believe you will save them from what's coming. That's where it starts." She patted my arm again.

I needed to change the direction of the conversation if I were going to keep my sanity. "Why does Baron Samedi think I've stolen something from him?"

"You did. The necromancer. He gave himself to the vodoun. Therefore, the Baron has the responsibility to collect his soul."

The necromancer. So this *was* about David Head.

"He's not dead," I said. "He's alive. In a coma at a Miami hospital, but he's very much alive."

She frowned. "You bound him to you."

I ground my teeth. This bullshit was getting old. "I bound his powers to keep him from killing anyone else. Do you know what he did at my brother's wedding? Hell, he sacrificed his best friend to Papa Ghede to raise the zombies that invaded my parents' backyard!"

"Yes, I am aware of what happened." She paused, and I stopped to face her. A shiver ran through me at her expression. One or more of Max's wedding guests had ended up in her realm. Or worse, they were trapped on the shores of the River Styx because they weren't buried with a coin for Charon, the boatman of Greek Hell.

She breathed deeply and nodded. "Binding his abilities and taking his soul are two different things. That is where your testimony shall start. You need to show the rest that binding him was all you did."

I groaned. How the hell did I end up in court twice in one day? The worst this morning's judge would have done is kill Lily's stand-up career, not kill my baby zombie.

"But how?" I whined. I wasn't proud of myself at this moment.

"SHE will question you. Just tell the truth, Sam." Persephone started walking again.

I didn't have a choice but to go with her. Damn, she was strong for her size. "Who is SHE?" Like when the supernaturals talked about Family, I could *hear* the capitalization.

This time Persephone giggled. "The oldest of us. You'll know when you see her. We're almost there."

I had the sudden urge to piss myself. For her claim to answer my questions, Persephone hadn't really told me a damn thing. If the monster Supay claimed I would face eventually was a dinosaur god, then what the hell was this SHE?

The awful odor of fresh tar and fresher death knocked away my fear. I gagged. The last time I smelled something close to this was when Caesar ordered me to make nice with the new Seelie queen at Hancock Park.

Just how far had we walked? If everything in Otherwhere had a counterpart in reality . . .

"Have you ever heard of the La Brea Tar Pits?" I asked.

"Yes, this is the same area in the mortal realm. It's the oldest concentration of death closest to your point of creation. Since you've been accused—"

"I have home court advantage," I finished with a sharp nod. I felt a little better, though I kind of wished I had worn one of my Sabretooth jerseys. Not that the Los Angeles pro basketball team really had anything to do with the big cats trapped and smothered in ancient tar besides the name.

Instead I still wore the business suit . . .

I looked down. My smart black jacket and skirt were gone as well as my blood-smeared white button-down shirt. A long black coat that reached my knees covered black slacks. My sensible matching pumps had been replaced by boots. I reached for my neckline. A high collar met my fingers.

Holy crap! I was dressed like Neo from *The Matrix*. Is this what I thought I should look like? And after Persephone's talk about my friends believing I could save them, did they think I was the One? Talk about being full of myself. Not to mention Neo died in the last Matrix movie.

Well, I had one up on Keanu Reeves's character. I died in the first reel.

All in all, I'd still rather be wearing one of my Sabretooth jerseys.

I glanced at Persephone. "Did my clothes change?"

"Yes." Persephone squeezed my arm. "Quit worrying. You'll do fine, Sam. You're one of us."

Her statement wasn't as reassuring as she thought. If it weren't for my cast-iron zombie stomach, I'd be puking right now.

A worse thought occurred. I couldn't really call myself a zombie anymore. But claiming I was a goddess didn't sit right in my conscience either. All I knew for sure was I could no longer claim I was human. And once again, I was subject to rules I didn't know.

We reached a rise in the black sand trail. A moat of burning tar surrounded a natural amphitheater below us, a basalt bridge the only access. I could see figures moving around the various levels inside the organic-looking structure.

"Looks like everyone is here already," Persephone said.

"Everyone?" I squeaked.

More laughter from her. I was so glad to be her personal comic relief. Not.

"It's a big deal when someone new joins the ranks. It's such a rare event." She tugged on my arm again. The woman was a serial tugger. "Usually, there's a huge party."

I dragged my boots. "Then why is mine starting with a trial?"

"If all you did was bind the necromancer, it's just a misunderstanding, Sam." She pulled harder on my arm. "We'll straighten it out and everything will be fine."

The walk down to the bridge took both forever and an instant at the same time. The path ended at an opening in the base of the amphitheater. I couldn't identify the new paving. It looked like diamond, but it chimed softly with each of our footsteps. When we strode onto the main floor, every head turned to watch us.

Race was a subjective term. Few of the entities, besides Persephone, appeared remotely human. Nor did they congregate in any method scholars would categorize.

Some I recognized immediately from my research. Kali's dark blue skin marked her as much as the belt of severed heads. Morrigan's flaming hair and pale skin matched the bloodstained shift she wore. Hela was as beautiful as the Eddas described her, at least from the waist up. The rest of her matched the rotting zombies I'd dealt with four months ago. The three of them whispered together where they sat four rows up.

From Phil and Alex's description, the Native American-looking man dressed in brilliant red, gold and black garb below them must be Supay.

A ghost of a smile crossed his lips, and he inclined his head as Persephone and I passed.

Next to him sat the Grim Reaper, complete with a scythe. He pushed back his hood. Instead of a skull, he had dark, curling hair to his shoulders and eyes so pale blue they were almost white. With a start, I realized he was the angel who collected Josh Williams' soul after the actor and I saved his son from Josh's killer. The angel winked at me and smiled. If my research was right, he would the archangel Azrael.

On the opposite side of the amphitheater, the ancient Egyptian's Anubis leaned on his staff as he spoke with a slim girl in goth make-up, her eyes done to resemble Horus's. It was a stark contrast to the black Victorian dress and hat she wore. I did a double-take. She wasn't my sister-in-law Tiffany, but the resemblance was damn eerie. The girl waggled her fingers at me and grinned when she saw me staring at her.

I finally noticed Persephone wasn't heading for any of the unoccupied seats, but toward the ruby dais where the stage would be in a human theater. Baron Samedi stood to our right. A man dressed like the proverbial liberal arts professor, including the tweed jacket and horn-rimmed glasses, stood to the left. His average, normal appearance stood out among this group because it was so average and normal.

But the woman seated, cross-legged, on the humungous jewel commanded the most attention. She reminded me of a model in the Neanderthal exhibit at the Museum of Natural Science. A thick brow ridge. Dark brown hair in heavy dreds. Ponderous breasts swung below her necklaces of bone. She clutched a gnarled stick that could be equal parts weapon and walking aid. The leather skirt she wore didn't hide her wide hips. Yet, she seemed familiar. Take away the skirt and accessories . . .

"You're Venus of Willendorf," I blurted.

She laughed, showing wide, blunt teeth. "That is mankind's latest name for me, yes." Her arm swept through the air to indicate the assemblage. "And each person here would call me by their own name for my role."

I blinked and heat rushed to my cheeks. "I-I'm sorry. I don't know your real name."

"My first name is long forgotten by mortals. Nor could you pronounce it." She sobered. "The rough translation is 'she-who brings-life-and-death.'"

The fake professor chuckled. "That's why everyone here simply refers to her as SHE."

I turned to him. "And you are?"

He held out his hand. "Call me Norman."

I took his hand and shook it. He had a nice firm grip and a Normal's body temperature. "Um, I didn't find a god named Norman in my research."

"That's because according to my adherents, there is no god." Amusement twinkled in his average brown eyes.

"O-o-k-a-a-a-y." I wasn't sure how to address his statement after all the deities I'd dealt with over the last few months.

"Consider Norman a spirit of intellect," SHE offered. Humor at my confusion danced in her visage.

"I don't understand the difference, ma'am." I figured a little politeness would go a long way here.

"I get the atheists, the agnostics, a few others who aren't quite sure about their beliefs." Norman shrugged.

"But if they don't believe—"

A wry smile tilted his lips. "The soul has to go somewhere. Basic principals of physics, such as the conservation of energy, still apply. Even here." He waved his hand, whether to indicate Otherwhere or the assembly of death gods I wasn't sure.

"So you have to take the stragglers?"

He chuckled again. In a way, he reminded me of my dad. "That's the paradox. They don't believe in an afterlife until they get here, but none of the rest of you can claim them unless they commit to a faith before they die. And when I collect them, they assume I'm a hallucination."

A dull ache behind my eyes started at the twists in his explanation, but I resisted the urge to rub my temples. Something I'd learned from Caesar was not to show weakness in front of enemies.

Or potential enemies.

"Are we finished with educating the thief?" Baron Samedi snapped. "Or can we get on with more important business?"

"Party pooper," Norman muttered in my ear. I suddenly liked him a lot more.

SHE banged her staff against the ruby three times. The sound the crystal and wood made was akin to a gong. The entities quieted and sought their seats.

Once everyone was settled, SHE climbed to her feet. "Another age has come. One who has died and is reborn has joined our ranks. It should be a time of celebration for her ascension and preparation for her final test. However—" She shot Baron an ugly glare. "There had been an accusation of theft. A soul pledged to the loa."

A rumble went up from the assemblage. Great. I wanted to run and hide. The accusation against me was the death equivalent of an Amish joining the NRA.

And my internal joke would have been a lot funnier if I didn't know an Amish vampire who was a better markswoman than the entire United States armed forces.

God, I wanted to puke.

"Who stands with the accused?"

"I do." Persephone's sweet voice piped across the amphitheater. It was a little reassuring that she kept her word to help me, but then she had sworn on the River Styx.

"As do I."

"And I."

I turned at the two masculine voices. Supay and the angel crossed the diamond floor and stood behind Persephone.

Kali rose. "I suppose I will, too. Otherwise, I'll never hear the end of it at home." The skulls on her necklace rattled in counterpoint to the chiming of her steps on the diamond. She stomped over to me and leaned close. "You owe me a night with Yama for this."

I jerked away. "What?" Was I that desperate that I'd pimp myself for my undead existence?

She merely grinned, a terrible smile with yellowish fangs and her tongue lolling, as if she already knew my answer before she went to stand behind Persephone.

"Who stands with the accuser?" SHE belted out.

"I-I w-will." A giant black, very hairy, spider on Norman's side crawled down, and over, the other observers. The deep vibrating timbre of its voice sounded like an overlaid soundtrack.

"And I," Morrigan shouted. She made a point of flipping a weird gesture in Kali's direction. I assumed it was rude from the Hindu goddess's scowl.

"You're just doing this out of spite, bitch." Kali glared at Morrigan.

"Maybe." The Celtic goddess gave me the same slow appraisal Duke Millanthropas of the Seelie Court had given me nearly seven months ago. "You don't have your worshippers nagging you about the child." She sniffed. "And I wonder why?" A horrible grin followed. "Overdoing the iron supplements, aren't you, kid?"

"It's steel," I shot back. "And I don't resort to nasty tricks with viruses like your fae do when they can't win against Normals and vampires in a fair fight." I realized shooting off my mouth like that may not have been in my best interest. The last thing I needed was more enemies here and now.

SHE snapped her stick against the ruby again. "Begin your statement, Baron Samedi."

Part of me was relieved I had twice as many people, gods, or whatever than he did, but I didn't think it mattered as far as SHE was concerned. Maybe the rest of the assembly didn't think he needed the help. Maybe it was a case of not letting the older kids beat up on the new girl.

"This isn't going to be trial by combat, is it?" I whispered to Kali, who still stood next to me.

"No. Now, shush," she whispered back.

Both SHE and Baron glared at me, but Norman and everyone else tried to hide smiles. A couple in the audience outright snickered.

Shit. Everyone could hear everything I said.

Then something else struck me. Everyone who'd spoken had an American accent. Even Baron, who extolled his side of the incident with David Head to the assemblage, sounded more American South than Caribbean like he had the first time we met.

He stabbed a forefinger in my direction. "She invaded my worshipper's home with her followers, including corpses she resurrected, and stole my worshipper's soul!"

"Wait just a fuckin' minute—"

SHE slammed the end of her stick into the ruby. In addition to the reverberating *gong*, blinding red light flashed from the jewel. "Silence from the defendant!"

"Down, girl," Kali murmured in my ear. "You'll get your chance."

I clenched my jaw to keep from getting into more trouble, but his twisting of the facts really was pissing me off. A warm hand wrapped around my left hand. I glanced down to find Persephone still standing beside me. She squeezed my fingers and smiled.

It was a little reassuring to know a couple of folks here believed me.

Baron finished his little soliloquy. "When I confronted her on the matter, she refused to release David Jebediah Head's soul. I have asked the required three times."

Silence reigned for a long moment. It could have been a couple of seconds or it could have been centuries. It felt like the latter, but I heeded Kali's advice and waited until SHE turned to me.

"The defendant may speak." She wasn't even going to give me the courtesy of using my name. Fine, I'd play her game. For now.

I released Persephone's hand, stepped away from my supporters, and turned to address the crowd. "My name is Sam Ridgeway. I didn't ask to be changed into a god. I was a human experiment. But what's done is done."

Taking a deep breath, I continued, laying out Head's zombie attacks during the week before, and day of, Max and Tiffany's aborted first ceremony. How he kidnapped Duncan in a final effort to kill me. How I accidentally restored Morty, Lily and Bill to life after Head had raised them from their graves.

I looked over my shoulder at Azrael. "They're yours. I swear I didn't intend what happened, and I definitely don't claim their souls."

He inclined his head. "Your word is sufficient for my Lord's claim."

I turned back to SHE. "Finally, Baron Samedi only asked me once. As I told him then, I don't have Head's soul. I bound his powers to keep him from hurting anyone else. And yeah, I admit I didn't know what I was doing and bound Head so tight he's in a coma."

I waved toward Baron. "His alleged second request was a threat. He inserted himself in a picture from my brother's wedding. His third request was kidnapping my brother Max. Neither changes the fact that I don't have Head's soul."

Another centuries-long pause filled the amphitheater. Finally, SHE stirred. "This is merely word against word. Neither of you has presented proof."

"Read my mind," I blurted.

From the wave of sound that swept through the assembly, you would have thought I told SHE to hike up her skirt and fuck me then and there.

Even she looked at me like I'd lost my marbles. Maybe I had. "You would allow me to see your thoughts and memories, and display them to the convocation?"

I realized total honesty may be going too far. "Well, if you could edit out the sex bits with my boyfriend, I'd appreciate that."

Laughter erupted from nearly everyone in the place. My request even drew a smile from SHE. However, Baron looked like an aneurysm had exploded in his brain.

"Come forward, Samantha Marie Ridgeway," SHE intoned.

I approached the ruby, and she placed the tip of the stick against my forehead. Part of me expected it to hurt, but it was more like the head rush you get when you stand up too fast. The memory of that godawful week and a half raced in front of my eyes. I blinked, but she was no longer looking at me.

Neither was anyone else. They all stared toward the center of the amphitheater. Where I heard familiar voices, including my own.

I turned. And blinked. Then blinked some more.

My memories were playing like some kind of holographic display from a sci-fi movie. Head's lovelorn gaze at Duncan when we crashed Duke Miller's soiree. Tiffany's bachelorette party that ended with us setting fire to the Clarke County morgue in Vegas. I winced at the slightly psychedelic images caused by Head drugging the stuffed mushrooms at the rehearsal dinner with some concoction that only worked on zombies. My baby zombies' restoration. Thank goodness, SHE's playback of my brain skipped everything after Baron's photo threat to his kidnapping of Max.

"Wait. Stop." Norman walked over to the holographic display. "Go back to the point where she enters Head's mind and binds him."

I tried to repress my shudder and utterly failed. I didn't like thinking about that night. David had already murdered Kensai. Buried him alive. Tortured Duncan. And I had wanted to return the favor.

Except I couldn't. Not when I saw him as a child, deep in his own mind. I tried to tell myself I was keeping my promise to David's sister and his boyfriend not to kill him. It didn't make swallowing my need for revenge any easier. Maybe that was the real reason I bound David so tight. So I wouldn't have to face the daily guilt that I left him alive when he'd committed so much carnage in his wake.

"There!" Norman jabbed an index finger and halted the playback. He made another gesture, and the image zoomed in on the child-version of Head.

Sounds of shock exploded from the assembly. Jabbering in a multitude of languages ended with every eyeball, or their equivalent, focused on Baron Samedi. I wouldn't want the look SHE aimed at him on me. A murderous expression filled her face.

"Explain yourself, Baron Samedi!"

He took off his top hat. "I-I-I can't."

"Can't or won't?" she growled.

My gut said something was wrong. Whatever she was blaming Baron for, he wasn't involved. His normal cockiness was gone, replaced with the same shock as the rest of the death gods.

"Wait." Like a dumbass, I stepped between them. I pointed at the holograph. "What was that stuff all over Head?"

"The marks of the mortal's alliance," SHE snapped. "I want an explanation, Samedi!"

The same feeling I had when I erased the cobweb writing erupted in me. "But there's more than one set of symbols." I turned to Norman. "I thought a mortal could only be bonded to one of us at a time."

His expression was thoughtful, and he slowly nodded. "Yes, normally that would be correct."

Something clicked in my head. "The red Afrocentric symbols are from Baron, from the loa, right?"

Again, Norman nodded.

"And that's why Baron thinks Head is still his." I didn't expect an answer to my statement, so I plunged ahead. "The black diamond pattern represents Head's power as a necromancer." Thankfully, the witches explained that part to me, and it made sense since my weird-ass magickal ability had the same coloring as Head's. "So who does the green alien writing belong to? Because it sure as hell isn't mine or Samedi's."

"It's the Ancients," Norman said.

I turned back to SHE. "That's the dinosaur gods, right?"

"Yes." Her mouth pursed, and from her change in expression, she was trying to follow my reasoning.

"My friends, Alex and Phil, managed to kill two of their minions a few months back. One of them imitated her mortal assistant so well, Phil didn't have a clue the bitch wasn't human until she took off for Peru. And Phil's dad is an Olympian."

Persephone nodded. "Yes, Phillippa is family."

I whirled to face Supay. "And another one disguised himself as one of your demons, but he made sure to do it when you weren't home." I deliberately left out the bit about how the dinosaur minions stole his tumi, his weapon of power. "They took some things to set you up for Ares's death, but my friends foiled their plans."

"That is the evidence I have recently pieced together," the Incan god admitted. Hopefully, I got a few brownie points for not exposing his weakness or his role in what happened at Nazca.

My gaze swept the assembly. "So what if one of the Ancients' minions disguised himself as Baron Samedi or Papa Ghede? If his people fooled a Greek demigoddess and the demons in Uku Pacha, he could have fooled a witch, even a necromancer like Head." I looked around the group standing next to the ruby, and finally up at SHE. "It's possible, right?"

She leaned forward, resting her elbows on her knees. "You knew there were *msopryx* on the mortal plane?"

I paused, but my mind couldn't wrap itself around the word she called the minions. So I shrugged instead. "If you mean the dinosaur demons, my friends found out when they kidnapped Phil's dad Ares. They planned to sacrifice him in order to break one of the seals, and if they couldn't break the seal, they hoped to sic us at each others' throats. The plan failed when my friends managed to kill two of the bastards, and they informed both me and Supay of what happened. But they know a third dino demon got away. I didn't know about these things until my friends returned to the U.S. I don't know if there's more than the one that escaped because I have no clue of how to search for them."

SHE blew out a deep breath. "This does not bode well for you, child. If there is even one of these creatures loose before your transformation is complete—" She shook her head, worry creasing her thick brow. "You must find it before it finds you." A sympathetic expression crossed her face. "I wish I could tell you how to find them, but I don't know either. None of us do."

Her statement left an awful feeling in the pit of my stomach. Not worry over my own safety, but anxiety of who might be with me when the dino demon bastard made his move.

With a wave, SHE restarted my memory. I watched as I brushed away what I thought were odd, dream-state cobwebs from the child version of David Head. SHE grunted when the holographic version of me wiped away the black diamond pattern that signified Head's necromancer abilities.

The ruby rang when she tapped it with her stick. "Baron Samedi, given the murders your priest committed of her associates as well as his direct attacks against her, Samantha Marie Ridgeway was within her rights to bind him. But I see no evidence she collected his soul. In fact, it appears that he still lives within his mortal form as she claims. When the boy awakes, it is his choice who he swears allegiance to. Not hers. Not yours." She glared at Baron. "Unless you have something else to add?"

"Yes." Baron replaced his top hat. Still none of his original anger or cockiness, but there was a measure of caution in his visage. "She did erase the original bargain he made with the loa."

Time for a little more diplomacy. I inclined my head to him. "I admit to that portion of Baron Samedi's accusations, and I apologize for my ignorance. Such a thing will not happen again, and I will make whatever restitution is acceptable. However—" I took a deep breath and faced SHE squarely. "Baron Samedi was remiss in taking my brother Max for I believe his allegiance is to Jehovah, and therefore Azrael's master has claim on his soul, not me."

Her gaze shifted behind me. "What say you, Azrael?"

"The child is correct in her assessment." The angel of death practically sang the words. "I'd prefer that any errors not be compounded. My Lord would be most displeased."

Baron Samedi's dusky skin turned a dark shade of olive. His discomfort made sense due to the merging of the West African religions with Christianity to create his pantheon. In a way, he'd stolen his cousin's toy, not the toy of the new bitch on the block. Nothing like family to keep things in check.

He tapped his cane three times on the diamond floor. Max popped into existence next to Baron.

"Sam?" Max glanced around, then shoved at the nosepiece of his glasses. Like that would clear up the problems with what he was seeing. "Where are we?"

"He is yours to return to the mortal plane," Baron Samedi intoned.

"Watch off first." I inclined my head toward Max's wrist. The gold watch detached from my brother's arm and dropped to the diamond floor. The weird thing was it didn't make a sound as it inched over to Baron Samedi, crawled over his shoe, and disappeared under the cuff of his trousers.

Satisfied that Max was free, I added, "There's also the matter of David Jebediah Head's sister, Yvonne." I glared at Samedi. "She tried to petition the baron on behalf of my brother since he didn't understand what the baron wanted and the baron refused to answer any of his questions."

"You hope to steal another soul from me?" He sneered.

"No, I want you to treat her fairly. She was innocent in the matter between us, and you took your anger at me out on her. All I'm asking is that you stop punishing her for something she had nothing to do with."

The expressions the other death gods gave him said, "What an asshole." The look SHE gave him was sheer parental disappointment.

Baron Samedi stared at the toes of his white loafers. "She is released and returned to her original condition."

"Thank you," I said, and I meant it. "And the form of my restitution?" I glanced between Samedi and SHE. The awful feeling in my gut was back full force.

A wicked grin spread across his face. "You shall host your coming out party. I haven't been to Vegas recently."

"Done." SHE tapped her stick. The weird play of lights from the holograph of my memories disappeared at the same instant.

"Uh, wait a minute." I frantically waved my hands. I should have been happy that this whole situation was ending with a party instead of a battle to the death or Max's head separated from his shoulders, but no, I had to push the envelope.

A collective silence fell on the amphitheater. A disapproving silence at that.

"Are you reneging on your word, Samantha Marie Ridgeway?" SHE's tone indicated there would be hell to pay if I did.

"No, ma'am. Can we push the party back a couple of hours?" I jabbed my thumb in Max's direction. "I need to get him home first, and set up one of the banquet rooms at the Karnak." Oh, shit. What was I going to say to the casino's staff? Duncan was going to have a cow when he found out about my impromptu gathering of death gods.

SHE smiled. "Two hours then, child."

I grabbed Max's hand as the assembly broke up. Making a claim on him before anyone got any funny ideas about taking his soul. He still wore a perplexed expression. As much as I wanted to reassure him, I didn't dare talk to him telepathically. Not with this group.

Settling for old-fashioned verbal communication, I whispered, "We'll talk as soon as I get you home." He nodded though I could see the millions of questions churning in his head, his attention sweeping the departing crowd. The floor sounded like insane Christmas bells with the beings who strolled out to the black sand trail. I turned back to the folks who stood up for me.

Persephone pulled us both into a hug. "I told you that you would defend yourself admirably, Sam." Max gave me a "what the hell is going on" look.

"Thanks." When she released us, I gestured toward her. "Max, this Phil's aunt, Persephone."

To his credit, he didn't bat an eye. He simply nodded. "Ma'am."

Before I finished making the rest of the introductions, both Morrigan and Hela joined Kali. Thankfully, the spider-thing had scooted off with the rest of the crowd. Even SHE and Baron Samedi had left though I hadn't noticed them walk by us.

Norman waited patiently to the side though he made no effort to join our little group. I waved him over. When he approached, his expression was a mixture of bemusement and concern.

"We need to return your brother to the mortal plane now, Ms. Ridgeway." He inclined his head toward the top of the amphitheater behind him. "There will be plenty of time for socializing later."

I looked up to where he indicated. A shadowy figure with glowing blue orbs watched us. But it wasn't the similarity to vampire's eyes that freaked me out. It was the waving feline tail with the tuft of feathers at the end.

From our side of the burning pitch moat.

"Um, yeah. That would be a good idea." I turned back to Persephone. "Can I trouble you for a lift back to the real Los Angeles?"

The other beings laughed, which set my alarm bells ringing. Had I saved Max from one fate to condemn him to another?

His fingers tightened around my hand. No doubt the same thought was in his mind without me transmitting it.

Norman shook his head. "Chill out, Ridgeway. I'll walk you through what you need to know, including how to shift between worlds."

My eyes narrowed. "Sure, because everyone's been so helpful and enlightening so far."

"Sam," Max hissed in my ear. "Do not piss these people off."

Norman's smile was warm, gracious even. "She's not, Mr. Howell.

There's a lot to take in, and it hasn't been a year for her yet. But I strongly suggest we leave the arena immediately. Your presence is gathering unwanted attention."

I glanced upward. More glowing blue eyes had joined the first set as well as orange, yellow and red. I tugged Max's hand. "He's right. Let's get you home.

Relief spread through Bill when the driver who picked them up after their second show set was Staci's brother-in-law Steve. He didn't have to worry about a werecoyote reading their minds on the drive back to the Karnak.

"Do we need to wait for Walter?" Steve asked.

Bill shook his head as he climbed in behind Lily. "He said he'll catch a cab back later."

The kid grinned, a gleam of white across his tanned skin. "So his coffee date this morning worked out?"

Bill froze. "Uh, yeah."

Lily stared at him. "You don't think—"

"Yeah, I do." Thankfully, she didn't say anything else as their driver slid into the front seat.

Steve glanced at them in the rearview mirror as he pulled into the heavy nighttime traffic. "Everything okay, man? Thought you two would be happier that the judge denied the restraining order."

Of course the gossip mill at the Karnak was working overtime. There was no way to keep a secret at that place even if the vampires weren't involved. Maybe he and Lily should think about getting their own place.

"Just a stressful couple of days with that lawsuit hanging over us," Bill said.

"I totally get it, man," Steve said. "If Lily Bell's kid succeeded, you know Faith and Stern's heirs would crawl out of the woodwork."

Lily leaned forward. "You're terribly jaded for someone your age, Steve."

He shrugged. "Normals react to the sound of money the same way vampires react to the scent of blood. It's life."

"So what spurs a were?" she asked.

The kid laughed. "Can't speak for every other were, but I'm saving my money to go to school. It's the reason I picked up the extra job driving for Mr. St. James."

"Good for you!" Bill said. He didn't add his opinion that Steve was a rarity among his generation. Most kids today expected everything to be handed to them. "What are you planning to study?"

"Hotel/casino management. Mr. St. James said he'd look at me for an internship if I keep my grades up."

Bill swallowed his other comment. Sam probably had more to do with the potential internship than St. James, but he wasn't going to point that out to the kid. Besides, Steve was intelligent. He probably already knew.

"Not casino security?" Lily asked.

Steve laughed again. "I'm not a 'wolf. I don't have to prove anything. We 'coyotes are adaptable to new environs just like our animal counterparts."

He brought the car to a smooth stop in front of the residential entrance to the Karnak before he jumped out and opened the passenger door. "You folks have a good night."

"Thanks, Steve." Bill climbed out before turning to assist Lily.

Once they were clear and the door shut, Steve climbed back in and sped off into the night.

"What do we do about Morty?" Lily whispered. "If he's run off with Molly . . ."

"Let's change first, then we'll check his room." Bill rubbed his nose. "If he has taken off, we find Sam next."

"What if she—" Lily's hands covered her mouth, and her eyes grew round.

He pulled her close. "You know Sam won't. As long as we get to Morty and Molly first." He didn't voice his own fear that their friend and his ex-wife may already be dead.

Chapter 26

Exactly two hours later, the party was in full swing in the Nefertiti ballroom. I had dished into my meager funds, but the staff had thrown in a bunch of extras. I guess there was a bonus to being the boss's girlfriend after all.

I'd requested the full supernatural buffet, which seemed the safest option. The blood fountain and raw meat table were a hit, though I'd overheard some grumbling about the lack of human steaks in the variety. Supay had asked for a newborn baby, but I swore to the terrified waitress that he'd been joking.

As I circulated among the guests, my pocket vibrated. I pulled out my new cell phone and thumbed through the notices. One voice-mail was from Marshall Wagoner. I frowned. Colin swore up and down he'd let the producer know that Lily could go on stage tonight. I'd have to give Marshall a buzz once my guests left.

I grabbed a cup of plain old punch when Mai approached.

She eyed the assemblage with suspicion. "Gods? Really? Your brain cells have finally died, haven't they?" She had a full security contingent at every door, including the one to the kitchen. The precaution was to keep innocent hotel guests out and the gods in.

The staff? Well, most of them were supers themselves. I'd insisted that no Normals be in here, even if they were Family. There's a limit to what a person could handle in a lifetime. Mai was the sole exception and she was glued to my side.

"Nope." I took a sip of my punch. "They really are." It was probably better for the enforcer's sanity if she didn't believe my guests were gods. But I never had lied to her before, so I wasn't starting now.

Thankfully, everyone was wearing a human form for this shindig though.

Kali swooshed over to us. The black and silver sari sounded like silk, but if I stared at it too long, the thread stars moved. "An excellent debut,

Samantha Marie Ridgeway." She smiled, human teeth a little too white against her dusky skin. At least, they weren't the yellow fangs of earlier.

"Please, call me Sam." I was getting a little tired of hearing my full name. And bad things had a tendency to happen when anyone used my full name.

Her smile brightened. "Sam." For some reason, that inordinately pleased her.

"Samantha." Duncan's voice wasn't loud but it carried over the buzz of the attendees.

I resisted the urge to wince, and waved to him. Kunal was on his heels. I leaned over and muttered in Mai's ear. "Did you tattle on me?"

She shook her head. "I assigned Kunal to guard Duncan tonight because someone needed to keep an eye on you."

My very tall, imposing boyfriend stopped in front of me, eyes glowing neon green. "Are Max and Tiffany home safe?"

Before I could say anything, Kali looped her arm around the Indian vampire's. "Kunal Saravati, it has been a long time."

He frowned. "Do I know you, madam?"

She sighed. "You used to dance for me."

"I beg your pardon—"

I sucked in a deep breath. "Kunal, this is my friend, Kali."

To his credit, his only reaction was the widening of his eyes. He inclined his head. "Forgive me for not recognizing you, my lady." A green tinge spread across his complexion.

"Come dance with me." She tugged at his arm. Whoever was DJing chose that moment to put on Miley Cyrus. Her song fit, but I wasn't sure who was the wrecking ball and who was the soon-to-be demolished lover.

Kunal shot a look at me.

"It's okay." I smiled at him before I glared at Kali. "No eating his heart."

"Just dancing." She saluted me before dragging the hapless vampire onto the laminate tiles that served as a dance floor.

"I'll walk the perimeter." Mai bowed to Duncan before she strode away, all business and efficiency despite the weirdness of my coming out party.

He crossed his arms. "Well?"

I matched his stance. "Pull your panties out of your ass. It's taken care of."

He surveyed the crowd. "Is Ares here?" The muscles in his jaw twitched as he ground the words through clenched teeth.

"Nope. It's a death-gods-only party." I wanted to get mad right back. I should be angry at him for his stupid jealousy bullshit. But I couldn't. Not after Caesar's little talk. "This isn't about Ares. Or Max and Tiffany. You've been freaking out since June." I swallowed hard. "Since Alex and Phil came back from Peru. Since you found out what these damn nanites were turning me into."

"That has nothing to do—"

"Let's go outside. I don't want to have this conversation in here." I turned to leave the ballroom, and Supay's gaze caught mine. I half-expected triumph on his face, but his expression was sad. Pitying even. The same look of commiseration Ares had given me when he tried to convince me to leave Duncan.

The Olympians words echoed in my head. *Samantha, vampires are not immortal.* They gave me a sick feeling in the pit of my stomach.

Doug Warner, Staci's husband, stood guard at the door to the pool area. He watched me with concern, but I mustered a smile and a wink. It didn't reassure him, but he backed off when Duncan held up his hand.

I swallowed the lump in my throat and shoved the exit door. Dry desert air mixed with the tang of chlorine. Any of the hotel guests up this late were in the casino, so we had the patio to ourselves.

Pulling out a couple of chairs the staff had neatly stacked by the towel cabana, I dragged them over to a table and sat down. Duncan followed, gingerly lowering himself into the other chair.

We looked at each other for a long time. Maybe we were both afraid to be the first one to speak.

"Samantha, I—" he said.

"Look, Duncan—" I started at the same time.

We both fell silent again.

"Ladies first," he finally said.

"Okay," I drawled. "I can't change what Mallory's boys did to me. I can't go back to being human. I wish I could. I just don't know if you can deal with what I am. What I've become."

He looked away, stared at the water rippling under the security lights, for a full minute before returning his attention to me. "I am scared you will leave."

"Leave Las Vegas, or leave you?"

A wry smile curved his lips. "Yes."

My turn to look away. I sighed. "It's not like people haven't been try-ing to talk me into it." I faced him again, really took in his pale features, his green eyes that had dulled, the length and breadth of him. I leaned forward and rested my elbows on the table. "And there's a lot of people talking me into staying." I swallowed hard. "Except you."

"I—" He actually had the grace to look embarrassed. "You are cor-rect. I am sorry." He cleared his throat. "What exactly are your reasons for wanting to leave?"

He deserved the truth no matter how painful it was. "I don't know if I can handle watching you die of old age."

He jerked. "I beg your pardon?"

"If I survive this test or whatever you want to call it, my lifespan is now longer than yours. Granted most vampires die from accidents, homicide or suicide." I sucked in a deep breath and released it. "In my case, I'd do anything to save you from those. But I can't stop you from aging." I shrugged. "Well, actually I probably could, but it'd be pretty ugly, and you'd hate me for it." I couldn't meet his gaze any longer.

He started to chuckle. It made me want to kick him, but with my luck lately, I'd accidentally put him into orbit.

"This isn't funny," I growled.

"It is." His grin was wide enough to show off his extra-sharp canines. "A little." He held up his thumb and forefinger. "In the last four centuries, I never contemplated being the one on the aging side."

"I guess we're both letting our fear get the better of us." I frowned. "But can you deal with a woman being the power in the relationship?"

He shrugged, but his arms were no longer crossed over his chest. "I honestly do not know if I can. I love you, but Selene . . ."

Old fury tried to ignite in my blood. His maker had been dead for nearly nine months, but she'd made his life miserable for four hundred years. It would be hard for him to shake his old emotions.

"I'm not her, Duncan." I reached across the table. "How I was made and how you were made are two very different things."

He eyed my outstretched palm. "They were both spawned by a twisted form of love."

"Then it's up to us to untwist it. But that's assuming you want to try."

Slowly, carefully, he laid his palm on top of mine. "I do want to try."

I squeezed his hand. "We are in Vegas. Want to hit one of the all-night marriage chapels?"

He blinked. "Are you serious?"

"I don't want to chance a repeat of Max and Tiffany's wedding." I smiled. "Well, the first one. Besides, getting hitched by Elvis would be kind of cool."

"You do know he is dead?" Duncan stood at the same time I did.

"Yeah, but wouldn't it be fun to freak my mom out?"

He pulled me into his arms. His kiss was hope and a promise. And it—

"Sam!"

Would, of course, be interrupted. We both turned to Mai as she jogged up to us.

"We've got a problem. Morty's run away."

Chapter 27

Duncan and I followed Mai down to what she and my fiancé referred to as holding rooms. Usually, they were used to keep Normals, when they were caught committing a crime on the Karnak property, until the Las Vegas Police Department arrived. Supernaturals didn't get that luxury.

The polite term for the rooms didn't change the fact that they were mini jail cells.

Mai said nothing until she paused before the door. "I'll warn you. Bill and Lily have not been cooperative." Her words weren't directed at me, but her evil death glare sure was.

"Unlock it, or I'll kick it in." I matched her evil death glare. To Duncan, I said, *Will you please let me handle this?*

Of course, darling.

When the enforcer didn't move, Duncan said, "Please unlock the door, Mai."

With a huff, she did as she was instructed. I pushed past her. Bill held Lily, who was crying, close to him.

"Go ahead and kill us," Bill snarled. "We can't tell you anything because we don't *know* anything."

I held up my hands. "No one's killing anyone."

Mai withdrew an envelope from her pocket and held it out to Duncan, but I snatched it before he could. I quickly scanned Morty's goodbye note to Bill and Lily. It was short, sweet, and not very forthcoming on details.

I looked up at my remaining baby zombies and took a deep breath. "Where'd he go and who's he with?"

"If you want to know, then read our minds," Bill snapped.

I sighed and sat down. "I've had a very long couple of days. Right now, I'm hosting a party of death gods upstairs, and you two interrupted mine and Duncan's attempt to elope." I could feel Mai's shock like a hot poker in my head.

"The last thing I want to do is dig through your ancient hash of resurrected brains." I looked over my shoulder at Mai. "Actually, anyone's brain." She got the message. The wave of emotion from her became slightly less suffocating.

I faced Bill and Lily once again, leaned forward and rested my chin on my hands. "But there're people out there who'd love to autopsy Morty, hoping to find out how I tick. If he were by himself, I'd say it's his own damn fault for getting killed. But my guess is an innocent Normal is involved, and I don't want her blood on my hands."

"B-but you said—Lilianne—our pasts—" With each syllable, Lily frantically waved her hands.

Oh, crap. I glanced at Duncan.

We need all the facts before a determination can be made.

I rubbed my hands over my face before I looked at the pair of resurrected comedians again. "Bill, please tell me Morty didn't hook up with the last bimbo he was married to."

"I can honestly say he didn't run off with Miss Nebraska." Bill's sarcasm could have cut an additional mile out of the Grand Canyon's basin.

I regarded my baby zombies. "Please, you two. I'm too tired to play Twenty Questions. And I promise I won't let Mai double-tap anyone."

"Party pooper," the enforcer muttered.

The two former superstars remained silent.

"Did he skip tonight's show?"

The guilty looks Bill and Lily exchanged told exactly why Marshall had tried to call me earlier.

I stood up, pushing back my plastic chair with a horrible screech. "I hope you two realize I can find Morty without you." I pivoted and pecked Duncan on the lips. "I want to resolve this without anyone dying. Do you trust me?"

A sweet, gentle expression crossed his gorgeous mug. "Yes."

I grinned. "Good. Keep an eye on my guests until I get back. Grab Norman if there's any trouble."

"Norman?"

"He's the one dressed like an English Lit professor. Mai can point him out." I concentrated on Morty and nodded like Jeannie because it seemed like the thing to do . . .

The first thing I noticed was the moon. And it wasn't the satellite orbiting the earth.

"Oh, my g—" I stopped myself just in time. "Morty! I was worried sick, and you run away with a chick to a cheap Tijuana motel?"

The woman underneath Morty's moon shrieked. He rolled off, and they desperately scrambled to cover themselves.

Pfft! Like I couldn't see every bit and piece in the dark.

"What the fuck, Sam!" Morty reached over and flipped on the tableside lamp.

The light did not enhance the nicotine-stained wallpaper and the who-knew-what-and-I-really-didn't-want-to-know stains on the shabby carpet.

I crossed my arms and tapped my foot. "And here I was worried the fairies might have grabbed you. If you wanted a weekend in Mexico, why didn't you just say so? I can't believe you skipped out on a contracted performance. So help me, you are still paying me my percentage for tonight!"

He glanced nervously at Molly. The jerkoff had forgotten I wrote his tribute for the *Scoop* after he'd died. I knew damn well who the woman with him was. I didn't need to read Bill or Lily's minds. Weiss Realty signs were all over fucking Clark County.

And I was a petty enough goddess to jerk Morty around for pulling this stunt.

I turned to her. "However, Ms. Weiss, I do apologize for the interruption." I shook my head. "And I know it's none of my business, but didn't you learn anything from the first time you were married to this asshole?"

She cocked her head as recognition dawned on her face. "You're the reporter—"

"Oh, like your love life's perfect, Ridgeway?" Morty interrupted. His jaw worked as if he were chewing on a stogie. "Who ran away to Los Angeles because she had a fight with her boyfriend last night?"

My eyes narrowed. "Do you mean the fiancé I made up with until your disappearing act interrupted our elopement?"

He opened his mouth like he was about to say something, but he must have reconsidered because his jaw snapped shut.

I turned to Molly. "I'll wait outside. You get dressed. There's a little cantina down the road that's still open. Just girl talk and margaritas, I promise." I jabbed my index finger at Morty. "You are *not* invited."

Molly started to get up, but Morty grabbed her arm. "Cowgirl, don't—"

She jerked out of his grip. "Stop it, Mortimer. If everything you told me is true, Sam and I need to discuss things. And frankly, I could use the tequila." She climbed out of the bed and gathered her clothes from the various places they had landed.

"B-b-but—" he spluttered.

"There's porn on TV," I said. "You can masturbate."

He glared at me, but Molly laughed, a low throaty sound. "Actually, a case of blue balls would serve you right," she said.

I was really beginning to like Morty's ex-wife.

Luckily, Molly's Spanish was way better than mine when it came to ordering. She nibbled on a taquito while I plowed through some seafood dish and two platters of nachos. We stuck to small talk about the housing and entertainment markets in Las Vegas until dishes were cleared and our second round of margaritas were delivered.

I took a sip of my drink before I asked, "What has Morty told you about me?"

Her expression went hard. "That you'd kill me because he told me about you. And if you didn't, the head of the Karnak's security would."

In other words, the idiot had blabbed everything.

I leaned back against my chair. "Well, if Mai had her way, then yes, you're right. Personally, I'm looking for a third alternative to this mess."

She crossed her arms over her chest. "And what does this third alternative entail?"

"There's exceptions for family members who can be trusted with our secrets—"

"What about ex-family?" Her rigid posture and scent said she was scared shitless, but her face said experienced negotiator.

I cocked my head. "You going to let me finish?" When she remained silent, I continued, "Or employees who can be trusted. Are you planning to marry Walter Kinney?"

She jerked at Morty's fake name. "We just met. We haven't been on a date yet."

"Puttin' out before the first date?" When outrage appeared on her face, I grinned and added, "You're my kind of woman."

I played with the stir stick in my margarita. "Personally, I don't think you should—"

"You also said it wasn't your business," she replied icily.

"It doesn't mean I don't have an opinion. Unfortunately, I accidentally brought him back to life, so I'm responsible for his behavior." I took a sip of my drink. "Let's approach this another way. Since the bottom dropped out of the housing market a few years ago, it's a buyers' market. What if I engage Weiss Realty in helping to locate and buy some of these properties?"

Molly relaxed a little bit. "So you can keep an eye on me?"

I shrugged. "Yeah, but I also need to look at alternate sources of income. You saw how much I ate. That's the equivalent of Grandma's cup of yogurt before bedtime."

Shock filled her face. "How do you keep it off?"

I grimaced. "The real problem is keeping me full. Otherwise, I go after the nearest fresh meat, and I'm not too picky if it gets to that point."

"Oh." She fiddled with her napkin. "That could work, I guess. Can we hammer out the details on Monday?"

"Sure."

"What do I tell Morty?"

I leaned my elbows on the table. "Tell him the truth. I can find you two anywhere on the planet. It's best if you both come home and live your lives."

"So does this mean you won't eat my brains?"

I pointed my index finger at her. "And that right there is how you get bitch-slapped by a zombie goddess."

We both laughed, and Molly shouted to the waiter for another round.

After I left Molly at the door of her hotel room, I returned to Las Vegas. I told her to enjoy the weekend before she and Morty drove back.

Mainly because I didn't trust my abilities to teleport her dad's car home intact. But Molly promised that they'd come home tomorrow to prove their good faith.

The Nefertiti Room was still packed when I returned, so I mixed and mingled with the guests. Once my coming out party broke up, Duncan and I had some pretty spectacular make-up sex back in the penthouse. After he fell asleep, my stomach reminded me I hadn't taken in sufficient calories after the insane day I'd had. I padded into the kitchen and examined the contents of the refrigerator.

I started pulling out items when a voice behind me said, "Hello, Samantha Marie Howell."

I screamed and dropped the orange juice. Luckily, the staff had learned to stock the plastic jugs. Otherwise, I'd have glass shrapnel imbedded in my feet and legs. However, the safety precaution didn't preclude the cap popping off and the contents splashing everywhere.

My bare feet made squishy sounds as I turned and found Morrigan standing in the middle of our living room. She was dressed in twenty-first century business clothes, a burgundy suit and matching shoes with an ivory blouse. Her hair was loose over her shoulders. The infuriating thing was her smirk as her gaze swept over my oversized "Dean Winchester for President" t-shirt.

"Shit." I glared at her. "Don't you people ever knock?"

She leaned over and rapped her knuckles against the side table piled with mail. "Satisfied."

"Not really," I muttered. Remembering what few manners I had, I asked, "Would you like to sit down?"

"No, thank you." She stared at the carpet a moment before her disturbing gaze rested on me again. "I came to apologize."

"Apologize?" Part of me knew I shouldn't appear confused to another goddess, but it was too late, so I forged ahead. "If this is about you taking Baron Samedi's side, that's over as far as I'm concerned."

"It's more than that. My daughter of Winter plotted against you even though her sister Summer told her exactly what you are. If I'd known that before she conspired with the loa regarding the abduction of your brother, I would have stopped it before the convocation."

It took me a moment to realize she was talking about the phone virus that took down all of Augustine Coven's communications. And that Winter meant the Unseelie Court.

I shrugged. "From what I've read about the loa, they like to tilt a bargain in their favor. I don't blame you for Winter's actions. However, I am . . . concerned that she will destroy herself and her people in her obsessive vendetta over how I was created. I have no quarrel with you, her or any of the fae." I gave her my serious bitch scowl. "But I will defend myself and my people."

Morrigan inclined her head and smiled. "Understood, Samantha Marie Ridgeway."

"Good." I smiled in return. "And it's just Sam—"

"Samantha? What are you—" Duncan stopped at the edge of the hallway. My guest's presence registered in his sleepy brain and he dived for the decorative afghan thrown over a chair.

Morrigan's smile grew into a lusty grin as my fiancé covered up his assets. "I don't suppose I could borrow your vampire for an evening."

"No!" Duncan roared. His eyes glowed in his mix of panic and outrage. "Sam!"

"I'm sorry." I rolled my eyes. "If I loan him to you, everyone will want a turn with him, including Ares. Then Duncan will be a bitch to live with."

His mood shifted to full-blown rage from the way his fangs protruded from his lips.

Morrigan chuckled. "I understand. Goodnight . . . Sam." The displacement of air made a popping sound when she teleported out of the living room.

"What the bloody hell was that about?" Duncan said.

"I don't think we have to worry about the fae anymore," I said as I unrolled paper towels to clean up the orange juice all over the kitchenette.

"Can we worry about our wedding?" he asked hopefully. He tossed the afghan on the couch and joined me in cleaning up the tile. I drew out the mopping process to enjoy the view.

"What about tomorrow night?

He paused in mid-wipe. "Tomorrow is your birthday."

"Then our anniversary should be easy for you to remember. I have only one request."

His eyes narrowed. "What?"

"I really do want to get married by Elvis."

Chapter 28

It seemed totally appropriate for a vampire and a zombie goddess to wed shortly after sunset on Halloween. Mai, Kunal, Quinn from Scheherazade, the Warner clan, and my baby zombies with Molly were our only witnesses. Leslie surprised me by offering to walk me down the aisle. She cried through most of the short ceremony.

And here I didn't think that 'coyote bitch had any tear glands.

Duncan and I got the call Tiffany had gone into labor as we walked out of the Hunk o' Burning Love Chapel with matching gold bands on our left hands. One teleport to Los Angeles and four hours later, our niece made her debut on the planet Earth.

Funny how when you're a goddess, no one argues when you want to be the first person to hold your niece. After the parents, of course.

I drank in the adorable bundle that was Eleanor Samantha Howell. She had ten fingers and ten toes. Cute little rosebud lips. A cap of blue-black hair. And best of all, we shared a birthday.

October 31. Halloween.

I hoped the date didn't bode the same things for Ellie it had for me.

It was only supposed to be family in Tiffany's hospital room. That meant Mom and Dad, me and Duncan, Phil with Alex since they were back together, and Ares. But no one was about to tell Caesar to leave.

Besides, with all the intermarrying between the Normals in the vampires' Families, he was probably a one hundred-twenty-ninth cousin to Tiffany somewhere along the way. With the recent chaos of the lawsuit, Max's kidnapping, and Morty re-finding love, my research into the coven's family trees had been set aside.

Bending my head to Ellie's, I inhaled. The sweet smell all babies have overrode the antiseptic odor of the hospital's maternity ward.

"Samantha!"

I glanced up. Mom had an expression of horror. In fact, everyone present had varying looks of discomfort.

Rolling my eyes, I muttered, "Oh, for the love of—" I stopped myself just in time. During my first death god tutoring session, Norman had mentioned that saying another deity's name was like a friend, or an enemy, shouting for you across a crowded room. "I'm not going to eat Ellie."

"Then give her to me. I'm her grandmother."

"No, me," Phil said, and inserted herself between us.

"You're not blood," Mom sniped.

"But I can throw lightening bolts." Phil smiled. "So Amazon demigoddess custodial guardian grandmother outranks the Normal one."

Only Ares had the balls to laugh at Mom's spluttering outrage.

I carefully handed Ellie to Phil.

"Support her head," Mom screeched.

"I've never dropped a baby." Phil glared at Mom, then swiveled to aim her look at Alex.

The Texas vampire glared right back at her. "I swear to God, Tiffany jumped out of my arms!"

Duncan snorted. "Even I know seven-month-old infants do not have that level of coordination."

"Really?" Caesar's dry tone left nothing to the imagination. "Then how do you explain Tiffany on my roof when she was eighteen months because you weren't watching her carefully enough?"

"How about you folks agree you all were irresponsible when it came to me?" Tiffany grinned from her hospital bed. She looked a little worn out, but otherwise, Bebe said it had been a textbook delivery.

Max sat next to his wife, an arm wrapped around her narrow shoulders. "In other words, I can't trust any of you with my daughter."

"Excuse me?" Ares drew himself to his full height. Flames flared in his eyes. "I've never put a child at risk."

"Really?" Phil smirked. "I seem to recall Mother having a fit because you let me pet the Nimean Lion."

"That's different," he grumbled.

"Depends," I said. "Was this before or after Herakles killed it?"

"What difference does that make?" Ares roared.

"Before," Phil mock whispered in my ear.

"Yeah, I kind of figured," I whispered back.

Ares made a studied effort to ignore us. His finger stroked Ellie's little head. "May you be as fierce as the other women in your family."

"No! No fierceness," Mom cried. "One girl in our family should be a lady."

Phil and I exchanged scowls before we turned them on Mom. Even Dad and Ares took a step away from her.

Mom propped her fists on her hips and lifted her chin. "You two know exactly what I mean."

Phil handed the baby to Duncan. "If Ellie wants sword lessons rather than dance lessons, then by Gaia, I will teach her."

"Yeah," I matched Mom's pose. "And if she wants to be a sarcastic bitch who can raise the dead, then I'll teach her that."

Mom put a hand to her forehead. "Why do I even bother?"

"Because you're a drama queen?" I offered.

"Sam, be nice to your mother," Dad said. For once, I listened to him and shut my big trap.

The next few minutes was spent *ooo*ing and *ahhh*ing over the baby. There's something oddly endearing about watching the Greek god of war and three vampires going gah-gah over Ellie.

Dad had finally gotten his chance to hold her when Bebe burst in the room. "Okay, mom and baby need their rest. Everyone out unless you were involved in the conception or you have a medical degree."

"What about one year of med school?" Alex asked.

"I said degree." Bebe jabbed a forefinger in the direction of the door. "Now, out." Not even Ares argued with the diminutive doctor. I'd heard through the grapevine she'd stuck a needle in his ass with enough sedative to take out a herd of elephants when he couldn't keep his hands to himself.

Dad placed Ellie back in Tiffany's outstretched arms and gave them both pecks on their foreheads. He hadn't said much the entire time we were visiting.

Once we were in the corridor, I asked, "You okay?"

"I'm fine, pumpkin." He wrapped an arm around my shoulders. "Just thinking about when you and Max were born." His breath tickled my ear, and he took my left hand in his right, rubbing his thumb across my brand-new wedding ring. "You know you and Duncan can always adopt."

I blinked away the sudden wetness in my eyes. Leave it to my father to ferret out both my latest and my darkest secrets. I was angrier Tyrone Mallory and Selene Antonius had taken away my choice to have a baby more than the fact that they had killed me.

I slung my arm around Dad's waist and hugged him back. "I'm okay. Besides, my job as favorite aunt is pretty full. Hype Ellie up on soda and sugar, buy her the noisiest toys on the market, and take her to get her first tattoo."

Mom whipped around which brought Dad and me up short. "Don't you even think about marking that beautiful child's skin!"

"I wouldn't worry," Phil called back over her shoulder. "Tiffany will take her long before Sam."

Duncan halted in midstride. "Wait! What?"

Phil shook her head. "Men. You are so clueless."

"Tiffany does not have—" Duncan started.

"Dolphin on her ankle," Alex said.

"A Japanese haiku Miko wrote on her lower back," Caesar volunteered.

"The double heart with an 'R' and 'E' on her right breast," I offered.

Dad squeezed my shoulders. "Doesn't he know about yours?"

I shook my head. "Lost it when the mad scientists injected me with the nanites. He never saw my naked butt before that." Hell, it'd taken me a month to realize my butterfly was gone.

The red alert sound from the original *Star Trek* series prevented Mom from adding her two cents. We all stared at Alex as he pulled his phone out of his pocket and answered it. I tried not to eavesdrop, but Waldo O'Malley's bass rumble was unmistakable.

As was the thread of worry in his voice when he mentioned multiple corpses.

Alex lowered the phone. "We've got a situation in Seattle."

"How bad?" Caesar asked.

"Bad enough he wants you and Duncan to go up with me." Alex's blue eyes shone, the slight glimmer that preluded the neon of a full-on vamp-out.

Caesar nodded. "Have Miko meet us at LAX."

"Wait." I waved my hands. "I can get you up there quicker."

"No!" Alex looked positively frantic.

"Teleporting is perfectly safe," I replied primly.

"You want an excuse to practice with people," he said.

"No, you're just afraid I'll leave your penis somewhere Phil can't find it," I shot back.

"Don't be vulgar, Samantha!" Mom snapped.

"She's right." Phil grinned and elbowed Alex in the ribs.

"Yes, she is." Caesar smiled as well. "Very well, Sam. We accept your offer."

Alex groaned.

I motioned for his phone. He reluctantly handed it over, and I chirped, "Where's Waldo?"

"That wasn't funny the first thousand times, Sam," the werebulldog growled over the receiver.

"Just tell me where you are, doggie breath." While he described the physical location, I followed the electric signal to his phone. "Okay, I got the lock. Be there in a flash. Unless Alex decides to act like a baby." I handed the phone back.

"I'm not acting like a baby," Alex muttered.

"Then take my hand."

He did, which I knew he would. He wasn't about to look like a weenie in front of his future father-in-law, who happened to be the Greek god of war, much less in front of his Amazonian fiancée.

Duncan grabbed my free hand, and Caesar took Duncan's other one. I did my Jeannie nod . . .

Mortimer traced Molly's curves. She lay next to him, her eyes closed, with the satiated expression he remembered.

"Mmmmm," she purred. "That feels good."

"I still can't believe you talked Sam out of killing us."

One of her eyes opened and peered up at him. "Like I said, it's conditional on me becoming Family. But since your damn-fool, running-away stunt already ruined her plans, we couldn't steal her spotlight a second time. So what about the Monday before Thanksgiving? You have that night off."

"You want an evening wedding?"

Both of her eyes opened, and one eyebrow rose. "How is Duncan going to escort me down the aisle if we don't have it after dark?"

A sense of unease stole over Mortimer. "I didn't realize you'd asked him."

"Sam did for me, but he said yes. He doesn't like killing innocent women if he can help it."

Mortimer's hand halted on her stomach. "Are you sure you want to be married to me again?"

Molly sighed. "It's not my first choice, but you don't want Sam or Mai to kill me, do you?"

"N-n-no."

"Good. It's settled then." A Cheshire-cat smile spread across her face. Why did he have the strangest feeling Molly had lied to him for the first time in their lives?

At the knock on Lily's suite door, Bill yanked it open. The person standing before him definitely wasn't one of the kids from room service. He really needed to start checking that damn peephole.

Lilianne Costas's grip tightened on her purse. "I know it's late, but is Ms. Tolley available?"

"You've given my girlfriend enough grief. Get out before I call security." Bill started to shut the door. Unfortunately, Lily chose that moment to come out of her bedroom, and Lilianne shoved by him. For someone her age, she was damn strong.

"Ms. Tolley, I—" She faltered. "I came to say I'm sorry."

Bill watched Lily carefully, but there weren't any tears on her face this time. Just a vague expression of regret.

"Very well, then," Lily said. "Thank you, but you need to leave now. The judge said—"

"Wait!" Lilianne gestured frantically. "I am sorry. My own children—"

It took her a minute, but she collected herself and continued. "Especially my daughter pointed out I was being a jealous shrew." She gave a weak smile. "I miss my mother, and part of me believed that her things were my only connection to her, but they're not. It's just . . . you remind me of what I lost, and I'm sorry I took my grief out on you."

She sucked in a deep breath. "Thank you for listening." She turned toward the door.

"Wait." Lily stepped forward and placed a hand on her daughter's shoulder. When Lilianne paused and looked at her, she dropped her hand and smiled. "I'd like to talk to you about your mother. If you're willing, that is."

Acceptance chased the surprise off Lilianne's face. "I—I'd like that."

"There's a Cuban restaurant two blocks off the Strip from here. Tomorrow for lunch? Around one?"

Lilianne nodded. "I know that place. My dad used to take my brother and me there after my parents split."

"Good." Lily nodded sharply. "Tomorrow for lunch then."

Once Lilianne departed and Bill closed the door, he faced Lily. "Are you planning to tell her the truth?"

Lily shook her head. "I can't do that to her. Not now."

"Not after the stunt Morty pulled?"

A wan smile tilted her mouth. "This has nothing to do with Morty and Molly. Lilianne Costas has a lot of mixed feelings about her mother." She chuckled ruefully. "And frankly, Lily Bell was not a good mother."

"Oh, Lily." Bill pulled her into his arms. Her melancholy mood made him glad he and Doris never had kids.

She patted his chest. "It's okay, honey. Right now, Lilianne needs a friend more than she needs a mother, and Maryann Tolley can be her friend."

"You sure about that?"

"Yeah, I'm sure." She wrapped her arms around his neck. "I just need you to start calling me 'Maryann' in bed."

"Really? Because you sure look like a ginger to me."

Lily groaned. "Oh, my god, you put that in your act, and I'll kill you."

"Then you better kiss me to shut me up," he said, and she did.

Chapter 29

We popped back into reality next to Waldo in an alley off Seattle's Pioneer Square. The city's head enforcer for the Augustine Coven jumped a good six inches at our sudden presence.

"Christ! Give a guy some warning!"

If the O'Malley triplets stood next to each other, you would have sworn they were three generations of the same family. Waldo was the lucky one. Unlike his brothers, he had the full range of were gifts, which meant he appeared to be in his late twenties.

"At least you don't have to deal with the nausea," Alex grouched. He did look a little green, but I wasn't about to let the slam slide.

"Hey, that's the smoothest 'port I've done to date."

"I can vouch for that," Duncan added.

"What's the issue?" Caesar asked. He used his serious dad voice. Whenever he did that, I'd learned things were about to get really nasty.

"You have to see this." Waldo's normally upbeat demeanor was grim. He led us to a door marked with University of Washington signs. "A graduate-level historical research team found the bodies late this afternoon. Luckily, the lead professor is one of us."

I grinned. Did he realize how much his tone gave away? "How long have you and the professor been dating?"

He glanced back at me while he pulled a flashlight from his pocket. "Ralph said you'd left the magazine."

"You presumed that would prevent her from asking highly personal and impertinent questions?" Amusement danced in Duncan's eyes.

Waldo grunted as he led us down a steel-grate staircase. "Libbie's students are excavating a section of the Seattle Underground."

"Any Normals in the group?" Caesar asked.

"Yeah. All of them." Waldo's irritation was understandable. "Not a damn one Family either. Libbie's second phone call was to Angela, a witch friend of hers. The kids' memories are blurred, and officially, there's a gas leak down here."

A growing unease filled my gut as the were led us through the tunnels that were the city's original ground level streets, and it wasn't about Waldo's new girlfriend or her witch pal. I had learned months ago to trust this weird undead sixth sense. It was the same feeling I got around the spot on our balcony in Las Vegas or the street in front of Caesar's mansion. Neither a Normal nor a supernatural committed these murders.

Waldo halted before a storefront. From the signage, it had been a haberdashery back in the 1800's. The scent coming from inside was better than Twinkies. The last time I smelled something that good had been when I'd insisted on a road trip back in September for a little alone time with Duncan. We passed roadkill on the highway between Las Vegas and Los Angeles.

Sometimes, I really hated my talents.

I plunged through the open door following the delicious odor. Weres and vamps could see really well in the dark, but they still needed some light source, no matter how faint. I'd discovered I didn't need a source whatsoever. Not that the halogens set up for the enforcers weren't appreciated when I reached the nightmare scene.

"Ma'am, you can't—" A were in the uniform of a Seattle beat cop reached for me. I could tell the instant she recognized my scent. "Sorry, Ms. Ridgeway. My mistake."

With the supernatural gossip mill, everyone knew I smelled more like a steak knife than a steak. I took a deeper whiff of the lithe, tall woman myself. Panther.

I smiled. "No problem, officer." I swallowed the huge amount of saliva the other damn odor triggered. Drooling in front of the rotting corpses was not going to make anyone more comfortable in my presence.

And there were fourteen of them from my count. Human ones anyway. I couldn't detect any scents from them to indicate a supernatural.

Secondary carcasses lay around or on top of the Normal corpses. They were much smaller, approximately the size of human babies, but the limbs were gangly, the heads grotesquely elongated. And in the gaps of rotting flesh, I could see needle-sharp teeth.

I took a couple of steps closer. Every single one of the humans had their abdomens ripped open. I wasn't an expert, but it appeared the damage came from the inside. A couple of the smaller bodies were partially embedded in the human corpses. I took another whiff. Underneath the delicious rot lay another scent. This one was almost reptilian, dry, alien.

A disturbing thought rippled through my brain, but I wanted Alex to confirm my suspicion. I expanded my awareness, but there was only Caesar's people down here and human pedestrians above us.

Two vampire enforcers took samples from the victims while another werepanther snapped pictures of the scene. Donna Whitefeather, the vampire who co-ruled the Seattle portion of the Western Vampire Coven with Waldo on Caesar's behalf, frowned at me from across the carnage. "I thought Master Augustine was coming—"

"I'm here." Caesar's cool voice echoed in the space. "Since Ms. Ridgeway is indestructible, she insists on taking point."

Well, that was a face-saving reprimand if there ever was one.

"And it's a good thing, too." I couldn't keep my tone respectful, nor did I try. "The asshole who did this could have still been here."

Donna nodded sharply. "Understood. I would also have taken the same precaution. These circumstances are unusual enough. It's definitely not a pattern we recognize from any known supernatural." Her support shocked the shit out of me, and I inclined my head to her.

Duncan and Waldo conversed quietly about procedure. I snatched a probe and a pair of latex gloves from one of Donna's techs before I waved Alex over to the closest tiny form on the two-century-old rotting floor.

"I'm catching a scent under the decay. Does it smell like Lizard Girl and her partners to you?" I flipped the body over. It had prominent ripping talons, similar to a velociraptor, on all four limbs.

"Shit," he muttered. He took a deep breath as he glanced around. "But the larger bodies are all Normals. With the dimensional barriers still closed—"

"The bastard tried to breed himself some new allies," I finished.

"But it didn't work." Alex gestured at the bodies. "I know he's not going to care about the women, but the little lizard demons didn't survive their birth either." He looked at me, and for the first time ever, I saw a well and truly frightened vampire. "If he finds a way for the babies to make it—"

I swallowed hard. "We are so fucked."

How much trouble is the world in? Alex's werewolf buddy Logan Polk finds out when the surviving lizard demon sets his sights on the gorgeous documentary film maker Logan wants for his own. Turn the page for a preview of *Ravaged*!

Also, please leave a review to let other readers know what you think of this book!

Ravaged

Chapter 1

The scent hit Logan Polk as he straightened with a bag of feed on his shoulder. She-were. Definitely she-were.

Wolf. His kind.

His canine libido stirred regardless of his human side, and he sniffed the air, trying to detect her location amid the cold, wet wind of the approaching snow storm. Montana was neutral territory for the various North American weres, but most of them visited in the summer and fall when hunting was good.

Not that the occasional loner didn't find it a good place to relax other times of the year. Or hide.

Like he did.

There. He admitted it like the therapist wanted.

It was fucking embarrassing for an alpha to have been kidnapped and tortured by a bunch of Normals. It was far worse to be treated for PTSD because of the experience.

But the therapy was working. He didn't have the nightmares like he used to. He owed Esther and Aaron a lot for insisting he talk to their daughter Sarah's doctor in Billings. Honestly, if another were had suggested it, he would've ripped their throats out.

But the witches understood. Sarah understood even more because she had been captured and tortured by the same assholes. The nineteen-year-old was talking about going to college next year. She was getting on with her life.

And he was killing time in neutral territory.

Pussy.

The internal insult was lost when he spotted the she-were. She approached a bright yellow Jeep. Even if the plates hadn't screamed rental, the color did. Not even Marvin, the town's librarian/theater operator would be caught dead in anything that bright as his camouflage-style nail polish attested.

The lady had long brunette hair pulled in a tight ponytail. Legs that went on forever. If only she would turn around . . .

"Dammit, Polk! Get a move on. Ed can't wait all afternoon for you to load his truck."

The she-were whirled around at Wade's shout. Mother Wolf bless his boss's bullhorn voice. The stranger was even better looking than his imagination had painted her. A perfectly proportioned rack and a face that would make angels weep.

She frowned when she caught Logan staring at her. Even though he was downwind from her, his unblinking gaze was unmistakably wolf. Instead of approaching him, either to take him up on his blatant offer or to warn him off, she tossed her shopping bags in her Jeep, climbed in and pulled away.

Ed and Wade flanked him as she headed down Main Street and out of town. Wade clapped his shoulder. "She's a looker all right."

"Yeah," Ed drawled. "We were all beginning to wonder which way your flag flew. Guess Marvin wins the pool."

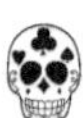

Alyson Tribideaux glanced in the rearview mirror. Nothing was behind her but the deepening twilight. Of all the things that could have gone wrong on this trip, another werewolf in town was not one she expected. Much less a lone alpha from the bold way he watched her.

Was he yet another beau Papa had steered in her direction? Damn, she knew she should have lied to him about where her next project was taking her.

Please, Mother Wolf. Let the were at the feedstore be the only one around. The last thing she needed was fighting off a bunch of suitors in Tuttle Creek while landing the biggest interview of her career.

The Reverend Ford Haight had taken over the Sunshine Believers four years ago. He moved the controversial group from Los Angeles to a ranch outside of the little Montana town. He was also credited with turning them into productive members of society after their leaders had kidnapped American TV actress Jessie Alton, the star of the hit comedy "Buddies".

For some strange reason, none of the media had run the story, not even the most notorious of the tabloids, *The National Scoop.* He'd brought the incident up first and emphasized that he wouldn't cooperate if Alyson only focused on his group's lurid past. When she said she strived to be even-handed about her subjects in her documentary on splinter religions, Haight agreed for the Sunshine Believers to be included.

She had left a message with Maddy, one of his adherents, at the general store to let him know she was in town as he had instructed. The teenager was far younger than Alyson had expected, but she promised to deliver the note when she went home after her shift. For now, Alyson had to be patient, something she'd never been good at.

Her real problem may be the alpha wolf getting in her way. This close to winter, she figured she would miss most of the hunting crowd. And he may take her rudeness as a reason to approach her.

Oh, hell. If he was one of Papa's plants, he'd approach her anyway. Maybe it would be best to do her own hunting rather than go back into town when she needed more supplies.

Except she couldn't hunt cherry amaretto ice cream in the wild.

Why couldn't Papa be as forward thinking as John Lannigan, the leader of L.A.'s werewolf pack? According to the grapevine, Lannigan's daughter was his beta.

Not that she wanted to be Papa's second. She wanted love, passion, respect for being herself, not because she was the pack princess. She definitely didn't want to be treated like a breeding bitch. She wanted to be swept off her feet by someone who adored her.

You're being as chickenshit and backwards as you accuse Papa of being. You're the wolf, not Red Riding Hood.

A flash of tan fur darted from the forest. She slammed on the brakes, and the Jeep's tires screeched as it slid on the asphalt. Thank Mother Wolf, the forecasted snow hadn't arrived yet, or the vehicle would have slammed through the guard rail and rolled end over end into the deep ravine on her right.

The acrid scent of burnt rubber mixed with the wet air as she opened the vehicle's door. A few flakes fluttered to land on the hood of the Jeep and her nose. The wolf had already disappeared into the thick brush on the other side of the road.

She took a deep breath. Werewolf. An unfamiliar pack. The one who had been staring at her back on Main Street? She hadn't been able to detect his scent in town with the wind coming off the surrounding peaks.

The road meandered around the river and up Mount Tuttle. He could have caught up with her if he knew the area better than she did.

Not if. Since. She'd been in Tuttle Creek long enough to pick up the keys for the rental cabin and supplies. Scouting the area should have been her first priority.

But then, she'd been mocked incessantly for being more human than wolf. Never in front of Papa though, and she hadn't been stupid enough to whine to him. Deep down, she knew he felt the same way as those who'd insulted her even if he never said a word.

Still, if it were the werewolf in town who'd been staring at her, there were easier ways to get her attention than running in front of her Jeep. She climbed back into the driver seat, shifted gears, and hoped she found the rental cabin before dark.

Golden eyes watched the vehicle as it disappeared around the bend. The shape-shifter would be strong enough to breed. She wouldn't survive any more than the weaker mammals he had experimented with on the ocean-side of these mountains, but she would live long enough. And in this isolated plateau, no one would discover she was missing until he had a score of his kind to prepare the way for his master by killing the usurper.

Ravaged is available at your favorite online retailer.

About the Author

Suzan Harden transitioned from writing information technology manuals for companies and legal articles for a law enforcement magazine to her first love, fantasy and science fiction in all their forms. She's the author of the Millersburg Magick Mysteries, the Soccer Moms of the Apocalypse series, and the Books of Apep series.

Contact Suzan Harden

Facebook: Suzan Harden
Email: suzan@suzanharden.com
Website: www.suzanharden.com

Sign up for Suzan's mailing list